SOMETHING VERY WILD

NEW ORLEANS LEGACY SERIES

SOMETHING VERY WILD

MARY ZELINSKY

FIVE STAR

A part of Gale, Cengage Learning

GALE
CENGAGE Learning™

Detroit • New York • San Francisco • New Haven, Conn • Waterville, Maine • London

GALE
CENGAGE Learning

Set in 11 pt. Plantin.
Printed on permanent paper.

LIBRARY OF CONGRESS CATALOGING-IN-PUBLICATION DATA

Zelinsky, Mary.
  Something very wild / Mary Zelinsky. — 1st ed.
     p. cm. — (Of the New Orleans legacy series)
  ISBN-13: 978-1-59414-719-7 (hardcover : alk. paper)
  ISBN-10: 1-59414-719-1 (hardcover : alk. paper) 1. Women college students—Fiction. 2. Government investigators—Fiction. 3. New Orleans (La.)—Fiction. 4. French Quarter (New Orleans, La.)—Fiction. 5. Art galleries, Commercial—Fiction. 6. Art—Forgeries—Investigation—Fiction. I. Title.
  PS3626.E36S665 2008
  813'.6—dc22   2008026749

Published in 2008 in conjunction with Tekno Books.

Printed in the United States of America
3 4 5 6 7 12 11 10 09 08

For Ken, always ready for late night research
on Bourbon Street . . .
as long as it includes live music and cold beer.
And for the beautiful people of New Orleans—
so generous in spirit as they rebuild
their homes and lives.

My thanks to many people: Peggy and Connie who helped me haunt the Quarter, Resa and Cindy who helped with art history, and Gray Line Tours of New Orleans who offered incredible post-Katrina information.

CHAPTER ONE

"Shall I take Chloe's bag to the guest room, ma'am?"

The warm, redolent texture of the maid's voice shattered the icy silence in the elegant living room. Guest room. That's what she'd become—a guest in her mother's home.

"No, Maxine, that won't be necessary, but you could bring us some lemonade."

Clotilde Galen turned her intense gaze on her only daughter as soon as the maid left. "You do occasionally drink non-alcoholic beverages, don't you? Or shall I get the bottle of gin?"

Sarcasm had never been her mother's style—this was something new. "Lemonade will be fine, Mama." Chloe tried to keep snippiness out of her tone since her mother had reason to be peeved. She would tolerate the afternoon mini-drama so Mama could get things off her chest, then she'd be on her way. She'd never been comfortable in the ultra-contemporary house on the far bank of Lake Pontchartrain where Clotilde had moved after Chloe's father died. It was too open, too airy, too clean-smelling. Give her the old neighborhoods any day, where the smell of boiled shrimp or simmering gumbos wafted from open kitchen windows. Chloe straightened her spine then added, "I drink plenty of non-alcoholic drinks."

"Oh, really? Not according to the campus paper. Seems your sorority holds the dubious distinction of beating one of the fraternities in a drinking contest." She tapped one perfect fingernail on the Ole Miss newspaper. Considering the disdain she conveyed in her voice, apparently Clotilde had never indulged in such pastimes during her four years at Mount Holyoke.

"How did you get ahold of that? Send poor James on a spy-mission up to Oxford?" Chloe smiled, remembering that particular campus party, although most of it remained a blur. "Don't worry. The frat let us win. They had ulterior motives," she added with a shrug.

Clotilde wasn't amused, reflected in her recently altered face. She hated the moniker Mama—it sounded low class to her refined ears—and hated Chloe's signature devil-may-care attitude even more. "What happened to you, Chloe? What happened to the girl who used to attend Mass with me at Saint Louis in the Quarter?"

Maxine silently entered the room and deposited a tray of lemonade on the sideboard, while Chloe fought back a wave of painful nostalgia. She remembered how safe and secure she'd felt nestled between her parents in the massive carved pew on Sundays. Her two brothers would sit at opposite ends so they wouldn't distract each other with their antics. Dear Grandmère and Grandpère would be in the front pew—she always in a hat, he always in a starched linen suit. Chloe shook away her emotions. "I'm not a little girl anymore. I grew up. I'm an adult now."

An unfortunate choice of words, to be sure.

"Is that what you think? That you're an adult?" Her mother's voice rose in increments in the rarified air of the high-ceilinged room. The gilt framed portraits of long dead ancestors seemed to join Clotilde in disapproval. "Hardly!" She spat the word. Her mother was rapidly losing her temper—not a frequent occurrence. "Adults don't get arrested for drunk and disorderly. Or for resisting arrest, like last year. Or for public indecency. You . . . you exposed yourself?"

A cartoonish picture of a balding, middle-aged man opening his raincoat to a group of unsuspecting women flashed through Chloe's mind. She suppressed a giggle then sucked in a deep breath. "No . . . I didn't expose myself. Not really, anyway."

Her mother's glare didn't waver.

Chloe felt forced to continue. "A bunch of us mooned a passing car on the way home from a frat party. How were we supposed to know they'd be a couple of off-duty sheriff's deputies? Those guys had absolutely no sense of humor."

An odd, uncomfortable stillness descended on the elegantly furnished room, then Chloe's mother, the Grand-Dame-Matriarch-Extraordinaire and Queen-of-her-Pontchartrain-Universe arched an eyebrow and spoke. "You are a disgrace. I am ashamed of you."

Chloe had no snappy comeback. No clever response to make everything right, at least in her own mind. Truth was, she was a little ashamed, too. If not ashamed, then tired. Tired of the partying and hangovers. Tired of going to class bleary-eyed—averse to bright sunlight like some kind of vampire, too strung out to do more than stare at her blank canvas. Tired of playing someone she wasn't, or at least, someone she no longer wanted to be. Maybe she wasn't the little girl in scratchy lace dresses with patent leather Mary Jane's anymore, but lately she didn't recognize the person staring back at her in the mirror.

Not that she could admit that to Clotilde Galen. Not in a million years. She chose to take an offensive stance. "Didn't you ever have any fun, Mama? Weren't you ever young?" Chloe lifted her chin and stared at the woman who held more than the purse strings in her life. "Or were you born wearing couture clothes, having hair and nails done on Tuesdays, bridge with the biddies on Thursdays and hospital guild every Wednesday afternoon?" She pronounced each word in a singsong mockery.

Her diatribe hadn't been planned. Attacking Clotilde on a

personal level had never gotten her anywhere in the past and always left her with the familiar remorse she seemed to have patented and mass-produced. Chloe watched her mother's nostrils flare as she contemplated her next foray.

"Yes, I was young once. I had plenty of fun in my day, since that seems to be of primary importance to you. But I never majored in making a fool of myself. I bet you're the Summa Cum Laude in that department."

Touché. Mama was getting better at sparring in her golden years.

Clotilde rose to her feet. "Although the trashy Phi Delta girls probably gave you plenty of competition. I heard the sorority lost its charter and has been forced to disband." She clucked her tongue in a fashion that never ceased to irritate her offspring. "I can't believe a club of ladies would behave so appallingly that the dean would have to step in."

Chloe couldn't help herself. She laughed. First a little snicker, then a full-fledged outburst. "A club of ladies? Are you serious? I'm picturing pillbox hats, white gloves and sensible pumps, with women's magazines spread across the coffee table and an honest-to-goodness housemother that looks like Alice on *The Brady Bunch.*" She chuckled some more. "Really, Mama, you're not that old."

"You associate personal dignity with being old. That's really too bad. I hope you don't wait to discover the truth until after it's too late."

Something on Chloe's face gave her away. Some minor flush or perhaps a quiver of a lip betrayed that Clotilde had won the volley.

Her mother swooped down for the kill. "You don't have a bit of integrity, Chloe. Not one ounce."

Chloe glared back with rigid features, willing herself not to cry, not to show weakness. Her fingernails dug painfully into her palm while she felt sweat run between her breasts, despite the intense air conditioning. Her mind tried to formulate a reply—something to turn the tables, something she'd always been able to do during these tête-à-têtes.

But the noisy arrival of Jack, her mother's gardener and handyman, preempted her comeback. "Excuse me, Miz Galen. Should I go ahead and bring Miz Chloe's stuff inside. Get it out of her hot car?"

Clotilde looked genuinely confused. "Chloe's stuff?" she asked the gardener, modulating her voice appropriately.

Jack shuffled his feet. "She's got that car loaded down with all kinds of trunks and bags and her computer, an' all." It was his turn to look confused and a little uncomfortable.

Clotilde turned on one high heel to face her daughter, her face blanching to paper white.

Not for the first time, Chloe wished she were a big, tall person, instead of five-one and barely one hundred pounds. She shot to her feet, but in her rubber flip-flops, her mother towered over her. "I got expelled, Mama. They told me I had to leave campus right away." She blurted out the words. The same words she'd rehearsed in her mind during the long drive from Oxford. Except during the rehearsal, everything sounded far more pitiable and less defiant.

The drone of the air conditioning and the buzz of an errant gnat were the only sounds for a full minute. Jack shifted a boot heel and cleared his throat, a reluctant witness to a family spat once more.

"No, Jack. Thank you, but you don't have to worry about Chloe's belongings. She won't be staying." Her mother's decorum returned, the melody restored to her tone, but her words held finality, not the usual wishy-washy pleading for improvement.

Chloe plunged ahead. "Look, I'm sorry that was the result of all this, but . . ."

Clotilde held up her delicately boned hand for silence until Jack exited through the French doors to the terrace.

"No, I'm sorry, Chloe."

"Mama, I didn't mean—"

"Stop!" Only Clotilde could put so much force into a single word without raising her voice. "Stop, please. I don't want to hear your excuses, your rationalizations or your promises. Frankly, dear, I'm sick to death of them."

Chloe stared at the icy creature that had given birth to her. There were no tears, no sniffling and no hand wringing.

Only cool, controlled contempt.

"You'll not stay here. You are not welcome. You refuse to follow my rules, so I therefore, refuse to continue to make . . . your . . . life . . . so . . . easy . . . for . . . you." She enunciated each word carefully as she walked to the sideboard and poured herself a stiff drink like a cliché from an afternoon soap, the tray of cool lemonade forgotten.

Chloe exhaled a snort. "My life easy? Is that what you think? You think it's easy to succeed in a Fine Arts program these days? The competition for grades, to achieve a private showing, to get anybody to see something worthwhile in your artwork becomes harder every day. Talent is apparently subjective to the observer."

"Poor Chloe," Clotilde cooed. "If you can't be the premier artist-in-residence, you might as well become the town drunk. Is that it?" She took a small sip of her drink.

Chloe inhaled deeply. Losing her temper wouldn't help the situation. And she knew her mom had a right to be angry; this wasn't the first time she'd been kicked out of college. "I regret . . . having to leave Ole Miss before finishing my degree. I want to graduate. I really do." She glanced up. Her mom was studying an ice cube in her glass. "I've decided to transfer my credits to Leporte. I've got some friends from high school who go there. They speak highly of the undergraduate art program." She straightened her shoulders and pushed her hair back from her face, wishing she'd toned down the fiery copper color with a rinse before coming home.

Her mother set her crystal glass down, then turned to face her. "I've made a decision, Chloe, one that should help you in the long run. I'll pay for tuition at Leporte—or anywhere else that'll accept you at this point—but that's it. No room and board, no allowance, and no access to your trust fund. As trustee, you'll not get one thin dime from me until you're twenty-two, as stipulated in your father's will. We'll stick to his original intentions that you grow up before assuming his legacy." She glared down her aristocratic nose at her child, waif-like in baggy jeans and cropped tank top.

"That's it? No shackles and leg irons? No public flogging in the stockade on Jackson Square?" Chloe couldn't believe her good fortune. Mama had "cut her off" before, forcing her to borrow from friends until the woman relented and returned her ATM card. Frankly, she had expected something far worse.

"Yes, that's it." A small smile turned up the corners of Clotilde's mouth, her first since her daughter's arrival.

"I could live at Grandmère's to save money. Her house is close to the streetcar line if I don't want the hassle of parking on campus. I know Ethan and Cora are staying there while Grandmère tours Europe with the Widow Brigade, but don't worry, I'll stay out of the newlyweds' way. Lord knows that house is big enough." She stretched her head from side to side to work out an uncomfortable crick in her neck, feeling a measure of relief.

"No, you will not live there. You must not have heard me, Chloe." A wicked glint sparkled in her mother's green eyes. "I said you are on your own. Living at Grandmère's, eating her food, while being pampered by Jeanette would hardly qualify as 'on your own.' Find a different place to live. I don't care if it's a cardboard box under the freeway overpass."

Chloe stared at her mother, speechless, then stammered. "Look, I said I was sorry about the expulsion. Can't we discuss—"

Clotilde continued as though Chloe hadn't spoken. "And I'll make sure Ethan and Hunter back me up on this. Don't even dream of turning your manipulative, poor-me routine on your brothers." She inhaled a half-breath. "Now, if you'll excuse me, I have dinner plans with some friends." She walked gracefully to the double doors to the hall then spoke over her shoulder. "And if you raid my pantry or load up your car from my liquor cabinet on your way out, I'll instruct my staff to call the police." She held open the door for her youngest to precede her from the room.

For a moment, Chloe stared at the immobile face, the rigid posture and the wrinkle-free designer suit and marched out of the living room, down the marble-tiled hallway, onto the front terrace toward her car, as quickly as her legs could carry her. She didn't want her mother to see tears streaming down her face, evidence that the elder Galen woman had finally gotten through to the younger.

Gotten through and brought to her knees.

Chloe started the engine then sped down the long driveway, spinning crushed oyster shells in her wake as the first drops of a spring shower began to fall. By the time she left the gated community in Mandeville, heavy rain lashed her windshield, making it difficult to see despite the wipers turned to high. Thunder rumbled behind her as though to underscore Clotilde's wrath. Chloe caught a final glimpse of a turbulent Lake Pontchartrain as she turned away from the lakeshore.

"She'll get over it," she said to herself, but she didn't feel so sure. She couldn't remember a time her mother had been mad enough for spittle to form in the corners of her mouth. But two expulsions in three years were pushing the envelope a bit. Chloe sighed heavily, trying to formulate a plan while the storm raged around the car like Dante's *Inferno*. She'd planned to spend a few nights with her mother and assess her options for higher education. She could do her laundry and restock her toiletries. And at least eat a good meal and sleep on clean sheets tonight.

"Oh, great," she said, pounding the dashboard. An annoying chime indicated the low fuel level just reached critical stage.

She wished she'd gassed up before the deluge hit New Orleans.

She wished she'd never gotten kicked out of Ole Miss.

She wished she didn't fight so much with her mother.

Pulling into a gas station, Chloe was soaked to the skin before she could get her credit card into the scanner and the nozzle into the tank. The rain slanted sideways under the canopy cover. "Hey," she called to the attendant. "Turn on the pump! Hey, Mister." No matter how she jiggled the trigger on the hose, the tank refused to give up any gas.

The young man in the booth seemed not to be paying attention. Chloe walked over, already soaked to the skin. Goose bumps raised the hairs on her forearms, while water ran under the waistband of her jeans. She wished she'd worn a bra under her nearly transparent top when she noticed the clerk's attention. "Could you please stop staring at my chest and turn on the pump?" she asked, as rain cascaded down her face in rivulets.

His gaze snapped back, then turned nasty. "Not much to look at, lady. And if you wanted to buy gas so badly, I recommend paying your bills next time." A smug, satisfied sneer pulled up the corners of his mouth revealing yellow teeth.

"I pay my credit card bills," she said through the streaky glass of the booth. Which wasn't exactly true—she'd never paid a bill in her life—but that was hardly his business. "Could you run it through the machine in there? There must be something wrong with the card reader on the pump." She slipped the card into the outstretched tray.

"There ain't nothin' wrong with the reader," he said, but took the card with an exaggerated sigh. He ran it though the machine then tried a second time and a third. "Says the account's been cancelled. You got that? Cancelled, and I'm supposed to confiscate it." He held up the piece of plastic with jubilation.

Chloe opened her mouth to argue, but caught only cold rain sheeting off the awning. Mama. She must've planned this, not just come up with the idea while they danced their familiar verbal two-step. Even she couldn't get an account blocked in the short time since she'd left the house.

She dug in her pockets and backpack, the console, the glove box, even looked under the seats, but came up with less than twenty bucks. *And all my friends think I'm rich,* she thought with wry humor. "Give me ten bucks worth," she shouted as lightning lit up the skies. Her cheeks colored with embarrassment when the clerk wouldn't authorize the pump until she slipped money into the drawer.

Chloe pumped her gas, then sped away, a sickening lump settling in her belly. It wasn't hunger, although it'd been hours since she'd eaten anything. It was fear. For the first time in twenty years, she was afraid. She had a half tank of gas, no money, nowhere to live, and no place to pursue her passion for art. Her teachers had told her she possessed real talent—a gift, her advisor had described it. If she would only buckle down and take her studies seriously, Chloe could develop into a significant watercolorist.

But that might be difficult living out of her car, eating what tourists throw into the trash on Bourbon Street. Tears welled in her eyes, then ran down her cheeks just as her nose started to run. She hadn't cried twice in the same day since her father died. She'd been his favorite. *M'amie petite*, he used to call her. Remembering her dad, who had spoiled and pampered her shamelessly, heartened her somewhat. An idea took shape as she neared the expensive, residential area of the Garden District and she punched a still familiar number into her cell phone. The other end picked up on the second ring.

"Sara? It's me." Then as an afterthought she added, "Chloe Galen."

"Chl-low-weee Galen? How the heck are you? Where the heck are you? Gosssh, it's been ages." Sara had the knack of dragging out words, adding at least one additional syllable to each.

"I'm in town." She laughed. "On Jefferson Highway as we speak." The voice of her best friend from high school reminded how much she missed her.

"Well, come on down, girl, as Bob Barker used to say. I'm at the Haiku Bar. Oh, that's right. You ain't a local anymore. You moved on and left us in your dust."

Chloe smiled into the phone, hearing blues music in the background and voices lifted in convivial chatter. "That all didn't work out so well."

"We'll make it right or die tryin'. The place is on Constance Street. You can't miss it. I expect you here in ten."

Then the line went dead. So like Sara, to speak her mind, then click off. And move on with the rest of her life. No need to waste airtime on superficialities. Chloe exhaled with relief as she shut her phone and shoved it back into her pack.

Who needed Mama with her manners and money and righteous indignation?

As long as a woman has friends, she's got everything she needs.

"What the heck are you knocking for, boy? C'mon in here." Lieutenant Charles Rhodes, Chief of Detectives of the New Orleans Police Department, slapped a hand on his favorite nephew's shoulder and dragged him across the threshold despite being shorter by at least six inches. "Why didn't you just come 'round the back and walk in?"

Aaron Porter, having no answers for the particular questions, grinned warmly at his uncle then shook his hand. "Good to see you, Uncle Charlie. It's been way too long."

"That is for sure. Sophie?" he called. "Sophie, Aaron's finally here." He led the way through the tidy living room into a kitchen looking like a cyclone just went through.

Aaron glimpsed his aunt standing by the stove in a spattered apron, her gray hair in disarray, and love seized his heart. Gripped it like a vise. "Hi, Aunt Sophie. What smells so good?"

Sophie Rhodes clamped him in a tight bear hug, even though she barely reached his shoulders. "You know what smells so good. I've been cookin' up a storm, all your favorites. It's not every day my Aaron finally comes home."

Home. Aaron glanced around the kitchen, every square inch covered with either something to eat or something used to cook with, realizing this house was the closest thing to a real home he'd ever known. "It's good to be back," he lied. But it was just a little lie, since he loved his aunt and uncle fiercely. He just hated the way he felt like a gangly teenager whenever he walked through the door despite achieving success since leaving New Orleans.

"This is your first genuine trip home, and you better be staying longer than the two days you spared us at Christmas." Gumbo dripped onto the tile as Sophie shook her spoon at him.

"I'll probably be here . . . a few days, until I find something to sublet. The assignment came up pretty fast. No time for the department to find me any short-term housing."

"A few days, my foot," Charlie thundered. "There is no housing in town since Katrina. Haven't you heard? Anyway, no sense running up expenses, yours or the government's, when you've got family in town. You'll stay right here with us. The upstairs guest room has a private entrance off the balcony, so you don't have to worry 'bout your comings-and-goings." He crossed his arms over his chest, challenging Aaron to argue.

Aaron smiled thinly. Uncle Charlie—the closest thing to a father he ever had. He opened his mouth to politely discourage them from getting the wrong idea, when his aunt announced, "Dinner, gentlemen. Ham and greens, plus fish gumbo, sausage jambalaya and hush puppies. Get 'em while they're hot, or I'll throw it all in the sink."

He exhaled a breath then rolled up his sleeves to wash off some of the dust from the ten-hour drive. There would be time to hammer out details. No sense disappointing them fifteen minutes after returning to the city that held all his memories, most of them unpleasant.

"How's the case going, Uncle?" Aaron asked while Sophie ladled another helping of jambalaya onto his plate despite his protest.

"It's not going. We've traced two of the forgeries back to New Orleans and that's all we got. That's why we asked the Feds for help." Charlie winked, his eyes a web of deep squint lines. "And I demanded the best agent to ever graduate from Quantico."

"You might be a little prejudiced," Aaron said, taking a sip of overly sweet tea. "And you tweaked the nose of an agent here in New Orleans anxious for the assignment."

"Nonsense, you've got art credentials, plus you grew up here. You know your way around. Easier for you to come and go undercover."

"A few courses in art appreciation and art history do not an expert make, and I haven't been a local for ten years."

"It can't be that long," Charlie insisted, spooning more wilted greens onto his plate and Aaron's. He stared off as though trying to create a timeline.

"Four years college, two years academy, then four years with the department in Atlanta."

"We hope you'll enjoy being back so much you'll put in for a transfer." Sophie's brown eyes glowed with naked sincerity as she pushed the platter of honeyed ham in his direction.

There was no way he could be truthful with her. No way and no point. He owed them so much—everything, in fact. He would complete the assignment his uncle had so graciously maneuvered him into, and then return to his own life in anonymous Atlanta. He ate another forkful of greens, watching his aunt beam with each bite.

I'll probably return to anonymous Atlanta twenty pounds heavier.

Sophie struggled to her feet to let out their dog. The scruffy mutt wagged his tail with dangerous enthusiasm. A rush of stifling, humid air flooded into a kitchen already overheated from her cooking marathon.

One more thing Aaron didn't miss—the oppressive humidity during the summer. And it was still spring. Everything always felt damp; anything left outside would mildew overnight. Forget about your clothes. You would break a sweat during the short walk from your car to an air-conditioned office. And since Katrina, the faint smell of mold lingered almost everywhere. Either mold or the scent of bleach. He didn't know which he hated more.

"You remembering the old days, honey?" Sophie asked, catching his disconnection as she returned to the table with the pitcher of tea. She topped off his glass without bothering to ask.

He sucked in a breath, pushing away his plate. How could he tell her this town was a reminder of everything he'd spent ten years trying to forget?

"No, actually I was wondering where I put all that dinner. Everything was delicious. Thank you." He reached over and covered her hand with his, feeling the warm papery-thin skin.

"Cut that out." Sophie blushed profusely, pulling her hand back.

"There's no call for thank-you's," Charlie said. "This ain't no bed-n-breakfast out in the bayou. This is your home."

"You want me to make a few sandwiches to take to the office tomorrow?" Sophie asked. "Can't see good ham goin' to waste." She tapped the platter with her knife. "I can't believe there's that much left with two strapping men at the table."

Aaron let out a sigh. This would be even harder than he'd figured. He was pushing thirty, yet these two could reduce him to kid status by evening's end. Before he carried in his suitcase, he'd better make sure there was no curfew or requirement to sit between them at Sunday Mass. Sophie loved to mother him and she was darn good at it, despite not having children of her own. He thought about jumping in his car and driving like a maniac back to Route 10 for the third time since arriving.

Instead he said, "No, Aunt Sophie. No sandwiches. Thanks anyway, but I don't eat much lunch. I really don't want to trouble you during the few days I'm here. If it looks like the assignment will last awhile, I'll get my own place."

"Sure, son," Charlie said. "We understand. You're used to living on your own." But the look on his wife's face indicated she didn't understand at all.

Aaron felt like a heel. And overly full. And tired from the long drive without any stops except for gas.

"We're really sorry about that mishap with Stacey," his aunt said without preamble.

Mishap. Like he'd accidentally shut a car door on her fingers or something, causing her to fly off and divorce him. He rose to his feet then carried his dishes to the sink. He didn't want to have this conversation right now.

Too much heat. Too much heavy food he wasn't accustomed to. And too much cloying attention. He had to get out of that kitchen before he said something he would regret to the two people he owed the most in the world.

"I'm going to get some air. Take a walk; work off some of that delicious dinner. I'll see you both later." He rushed out the back door before his uncle offered to walk with him, or his aunt insisted he take the umbrella in case of rain.

This had been a mistake. He should've declined the assignment when it came up. He should've made up an excuse. Chanced hurting Charlie's feelings by passing up the opportunity to work together.

Better that than breaking their hearts when he couldn't resume the life he left without a backward glance.

Aaron closed the garden gate behind him feeling relieved, despite the heavy night air. He didn't like people watching his expression while he ate, ready to jump up for whatever necessary to make him happy. They couldn't understand he was happy just how he was—alone. Alone to do the job he trained for without a lot of baggage—literal and figurative.

It didn't take long for his agitation to evaporate. Walking in the Garden District always had that effect on him. Despite the heat, humidity, hurricanes, termites and taxes, those beautiful ornamented homes looked like they'd stand another two hundred proud years. Some needed a coat of paint. Some wouldn't look quite so magnificent in stark daylight, like aging film stars who only used forty-watt light bulbs. But tonight, each house stole his heart and reminded him why tourists still flocked to the nearly destroyed city, twenty feet below sea level.

In homes with lights on and drapes not drawn, he glimpsed people doing things people do in the evening. Families revealed a very different lifestyle than the one he'd known. But he experienced not an ounce of envy—he never had much use for families. Everything he saw came with a price tag he wasn't willing to pay.

Magazine Street took him away from wrought iron fenced yards into a commercial area of offices and warehouses. Some had been abandoned after the hurricane, but many had been rebuilt. Aaron turned down a side street, drawn by a blues-y ballad carried on the evening air like fog. The music waxed and waned, sometimes barely discernable as traffic noise drowned out other sounds, but the singer's soulful voice drew him to the flame. The blues emanated from a bar with tall windows outlined with twinkling white lights—an oasis among the stark warehouses. He stood across the street for several minutes watching people come and go. They looked so young, yet in years probably weren't much younger than he. Their animated chatter into cell phones, their tastefully grungy clothes, their ambivalence about where to go, what to do next indicated carefree lives.

Now that was something to be jealous of.

"What the heck," he mumbled to himself. "Might as well have a cold one before starting back." His aunt had probably set milk and cookies next to his door for a midnight snack. He waited until three chicly dressed women jumped into their sports car parked in front before climbing the steps to the yuppie watering hole.

Haiku Bar. Even the name smacked of artsy-fartsy.

Chloe spotted her friend easily even though the place was packed. Sara Klein commanded attention wherever she went, yet in her case, that wasn't always a good thing. Her method of passing notes in class was to wad them up, then bounce them off the ceiling when the teacher's back was turned. Sara was sitting at the bar, cross-legged and mini-skirted, drinking something blue.

"I'll have a beer," Chloe said to the bartender as she slipped into the space next to Sara's stool.

"A beer? Chloe Galen is that you in there?" Sara pulled Chloe's overly large jersey almost off her shoulder, something Chloe had grabbed in the car to replace her wet clothes.

"It's me in the flesh."

"One hundred, count 'em, a hundred of the most lip-puckering, reality-adjusting martinis on the menu here, and you want a beer?"

"Whatever you've got on draught is fine," Chloe said to the waiting bartender. "A draught is what I can afford, Sara," she said to her friend's skeptical face. "At least till I get to an ATM." No sense dropping everything on her at once. She might run in the other direction.

"Well, well. Never thought I'd see the day as your Grand-mère would say," Sara said with an exaggerated southern drawl.

Chloe picked up the cool mug set before her and took a swig. She wrinkled her nose and grimaced. This would take a bit of getting used to. She hadn't had beer in a long time. "Cover me if this isn't enough." She set her remaining wadded bills and loose change on the bar, pushing them toward the rail.

"Stop, girl. A draught's only two bucks. You're appearing pathetic. Not a smooth move in a place filled with excellent looking men for a change." Sara swept back the coins and smiled brightly at the man behind Chloe.

"I am pathetic. That's all the money I've got." She took a second sip. The stuff already tasted a bit better.

"I don't believe it. Chloe Galen reduced to groveling like the rest of us common folk? What happened? I smell a story here."

Sara's blue eyes grew round with excitement.

"My platinum credit card has been cancelled."

"No! What is this world coming to?" Sara fluttered her lashes then sipped the blue martini.

"And I've been kicked out of Ole Miss."

"Again? What else is new?" Sara's eyes flitted back to the guy on Chloe's other side.

He must be drop-dead; Sara usually didn't act this obvious, Chloe thought.

"Expelled. Not just suspended this time. They told me to pack up and go home. And never come back. That was after I did ten days of community service to avoid jail time. Mama doesn't know about that part."

"What did they make you do, pick up litter again? Mop the hallways in Oxford City Hall? Mold control on the statues in the park?"

"I had to set up a watercolor painting program with the trustees in the women's correctional facility."

"No kiddin'?" Sara finally pulled her gaze back to Chloe.

"No kidding. And the dean said, 'Don't come back' as I drove away. My sweet, understanding mother blew a gasket. She wouldn't even let me spend the night in her precious lakeshore house." Chloe was too embarrassed to add the warning about raiding the pantry even to her best friend. "If you don't take pity and offer your couch, I'll be sleeping in my car tonight." She looked into Sara's eyes, which stared back with tender emotion, then Sara's focus narrowed slyly.

"You had me feelin' sorry for you, girlfriend. Right up till you mentioned the car, and I remembered what kind of wheels you drive." Her attention returned to the person over Chloe's shoulder.

"I'm serious, Sara. I've got no place to go. Tomorrow, I look for a job." She took a long swallow of beer.

"Would you please stop? Of course, you can stay. Don't be a goose. For as long as you like. As a matter of fact, I just kicked my previous roommate out. That worthless bum ate up my food and didn't pay half of anything!"

"I might not be much improvement," Chloe said softly.

"At least you won't try to get into my pants every other day. That much I know. What are you gonna do? Try to get Henderson to take you back? They might have cooled down by now. And that is one great art school."

"Can't afford it. Mama's willing to pay tuition and zilch extra. She said I could live in a cardboard box under the freeway."

That got Sara's attention. "Clotilde said that? You did chank her chain this time."

"Apparently so. I'm thinking about enrolling in Leporte, if they'll take me," she said, holding her breath for the reaction.

"Are you serious? That's great!" Sara wrapped her arms around Chloe's shoulders and hugged with sincere emotion. For the first time in days, Chloe felt a little less worthless. "We can be roommates until graduation . . . or expulsion. Whichever comes first."

"That's not funny, Sara." Chloe finished off the rest of the beer.

"Yes it is. You just don't see the humor right now. But you will; trust me. Now, where will you look for a job? I never thought I'd hear those two words in the same sentence."

Chloe slanted her gaze. "What two?"

"Chloe. Job. Chloe. Job," Sara chanted, tossing her blond curls from side to side. "Does have an interesting ring to it. What are you going to be? A living mannequin in a designer clothes shop?"

"You are so funny, Sara. I can't believe you haven't been invited to appear on Leno yet. I just had the rug pulled out from under me and you see humor in my misfortune."

"Sorry," Sara whispered. "Tell me about your prospects. Got anything in mind?"

Chloe nodded. "La Bella Gallery on Rue Royal in the Quarter. World renowned fine art and collectibles," she said, sounding like a radio commercial. "The guy who owns it was a friend of my dad's. He always said he'd hire me on the spot with my art background if I wanted to work summers." She exhaled a deep breath. "I never did before. I hope the offer's still open."

"I hope so, too." Sara hugged Chloe's shoulders once more before focusing her gaze behind her.

Chloe couldn't help herself. She had to see what this person looked like. Pivoting around, she came eye-to-eye just inches from a nice looking man. A very nice looking man.

He blushed since their noses couldn't have been more than six inches apart.

"Hello," he said, leaning back on his stool.

"Hi, I'm . . . sorry. I was just . . . curious about . . . something." She'd been ready to joke about Sara practically stalking him, but changed her mind the moment she looked into his eyes. And hadn't the foggiest notion why.

"Is your curiosity satisfied?" he asked in a soft, sexy voice with a hint of drawl beneath the surface.

"Oh, yes. I'm fine now. Thank you. This is Sara, by the way." Chloe sat back so he could see past her.

"Hello, Sara. Aaron Porter. How do you do?"

Sara stretched out her hand. "I'm fine, although I'm never quite sure how to answer that question. I can answer 'what do you do' or 'how are you', but 'how do you do' always stumps me."

Aaron Porter grinned and shook Sara's hand, then his attention returned to Chloe. "And you?"

"I do fine, I guess." Chloe didn't like the way this stranger made her feel somehow adolescent.

"I was hoping for your name." He smiled, revealing perfect white teeth and tiny squint lines around his eyes.

Must not wear his shades, she thought, trying to calm her fluttering stomach. She really must stop skipping meals. "Chloe Galen. Hi." She picked up her empty glass to sip, then set it back down, feeling color flush up her neck.

"Would you two join me for another round? I'd like one more before I start back."

"Sure," Sara answered, a little too anxiously.

Chloe sat mutely, but nodded her head while sweeping quarters and dimes into a neat pile. "Start back to where?" she finally asked when two beers and a blue martini were set before them.

"Philip Street. I'm new to town. I'm staying there until I find something decent."

"Oh, in the Garden District, my grand . . . mother lives in that area." For some reason, she couldn't refer to her beloved Grandmère with the usual French endearment. It seemed pretentious for a woman lining up dimes on a bar top.

"You're from around here." It was a statement, not a question. "Perhaps you can point me in the right direction to the famous sites. I'd like to get a feel for the place before the next hurricane puts this lovely city back under water."

"You don't look like a tourist."

"What do they look like, Chloe?" he asked.

Chloe. A deep, rich voice uttered her name with the barest "e" sound at the end. Just like her father had pronounced it. She stared at him, noticing his dark, straight hair. It skimmed his collar in the back, yet was fairly short on the sides with the start of silver at his temples. He had dark eyes too, almost black, in the bar light. Yet, his skin was creamy, not olive, as one would expect.

"Hello?" He dipped his head to position himself in her line of vision.

"Sorry," she mumbled. "I was contemplating a description of the average tourist. Let's see . . . Bermuda shorts, screen print t-shirt advertising their last vacation, and huarache sandals with black socks."

He laughed easily. "Since I don't even know what huarache sandals are, I guess I'm not that average, but I did arrive from Atlanta tonight. So what do you say? If you don't have time to give me a tour of New Orleans, can I at least call you if I get lost?"

"Oh, she's got time to give you a tour. She's got nothing but time right now," Sara interjected with bubbly enthusiasm.

Chloe feigned a thin smile at her friend. "I believe I mentioned I need to find work tomorrow, Sara."

"Coffee, then, say . . . in your famous French Quarter? A cup of coffee shouldn't take too long. Then you can point me in the direction of the must-see attractions."

Chloe gazed into his heavy lidded eyes. Are these what her mother referred to as bedroom eyes? The thought triggered a chuckle.

"Did I say something funny?" he asked. The warmth of his tone had fallen thirty degrees. "Maybe you'd rather not give your number to someone from Atlanta. Hey, I understand." He stood, draining the rest of his beer. "Here's mine in case you decide to be hospitable after all." He jotted a number on a Haiku coaster while glancing at his watch.

"No, I've got nothing against Atlanta. My brother's a big Braves fan," Chloe said quickly. "Call me tomorrow afternoon. I'm sure I can squeeze in coffee." She jotted her cell number on the coaster and pushed it back toward him.

He took a long look at the number, then at her. "All right then. Nice meeting you, Sara. I'll call you, Chloe." He dipped his head ever so slightly, turned, and disappeared into the crowd milling up for drinks. The coaster remained where it was.

"Wow, do you think he'll remember your number and call?"

"Sara, are you feeling all right? Remember our pledge? If they don't come beggin', there's plenty more dogs at the pound."

Sara burst into hysterics. "I did forget that one. Girl, where have you been? I've missed you." She held up her glass in salute and said with an exaggerated slur, "To friends," then finished the blue liquid in one long swallow.

Aaron stepped out into the spring night, thick with a warm mist crowding in. It would rain later, but something other than rain dampened his spirits on the walk back. Tonight he hadn't liked lying, and that didn't make sense. He'd gone undercover many times and spun too many tall tales to even consider the few lies he'd told tonight. Philip Street had been one he'd passed along the way, though two pretty women in a bar posed little threat to his uncle and aunt's security.

Aaron had noticed the blonde watching him from one eye while talking to her miniature friend. Both girls, although attractive, seemed decades too young to interest him. Up until the one mentioned La Bella Gallery, that is. Charlie had named that particular shop as the one selling two mega-buck fakes. Unfortunately, the soulful singer who'd drawn him into Haiku had gone on break, replaced by a jukebox that made conversation—or eavesdropping—impossible. Just when he decided to get away from the raucous rap music, the crimson-haired woman had turned on her stool and looked at him.

He was taken aback to see something he hadn't seen in awhile—innocence. Her cat's eyes held a shy sweetness. When was the last time he'd met anyone bashful in a bar? She'd held his gaze, blushed, then looked away demurely. He'd found it hard to lie to the innocent face, but lie to her he did. Since he was working undercover on assignment, he might as well start tonight.

Chloe Galen could be helpful if she got hired in the gallery, and she sounded confident that she would. An art student with substantial background could prove useful, especially one working at La Bella. His interest had nothing to do with her luminous green eyes or the hint of a lush figure beneath the baggy clothes.

As he crossed back into the Garden District, a cool rain began in earnest. Now his foul mood was complete. He wondered why a man who prized honesty so much loved to work undercover so often.

And he wondered, too, why the incongruity had never bothered him until now.

CHAPTER TWO

Aaron awoke in the familiar room still sporting the same flowered wallpaper his mom selected when she'd lived with Sophie. Charlie had moved the old iron bed into the larger of two guest rooms when Aaron's temporary assignment had been approved by the Bureau. Sunlight filtered through the slats of the shutters while the traffic noise on St. Charles Street could be heard a block away. Somewhere a dog barked, car horns blared, and the smell of frying bacon brought him to full alert.

What time was it? He bolted upright and grabbed his watch from the nightstand. Eight-fifteen. He could've sworn he'd set the alarm for six-thirty. In full daylight, he saw that no cord connected the clock to the wall. He hadn't wound the thing since he didn't think they even made wind-up clocks anymore. He jumped into the shower without allowing the water to reach a comfortable temperature. His first day on the job, and he would be late. Not a great how-do-ya-do.

"Good morning, Aunt," he said cheerily, pouring himself a cup of coffee.

"Good morning," she chimed, her skin already pink from the hot stove. "Charles thought he would let you sleep in. Allow you a little time to acclimate. He said he'll see you at the precinct."

"Atlanta's only one time zone different, but that was . . . nice of him." Home for a day and he already felt he should apologize for being an adult. He needed to set boundaries or this wouldn't work, no matter how temporary the assignment. "No breakfast for me," he said, noticing the spread of food. "I need to get going and don't like being late." He gulped his coffee and tried to ignore his aunt's crushed expression.

"Sure, honey. I understand." She buttered another slice of toast and added it to the stack.

"I know; I'll make a sandwich to eat on the way." Aaron grabbed a piece of toast, smeared it with scrambled egg, added two strips of bacon, then topped it with another toast. He took an appreciative bite.

Sophie puffed up like an ostrich. "That's better. Now you don't take no sass from the 'Orleans boys. You bein' way up on the gov'ment food chain, an' all." She lapsed into her Cajun backwater slang, usually kept in check since she'd married Charlie and moved to town.

"I take no sass from no one. Thanks for breakfast." He brushed a kiss across the top of her head then headed for his car, finishing the sandwich en route.

He wasn't sure how long his no-sass avowal would last. His first morning in the NOPD included more bureaucratic paper shuffling than his office in Atlanta. Everything would be a savvy try-not-to-step-on-too-many-toes dance as he tried to solve a case of art fraud. The Bureau held jurisdiction since forgeries had been passed as real McCoys across both state lines and international borders. He spent the bulk of the morning studying reports supplied by Interpol. These copies of paintings were good . . . frighteningly good according to the art experts hired to appraise for insurance policies. The experts had never seen better fakes. Two paintings had been sold by a posh gallery in the French Quarter, La Bella, a shop frequented by well-heeled tourists and art aficionados alike. The gallery, which specialized in turn-of-the-century American work, might be an innocent victim—duped by whoever sold the paintings to them—or could be at the heart of a sophisticated ring. Either way their reputation would suffer if word got out they'd passed fakes as originals.

Aaron knew the art business was rife with dishonest men, but this wasn't the same as inflating values to a moneyed collector who didn't know the difference between great art and not. Authentication documentation had accompanied both sales, provided by an independent appraiser from Baton Rouge. Aaron had been invited to head the case since Interpol suspected this might be the tip of an iceberg. How many forgeries had made their way into small museums and independent collections around the world before the initial complaint alerted the authorities? Wheels turned slowly in the world of art fraud detection. The criminals possessed a definite edge over law enforcement. When you threw the Feds in with local police departments, the jurisdictional gumbo thickened. Having the chief of detectives for an uncle would help, at least on the surface. His reports would get typed, his evidence promptly processed at the lab, but the amount of real cooperation he received remained to be seen.

With an escalating violent crime rate, many cops viewed art fraud as victimless. Rich people ripping off other rich people failed to garner as much interest as a bayou strangler. But rich-people crime happened to be Aaron's pet project. The street punk robbing a convenience store receives twenty years for less than a hundred bucks in the cash register, while a designer-suited businessman could rip off a Paris gallery for millions and get away with it. Crime pays for those with expensive lawyers on retainer, offshore bank accounts and bookkeepers to create a labyrinthine trail no one could follow. Two scales of justice existed in the world, one for the rich and one for everyone else. And Aaron would do everything he could to even things out. Whoever was behind this fraud deserved jail as much as the poor fool writing bad checks to buy groceries. More so, he felt, due to the crime of arrogance.

And he'd never met a rich person yet who wasn't guilty of that.

Aaron had caught a lucky break meeting someone with a connection to the gallery suspected of selling the fakes. Now if his luck held, the owner would hire the little pixie. He smiled, remembering her reticence when he'd asked to meet for coffee. But she'd said yes, and that's all that mattered. She might be a way in, the all-important link. He tried to forget the upturned nose, the high, elegant cheekbones and the rounded curves, almost hidden under her oversized clothes. Her voice, soft and sexy, sounded cultured, but sophisticated women seldom paid for beer with pocket change. He liked the sound of her voice, too, like the cool notes of a saxophone carried on the night breeze when sleep wouldn't come. Chloe.

Not that any of it mattered. She was his connection, nothing more. He had come home to solve a crime and put the rich bad guys behind bars, then get out of the Big Easy before something small, and not so easy, changed his mind.

He punched in the number from memory that she'd scribbled on the Haiku bar coaster. "Hello, Chloe? Aaron Porter. I'm at the corner of Canal and Bourbon. Am I close to the French Market?" he asked, even though he'd gone shopping there every Saturday morning as a child. "I'm not sure if I'm headed in the right direction. I thought we could meet for coffee."

He heard the hesitation before she answered. "You're not too far away. Stay where you are. I'm close by. I'll take you the scenic route and begin your tour of the Quarter properly."

He clicked his phone shut and began to relax. True to her word, she materialized out of the crowd of tourists within minutes. Dressed in a dark suit and white blouse, she would look downright conservative if it wasn't for the almost indecent skirt length, flaming crimson hair and dark lipstick. Her cat eyes

35

sparkled with excitement.

"I got the job. I got the job." She squeezed his arm, blushed, then released her grip, but her smile remained.

"You sound surprised. I'll bet you were a shoe-in. Let's celebrate your good fortune. Coffee? Champagne? How 'bout a couple of those monstrosity drinks I see everybody carrying around?"

"Those are called hurricanes, and you better beware. They go down smooth and sneak up in a hurry. Let's stick to coffee."

"Lead the way. I'll follow you anywhere in that skirt."

She made a face at him, but her eyes still sparkled. "Let's head down Canal and avoid Bourbon, which you'll want to do in the future unless you prefer to get jostled by tourists, flashed by women on balconies, and have drinks spilled on you by drunks. In which case, have at it. Just watch out for pickpockets."

"Sounds absolutely delightful." He liked seeing the city from her eyes, but didn't relish pretending to be someone else. It came with undercover work and he'd grown used to it, but this time he felt a little guilty.

"Where's your new job?" he asked, already knowing the location of La Bella Gallery. He'd gathered available information on-line that morning.

"I'll take you down Rue Royal so you can see for yourself. There're lots of great shops and galleries on that block, but La Bella is the nicest." She tugged his sleeve to maneuver them around picture-takers stalled in their path.

"Should I buy one of those disposable cameras?"

"Not if you want me to stick around. I don't like people taking my picture. We'll take Royal to St. Peter onto Jackson Square, then Decatur to the Market. You'll get a crash course on the French Quarter."

"I hope I remember all this without a map," he said, stepping around two elderly people sharing an ice cream cone.

She pulled him to a stop three shops later. "Here's La Bella, where I start work tomorrow." Pride resonated in her voice and glowed on her fresh-scrubbed face.

"Looks hoity-toity," he said, peering through the lead-paned windows.

"Of course, it's hoity-toity. How much money do you think poor people spend on art?" she whispered, tugging his upper arm again. "Let's go, before I'm caught spying through the window. Not a good first impression."

Aaron allowed himself to be dragged along on her impromptu tour, but found himself watching Chloe more than the famous sites she pointed out. Partly because he'd seen these sites his whole life, but mainly because he loved her enthusiasm as she spoke. Her mini-history of St. Louis Cathedral made him want to attend Mass, and he wasn't even Catholic.

Finally, they settled themselves at a table in the famous market. "Café au lait? Cappuccino?" he asked, scanning the coffeehouse menu. Everything sounded the same, giving him no clue what to order.

"A latte, please, and two beignets, if you don't mind. I'm starving." Her cheeks heightened with color.

"Don't mind at all. Job interviews are exhausting work." He doubled her order to the waitress and settled back in the chair to watch his newfound connection. Never had one been so attractive. The breeze through the open-air market stirred her coppery curls into a flurry as he smelled a hint of her cologne. "How did the interview go?" he asked.

"It went pretty well. The owner, Mr. Shaw, gave me a packet of confusing forms to fill out. He said he would schedule hours around my classes and on weekends. I'm transferring to Leporte. I'll take care of that tomorrow." The waitress set down two large mugs and a plate of sugary donuts.

"A week of big changes. Why are you transferring colleges

during the middle of the year?"

Something flickered in her green eyes; the lively sparkle faded. "I wasn't getting the preparation I needed at State. Competition to get into grad school is fierce," she said, taking a bite of beignet. "Whoa. These are great. Try one." She proceeded to eat as though her previous meal had been days ago.

He ate half a powdery pastry. "What else is good to eat in this town?"

"Are you serious? Anything Cajun or Creole, blackened seafood, red beans and rice, crab boils, étouffée, jambalaya."

"Oh, yeah. I bought one of those jambalaya box mixes once. It tasted pretty good." He struggled to look sincere.

She wrinkled her nose with a sniff. "A box mix is fine if you live in Omaha, but while you're in 'Orleans; you must try the real thing." She slowly licked powdered sugar off one fingertip.

The gesture momentarily mesmerized him. He finished off the other beignet in two bites and tried to get his mind off her inviting mouth.

"Why are we talking about food?" she asked. "Are you still hungry? You practically devoured that baby." She licked another finger.

"Thinking about later tonight. A man's gotta eat." He shifted uncomfortably in his chair. The fingertip lavation affected him more than he thought.

"Well, we can get great sausage and shrimp jambalaya at Chaz's on Chartres. For five bucks they'll give you a plateful, with warm baguettes baked fresh every morning."

"Why don't we go there for dinner?" he asked, sipping the overly sweet latte. He needed to remember this date was strictly business.

Her expression turned suspicious. "Why do I suddenly feel set up?"

"Are you my tour guide or not?"

"I didn't sign on for a permanent position. I promised you coffee at the French Market. Here we are." She opened the palms of her hands in gesture. "Do I look like the local tour guide?"

"I'd have to guess no, but why don't we make a trade? I'll help you fill out those forms if you'll have dinner with me."

She appeared to ponder this for a moment. "I don't think so. You could be an ax murderer, for all I know."

"An ax murderer wouldn't hang out at a place called Haiku Bar."

Her smile revealed small even teeth. They were perfect, like everything else he'd seen so far. "I believe you were lost at the time. You just happened to wander in."

"If you're nervous, we'll invite along your friend. Even an ax murderer couldn't handle both you and Sara."

She pondered once again while spreading several papers across the table. "Maybe. Let's see how much help you are first. Look at these forms I have to fill out—an application, a health insurance form, a . . . a . . . W-4. What do you suppose that is?" Her forehead wrinkled as she peered at the paper.

"It tells the IRS how many exemptions you wish to declare."

The furrows deepened. "Exemptions?"

"How many dependents you'll claim on your return, so they know how much tax to withhold."

"Oh, yeah. That." Her expression of confusion didn't change. "What do I put here?" She tapped a box with her pen. "Do I count myself?"

"Yes, you count yourself. Haven't you ever worked before?"

"Of course, I've worked. But until now, it's . . . been under the table. You know, landscaping, waitress for tips, babysitting. That sort of thing."

Aaron took another sip of the sweet latte, then ordered black coffee from the roving waitress. Chloe looked too small to be much of a landscaper, but appearances could be deceptive. "Under the table? You'd better be nice to me, or I'll turn you in to the IRS."

"I was planning on being nice to you, but if you don't help me I might change my mind. Anyway, isn't there a minimum you must earn before you owe taxes? I've never made that much in any given year."

"You've never filed a tax return? How old are you? Should I be worried about your daddy showing up with a shotgun?"

"Just worry about me with a shotgun. Will you help me or call the IRS snitch line? That 'being nice' business is still up in the air." Her hands fisted on her hips as she glared down her nose.

He laughed. "Name, address, social security number on those lines." He tapped the form with his coffee stirrer. "Then check that box there—single. Put a "1" in that box. Sign there, date it, and you're done."

Chloe did as instructed. "That's it? That wasn't too bad." She studied over the paper.

"You are single aren't you?" he teased.

"Yes, Mr. Porter. I am single, or we wouldn't be having coffee on this fine spring morning. What kind of woman do you think I am?"

"I can't even imagine."

"That's it." She threw the pen down on the table. "The nice part is definitely off. The next direction I point you is over the levee and into the river."

"The Mississippi River is right over that hill?" he asked, feigning surprise. He drank his coffee, trying to ignore his beeper and cell phone, both in vibration mode.

"Whoa. You are too much for me. The bus tour office is straight down the Moon Walk. Sign up for the mega-tour. I've gotta run. Thanks for the coffee." Chloe swept the papers into her backpack as she scrambled to her feet.

"Moon walk? What moon walk? Wait, can't I drop you somewhere?"

"No."

Aaron dug in his pocket for a tip, but Chloe was already halfway across the coffee shop terrace. "What about dinner tonight at Chaz's?" he called, drawing the attention of nearby patrons.

She stopped and pivoted. "You may call me. But if Sara can't join us, the date's off. And it's not a date. It's just part two of my Welcome Wagon shtick. You got that, Atlanta?"

"Got it," he called, but Chloe had disappeared into the throng. Something unsettled him. He didn't like how his heart lurched whenever their eyes met or the way his blood pressure spiked watching her every movement. When he got back to Georgia, he would call his doctor for a complete physical.

He seemed to have developed a mysterious disease or nervous disorder. Or something.

Can I drive you somewhere?

I think not. Aaron's words ran through her mind as she rode the streetcar back uptown. There was no way she'd let him drive her back to Sara's, and not because she feared a hidden ax in his back pocket. She'd rather not have him see where she lived.

And what kind of person did that make her?

Sara had been kind enough to take her in or Chloe would be living in her car, yet she felt a tinge of shame at the tiny, off-campus apartment. The balcony railings had rusted, the stucco faded to a dirty pink, and the trashcans in the alley prevented opening windows even if there was a breeze. Yet Sara saw—or smelled—none of it. Pride had shone in her eyes when she'd given the grand tour last night. The place was downright tacky

41

from her faux silk lampshades, to her fake Persian rugs, to her bordello brass bed. Chloe's grandmother had more serviceable pieces crammed in her attic, never to be used again. But Chloe would die before she hurt Sara's feelings, so she'd oooh'd and ahhh'd appropriately.

The thought of Grandmère made her heart clench in her chest. She missed the woman fiercely and couldn't wait until she returned from Europe. She yearned to hold the wren-sized hand, smell her signature perfume and listen to her whispered French endearments. She wouldn't allow the estrangement with her mother to affect the relationship with her beloved grandmother.

Chloe let herself into Sara's apartment with her new key. Dust motes swirled in the slanted sunlight through the window. The living room held a sofa, two unmatched stuffed chairs, a TV on a metal stand and a wicker planter with an overgrown pink hibiscus. The kitchen contained a small fridge, stove and microwave. No dishwasher, no washer, no dryer. Not even a table. Just two stools pulled up to a plank bolted on the windowsill provided the only dining area. A small vase sported a wilted gardenia. It all looked very sad.

At least the view from the window commanded the street, not the alley. From the corner of her eye, Chloe saw something scuttle across the linoleum, but refused to acknowledge it. She had her own room, for which she would remain eternally grateful. And Sara said she could throw out the former roommate's maple bed and replace it with whatever she chose. She needed to call her brother. If Clotilde got word to Ethan before she did, Grandmère's attic would be off-limits, and she'd be stuck with multi-recycled furnishings for the rest of her college education.

"I'm home," Sara called from the other room. "Whew. What a day. I'll be glad when classes start and I can break up my restaurant shift." She walked into Chloe's room and sprawled across the bed.

"Sara, I want to thank you again for letting me stay." Chloe opened one of her trunks and lifted out folded sweaters and jeans.

"Are you kidding? This will be so cool—us rooming together. I kinda hoped we would when we left high school, then you went off to Henderson." She propped up on one elbow. "How much did that place cost? Ten thousand dollars per credit hour?"

"I don't know," Chloe said softly. "I didn't pay much attention to that stuff then."

"And I went to work, taking night classes at community. Now I can afford two classes per quarter at Leporte. At this rate, I'll graduate at thirty-five."

"You should be proud of yourself. You're making it on your own," Chloe said, stacking socks in the rickety bureau. "You've got your own place." She threw her arms wide as she walked back into the bare-bones living room.

"What have you been sippin'? It's not much of an apartment." Sara rose from the bed to follow her.

"But it's yours. And everything in it."

"You're right. This couch that I dragged home from someone's lawn on trash day? Mine!" Sara plopped herself onto the middle saggy cushion. "This lamp, a bad imitation of art deco? Mine!" She shook the base of the monstrosity.

Chloe giggled.

"These works of fine art?" Sara flattened herself against the wall, her arms stretched over several prints in mismatched frames. "Mine! All mine. Everything is mine."

"It's a lot more than I have since falling out of Mama's favor. I've got a computer, my art supplies and two trunks of clothes. That's it."

"Yeah, but the computer is state-of-the-art and your clothes are designer. And are you forgetting about your car?"

"But you've got a place to live."

"Chloe, you should get your eyes checked before Clotilde cancels your health insurance. This place is a dump, filled with other people's castoffs."

"So what? You're beholden to no one. And I love it here. I'm glad you're letting me stay. You'll get money toward the rent out of my first paycheck."

"Paycheck?" Sara asked, lifting one brow.

"Paycheck. I got the job!" The two women joined hands and jumped up and down like children on a playground. "My first job. Mr. Shaw hired me on the spot," she enthused, even though Shaw only hired her because of family influence. It was still a job, and she'd gotten it without Clotilde laying the groundwork. "I didn't even know how to fill out a W-4 form, until Aaron helped me."

Sara stopped jumping. "Aaron? That hunk-of-burning-man flesh we met last night? He works fast. Or you do."

Chloe held up a hand. "Easy girl. I met him for coffee after my interview. He wanted to find the French Market and I agreed to show him around a little."

Sara wiggled her eyebrows like a bad Groucho Marx imitation.

"Stop. Nothing is happening here and nothing will. I got more important things on my mind than men. I gotta get my life on track—learn to live without trust fund intervention. 'Sides, he's not my type."

"What part of tall, dark, and gorgeous isn't your type?"

"He's too . . . serious."

"Uh-huh. Seems like a Chloe excuse to me."

"Here's a novel idea for you, Sara. It might be nice to have a friend. No spit-swapping, no heating-the-sheets, no steamy late night phone calls."

"Uh-huh."

"He just moved here from Georgia and needs someone to

44

show him around."

"Uh-huh . . ."

"Would you stop saying uh-huh like that?"

"Like what?"

"Oh, never mind." She chucked a pillow across the room at Sara's head. Sara dodged it with athletic grace. "He wants to take us to dinner tonight. You know, sample some regional cuisine. I said I'd let him know." She felt a flicker of heat spark inside her belly.

Sara pulled open the refrigerator door, then stepped back to assess. "Half a bottle of catsup, a week-old carton of Chinese, one quart of milk well past prime, and an unexplained brown bag in the back. I'd say that would be a big fat yes."

Chloe clutched her stomach, smelling something foul emanating from the interior. "Maybe I will give him a call," she said, trying to keep the excitement from her voice. Everything she'd said to Sara had been true. She didn't need anybody complicating her life right now. For once, she had to figure things out for herself.

So why did she feel so giddy about seeing Aaron again?

Sara didn't let the woolgathering last for long. "Since you're afraid to see this guy alone, why don't you call up your old friend Jason Hightower and ask him to join us? Just casual, no big thing. I'll bet he doesn't even know you're back in town."

"Absolutely not." Jason Hightower evoked feelings of shame and regret, the kind brought on when one person wishes platonic friendship and the other pledges undying love forever. They'd been friends since grade school, until one day he decided he was in love with her. She'd tried her diplomatic best to let him down easily, but their friendship had been strained afterwards.

"Please, Chloe. Please? You know I always liked him. Once you dumped him and all."

"There was nothing to dump. The relationship existed only in his mind, and I'd rather not wake that sleeping dog again. No. Final answer." She stamped her foot on the threadbare rug. She'd forgotten how persistent Sara could be.

"You're probably right." Sara switched on the TV with the remote. "We'll just split the green moo shoo pork and forget about Jason and mysterious Aaron from Atlanta." She surfed through the channels with growing interest.

Chloe remembered the bizarre smell in the fridge as her stomach growled once more. "Okay. Okay," she said, grabbing the TV control. "You win. I'll call Jason, but you'll probably hope Aaron is an ax murderer by the end of the night."

Calling Jason Hightower after no communication whatsoever for two and half years proved easier than she expected. She only needed to tell two little white lies and one big whopper. Spinning a deceitful web didn't fit with the new image of Chloe Galen as an independent woman answering to no one, but she couldn't exactly say why. She told Jason she'd transferred to Leporte because of their excellent graduate program and mentioned nothing about her expulsion. Jason, two years older, had already been accepted into grad school, and was busy preparing for his first one-man show in the fall.

She'd explained moving in with Sara as a long-overdue quest for independence, away from Mama's controlling influence, with nary a word about being cut off or the newly cancelled ATM card. She'd discovered her ATM didn't work on the way to the interview, and luckily had enough pocket change for the streetcar. Jason's response had been a nasty string of invectives toward Clotilde, "domineering witch" being the mildest. Discovering that the sweet boy from her youth had soured into an acerbic man surprised Chloe.

The big lie she told Jason involved Aaron. She described

Aaron as a long-lost cousin from Georgia whom she'd agreed to show the sites as a favor to Grandmère. No way could she expose her true motive for rekindling their acquaintance without incurring Sara's wrath. Jason was invited along since "backwoods" Aaron was uncomfortable in the presence of strange females. Whew. Chloe's new penchant for fabricating stories might land a career in tabloid journalism if the art world fails to embrace her watercolor interpretations.

Sara and Chloe fought for mirror space in the tiny bathroom as they readied for their double date.

"Can I borrow this?" Sara exclaimed, pulling a black silk sheath from Chloe's closet.

It had been a gift from her parents, a designer original, during happier times in the Galen household. "You can, if you get invited to a gala. This is dinner in the Quarter where we'll eat gumbo and drink hurricanes with the tourists. Jeans and a t-shirt would be a better choice." Chloe pulled the dress from Sara's fingers and replaced it with a soft cashmere sweater. "Here, try this. Peach will look good with your blond hair."

"Wow. It's fun having a rich roommate." Sara pulled off her shirt and slipped into the sweater.

"That's something I wanted to discuss with you." She waited until Sara's head reappeared from the neckline before continuing. "I'm not rich anymore, remember? I've been cut off."

"Yeah, yeah. This has happened before, but Clotilde comes around eventually." Sara held a pair of sterling hoops next to her earlobe.

"She's not going to this time. And I don't want her to. I want to break it off with my family. The time has come. Papa's dead, and I have no desire to be under Mama's thumb anymore."

"You think poverty is chic, Chlo? You think it's fun not having money in your pocket? Like a fad or something?" A hint of resentment laced Sara's words.

"No, I don't think it's chic. And I'll admit, the adjustment period will be tough, but it's something I must do. And . . ." Chloe paused, seeing that Sara's attention had faded back into the jewelry box. She grabbed her by the forearm. "And I don't want you to say anything to Aaron about my family or their money, or anything of the sort. That's past history. I want him to see me as I am now . . . a struggling college student trying to get by."

"With a Lexus SC™ and designer clothes?"

"Men can't tell the difference between designer and discount house clothes. And he won't see my car. I've decided to garage it at Ethan's. I'll never be able to afford the insurance living in the city, plus parking on campus is a hassle. You get around just fine without wheels, and so will I."

Sara exhaled through her nostrils. "We'll see 'bout that, Cherie. I'm used to toting groceries and dirty laundry on the streetcar. I don't care what people think of me when I haul stuff like a bag lady. We'll see how you like it."

Chloe opened her mouth to argue, but Sara held up both palms. "I'll say nothing to Atlanta Aaron about your vast quantities of conspicuous wealth, readily available for a mere groveling." She picked a bracelet from the box and snapped it on her wrist. "Let him think you're the queen of shoplifting at the mall. I just can't wait to see how Chloe Galen does poor."

There was no point in arguing. No way could she explain that she wanted to date someone who didn't know about her past excesses, her misjudgments and a few indiscretions—a man who had no expectations of her due to family money. A clean slate. Something about that was very appealing. "Let's go. I told Jason we'd pick him up, then head downtown to the Quarter. Chloe glanced at her reflection in the mirror one last time. Tight capris, a loose cotton top, high-heeled wedge sandals, and small gold hoops. She'd held her hair back with a thin plastic band, making her eyes look even larger than usual and her cheekbones more pronounced. Was she mistaken, or had she lost weight? Her jaw looked sharper, her cheeks more hollowed out. She thought it her imagination, until her stomach delivered a nasty rumble.

"Let's go. I am starving." Chloe pulled her friend away from the mirror and out the back door. From the top of the stairs, they had a bird's-eye view of the back end of Chloe's classy wheels being lifted by a wrecker.

"Stop! What are you doing? That's my car," she shouted, then fled down the steps and pounded on the truck's window.

A man with a greasy cap lowered the window and looked down his nose with scorn. "That was your car, Miss. Not anymore. The lease has been cancelled. Sorry," he added without an ounce of pity. A second man finished hooking the car to the lift then crawled in on the passenger side.

"Lease? The car was leased?" She'd assumed her mother had bought the car. "Don't I get thirty days or something? I need that car tonight and tomorrow to get to work."

"Normally, yes. But the lessee paid a service fee to have the car brought in early. Something 'bout fear of interstate flight."

"Wow. You really did piss off Clotilde," Sara said, her mouth agape.

"But I'm not going anywhere! I swear to you," Chloe pleaded, her face nearly inside the truck. Her efforts proved fruitless.

"Sorry, kid. I just do what I'm told." The tow truck driver shook his head, rolled up the window and drove off. The hazard lights of her beloved SC blinked forlornly in the fading twilight.

"Guess you don't need to worry 'bout your wheels giving Aaron the wrong idea," Sara said, wrapping her arm around Chloe's shoulders.

"See? There's a bright spot to everything." Chloe turned her back on her car as it disappeared around the corner.

Along with her old life. Good riddance to the gas-hog. And good riddance to being someone she didn't want to be.

She punched in Jason's number. He picked up on the second ring. "There's been a change of plans," she said without explanation. "Could you pick us up instead?"

Within fifteen minutes, the three of them had crowded into Jason's sedan and were headed down St. Charles Avenue. Jason hadn't seemed too surprised by her phone call. She'd invited him along to "help entertain her out-of-town and out-of-his-element cousin." He had accepted the invitation with few questions and cool detachment—a new mode of behavior from the man who once loved to probe her psyche about everything.

Chloe happily observed her two friends from the backseat during the drive downtown—observed and planned her strategy for the evening while Sara kept up a steady banter of conversation. She chewed her lower lip, thinking about Aaron and what they would talk about. Never in her life had she felt short on things to talk about with a man.

Never before had it felt important for her to find something interesting to say.

Aaron stood waiting on the street in front of Chaz's as they arrived and parked next to the curb. Chloe scrambled out of the backseat as soon as Sara's sneakers hit the pavement.

"Hi, Sara, nice seeing you again. Hello, Chloe," Aaron said. He looked cool in chino slacks and un-tucked white shirt.

Something in Chloe's chest tightened, making it hard to catch her breath. "Hello, Aaron. This is my old friend, Jason High-tower, and you've already met Sara. Jason, this is my cousin Aaron Porter from Atlanta."

Chloe winked her eye dramatically behind Jason as Aaron reached to shake hands. "How you doing?" Aaron said to Jason then spotted Chloe bobbing like a wind-up toy. "What's wrong with your eye?" he asked. A grin turned his eyes into a web of fine lines.

"There's something in it," she said, stepping toward him. "Maybe a piece of dust."

"Let me see." He tilted up her chin and peered into her eye, bending down to accommodate her stature.

Chloe stretched up on tiptoes then said softly, "Play along with me." She tugged at her lashes.

"What game do you have in mind?" he whispered back into her ear.

"That you're my cousin," she hissed under her breath.

"Why?" he mouthed, pulling away her hand. "Stop rubbing it. You'll make it worse. Something has probably scratched the cornea." He studied her eye inches from her face.

She could smell his spicy aftershave and something minty on his breath. Her stomach took another tumble. "Yeah, it must be some dust."

"And why am I your cousin?" he whispered into her hair.

"I'll explain later," came out disguised as a cough as she wiped her face once more. "Let's go inside. I'm hungry enough to eat a gator."

"Knowing Chaz, that can be arranged," Jason said, holding the door and studying Aaron curiously. "How long will you be in town?"

Aaron took Chloe's arm as they entered the dimly lit restaurant. "That depends. I just finished eight years in the Marines. I'm thinking about taking some classes—maybe Leporte, maybe Loyola. I gotta look into how much the GI bill will pay."

"Those are expensive schools. Maybe New Orleans or Delgado Community College would better suit your bankroll."

Jason's voice sounded haughty, pretentious. Not at all like the sweet, sensitive boy Chloe remembered from high school. If

Aaron really were her cousin, she'd be angry at Jason's arrogance. And since he wasn't, she found she liked it even less. Aaron didn't seem to notice.

"Delgado? Haven't heard of it, but I'll look into it. I'd hate to hobnob with a bunch of rich brats, but my Aunt Sophie said I should check out the best if I'm making the move." He clamped his hand around Chloe's shoulder. "And I plan on getting to know my favorite cousin again."

Chloe smiled up at him, pinching skin through his shirt as they slipped into a booth. "I'm enrolling in Leporte tomorrow. Give that one special consideration."

"You are?" Jason asked, his voice no longer ambivalent.

"She is," Sara interjected. "And we're roommates. Ole Miss was a bore. Their loss, our gain. Let's all have Margaritas!" she said to the waitress, then proceeded to order almost every regional dish on the menu.

"Not for me," Chloe said, remembering her last tequila hangover and desiring no repeat performance. "I'll have wine." She reached for the wine list, one of the most extensive in the Quarter, then thought better of it. "The house white will be fine."

"For me, too," Aaron said. "Tell me, Chloe, do you still eat modeling clay and wear a shower cap when you go swimming?"

Jason and Sara broke into hysterics. Chloe tried to kick him under the table, but connected with the table leg instead. "I was very little then," she said, trying to act irritated. "Those memories are best forgotten." She slanted him a glare. "Or I'll bring up some recollections of my own."

"In that case, the rest of my memories will remain a secret," he said, placing his massive hand over her smaller one. His touch filled her with warmth and tenderness, as though they really had a history together.

As quickly as their sensual connection began, it ended as

bowls of gumbo appeared with long baguettes and platters of boiled shrimp and steaming mussels. Sara took over, doing what she did best—monopolizing the conversation and directing the consumption of a vast quantity of food. The pressure was off Chloe. She could sit back, sip her wine, eat her dinner and enjoy the evening without nervous anticipation about what to say.

A warm breeze blew in from the open window, carrying mournful blues music from blocks away. Voices of the other diners rose in laughter then faded into the street cacophony. Foghorns from freighters sounded mournful on the river. Chloe felt comfortable in Aaron's company, despite their brief acquaintance and the silly subterfuge of being cousins. When he slipped something tasty onto her plate, she ate it with relish. When she insisted he try an alien new food, she laughed with abandon at his reaction. When they both reached for the hot sauce at the same time, their fingers stayed entwined longer than necessary. And when his leg brushed hers under the table, he held it there for a long while. The contact sent a shiver of anticipation up her spine—a little *frisson* of energy.

Jason didn't seem to notice.

And Sara wasn't aware of anything in the room except Jason.

But Chloe felt it. Emotion and heat stirred within her that didn't feel the least bit cousin-like. In fact, it felt like nothing she'd ever experienced before. And that scared her more than tow trucks, or poverty, or even the wrath of Mama.

CHAPTER THREE

After a day and a half of hunching over his laptop in his new cubicle, Aaron was ready for a break. He'd been tracking the sales for the past two years at the largest auction house in New York and needed to get out of the precinct. Not that he hadn't made some interesting discoveries. An amazing number of Irving Blakes, an early twentieth century watercolorist, could be traced back to La Bella Galley, most not directly bought through one or two intermediaries. La Bella had then sold or consigned them to galleries all around the country, but the result seemed to be the same: the works ended up on Madison Avenue, where they were auctioned to foreign collectors and small museums. None had fetched seven figures, so nothing had attracted much media attention, yet the sheer number of Blakes becoming available during a three year time period astounded him. Where had all these originals been hiding for decades? In some elderly lady's dusty attic? An art discovery of that quantity would have made the papers. He found no reference to it in any newspaper archive or web search he conducted.

Aaron knew the art world moved often along the lines of manufactured interest and generated hype. If dealers could elevate one artist or one style to fad status—the coveted collectable of the moment—a fortune could be made. Current market value was an ephemeral if not meaningless concept. Appraisers could be hired and advance publicity arranged since collectors, both new and sage, loved seeing their recent purchases in oversized coffee table books. Often experts would offer their opinions regarding value in return for the same courtesy in the future. It was a buyer-beware business like no other, yet outright signed forgeries were rare. And Aaron couldn't imagine these paintings were anything but. Their provenance all seemed to stop at La Bella as though the artist, Blake, had painted on the upper floor eighty-five years ago. The gallery was in business back then, but Aaron doubted the New Englander ever visited the French Quarter. Proving this wouldn't be easy. And a man as rich, influential, and respected as owner Kurt Shaw had a team of expensive lawyers to protect him. Aaron didn't want his lackeys. He wanted Shaw, if he was behind this. And a plan so well executed, a manipulation this intricate, it couldn't be anybody but someone at the top rung of his profession.

Kurt Shaw was Ivy-league educated, with a pedigree longer and more impressive than the artwork he sold. He came from old money, and then amassed a sizeable fortune after inheriting the gallery from his father. The elder Shaw had notable integrity in a business where his peers often didn't. However, the current owner and proprietor traded on the family's reputation without doing much to earn it on his own. Several shady deals with artificial pricing for insurance valuations had been quietly settled out of court, and out of the papers. Shaw had apparently insured an acquired collection at inflated prices, printed a glossy catalog showcasing the collection, then loaned it to a small museum where it was reported stolen within weeks. Not a bad way to parlay two million dollars into eight. But one couldn't do that too often. What Shaw had hit on was a steady, regular income, and relatively under the radar. Sort of like having a day job.

Aaron worked the kinks out of his neck then reached for his sport coat. He needed to stretch his legs. He wanted to experience the ambience of La Bella and meet Kurt Shaw firsthand. And most of all, he wanted to see Chloe again. He hadn't talked to her since their odd little dinner at Chaz's. She'd said little, but her eyes did plenty of talkin', as Aunt Sophie would say. He hadn't liked the way Hightower practically pushed Chloe into his backseat then waved Aaron off with a "Watch your step in the Quarter. This ain't no Peach Street."

The pompous little fool.

Hightower wasn't his concern. Ms. Chloe Galen of Avalon Lane was. He'd located her residence via her friend Sara Klein. According to his sources, Ms. Klein paid her rent and utilities late, but her tuition on time. She also was a student at Leporte, but majoring in elementary education. Chloe, true to her word, had enrolled that morning as a junior in the Fine Arts program.

He'd done no further delving into her personal information. He felt bad enough spinning a tale about pursuing a bachelor's degree with the GI bill when he already held a Master's in Criminology. This was his job, what he was paid to do. He couldn't let his testosterone interfere just because a man could get lost in her eyes and never be heard from again.

He'd seen prettier women in his day, but he couldn't remember any at the moment.

He'd certainly talked to wittier, more engaging conversationalists, but couldn't recall their names. What had stuck in his mind was his urge to arrange for dinner to be delivered to their apartment. Every day. Both girls, thin as wraiths, had been famished when they'd arrived at Chaz's. Chloe apparently went without food in order to buy books and supplies on campus. He kept his opinion that she should eat more to himself, since something in her eyes spoke of a strong will. And something in his heart told him to give her a wide berth. He didn't need any complications on the case right now.

And didn't want complications in his perfectly satisfactory personal life. He'd gone the relationship route before, and it hadn't produced many fond memories.

Aaron drove downtown as fast as afternoon traffic allowed. He parked on Rue Royal and followed a group of tourists into the gallery. One foot inside reminded him why wealthy collectors parted with their hard earned dollars so easily. He entered a rarefied atmosphere of hushed voices, soft lighting and beautiful objects d'art. Polished antiques, rare porcelains, oil portraits depicting beloved spouses, and pastoral watercolors offered a glimpse into a bygone era. When you stepped inside this world, you left the bustling twenty-first century outside. Those willing to spend some money could buy a piece of life sweeter, gentler, more serene than their own.

If Aaron didn't know better, he might get sucked into the undertow himself. His art background had taught him to appreciate the finer things in life. But criminology had taught him most things were not what they appeared to be.

He wandered unobserved while a tall, silver-haired man in three-piece Armani hovered close to some expensively dressed ladies. Shaw. He would've recognized him without help from a DMV photo. A long-legged blond woman with a great smile, apparently his assistant, worked the husbands in the group. The two created a formidable pair. Aaron watched their sales presentation from behind a bronze urn that was large enough to hold the remains of a departed loved one.

"Aaron. What are you doing here?" A soft voice emanated from a potted hibiscus separating the two rooms until Chloe stepped out. She wore a short skirt, starched white shirt and a paisley scarf knotted as a necktie. She probably thought she looked professional. He felt a twinge of something carnal from the brevity of her skirt. Her tanned legs were sleekly athletic.

"I'm admiring the masterpieces," he said, focusing on her fresh scrubbed face.

"I didn't know you liked art. Do you want to see the Fritzches in the backroom? They're not officially on exhibit yet, not until consignment papers have been signed, but they're my favorites."

She sounded breathless, enthusiastic, and so very young. Aaron couldn't imagine he ever sounded that youthful in his life. "I'd love to see them. Is it okay? Do you have to ask your boss?" He hooked a thumb in Shaw's direction.

"No, don't worry about it. I've got carte blanche." She laughed.

"So soon? Isn't this just your third day on the job? You must've made quite an impression."

Chloe's cheeks pinked with embarrassment as she glanced away quickly. "Mr. Shaw is a . . . trusting person and a very nice man. But you're right, I probably shouldn't take you in the backroom."

Aaron could've kicked himself. In the sixty seconds he'd been in her company, he'd forgotten he was undercover and not here to flirt with the clerk like a hormonal high school kid. "How 'bout a quick look? Fritzche is one of my favorite artists, too." At least, that part wasn't a lie.

"Follow me," she whispered, crooking her index finger. "We'll just take a peek."

As promised, four matted Fritzches lay on a large worktable, awaiting new frames. Frames could make or break a painting, and those that had been pried off added nothing to the artwork. He stepped closer to peruse, wishing he could examine with his magnifier, but he restrained himself. "They're beautiful, Chloe. Thanks for letting me see them." He stepped back from the final piece, a still life done in oil that looked recently repaired.

"You're welcome. I didn't know you were interested. Well, we didn't get much of a chance to—"

"Chloe! What are doing back here?" Whatever she was trying to stammer as her cheeks flushed with color was cut off by the crisp voice of Kurt Shaw. "I thought I mentioned yesterday this area is off-limits to customers."

"Mr. Shaw. I'm sorry, sir." She turned so quickly she almost fell off her platform sandals. "I just wanted my cousin, Aaron, to see the Fritzches while he's in town. He loves art like I do." She flashed a mega-watt smile so stunning a man would have to be moldering in the grave not to be affected.

"Your cousin?" Shaw's question sounded cool, but no longer so angry.

"Yes, from Atlanta. I know I should've asked you first." Her blush shot up to her hairline.

"How do you do, sir," Aaron said, glad she hadn't added his last name. "Nice to meet Chloe's boss." He conjured up an ingratiating smile.

"And you, son." Shaw shook Aaron's hand briefly, then guided them back into the showroom. "No harm done. I know Chloe is excited by the Fritzches." He closed the door behind them with a click of the lock.

"Chloe, would you mind getting some refreshments for our clients? I belief the '48 Rothschild would do nicely." After Chloe left the room, Shaw added to Aaron, "Thanks for visiting our shop. Enjoy your look around, young man." Then Shaw glided back to his customers without another thought for a non-buying visitor.

Smooth as silk. This was a man who could sell scuba gear to an Eskimo.

Aaron knew the type. With a voice like aged brandy, he could lie for hours about the pedigree of something he'd picked up for a song from someone desperate for cash for last-ditch medical treatments. At the same time, he could convince a naïve couple looking to sell a piece that its poor condition rendered it almost worthless. He would have a master restorer strip and refinish, then sell to a museum at an astronomical profit.

As Chloe searched for the vintage wine, Aaron watched Shaw at work. The group of elderly tourists seemed ready to sign on the dotted line. Aaron would take great pleasure in bringing this pretentious man to justice, despite many in the department who saw this crime as inconsequential.

He knew better.

"How do you like the job so far?" he asked Chloe after she finished serving the clients champagne.

"I love it! I didn't think it would be so much fun. My worthless art background—as my daddy used to call it—is coming in handy." She bounced up and down on her toes like a child waiting for a special treat.

Maybe it was her innocent enthusiasm, maybe it was the damn short skirt, but Aaron knew he had to get out of there before he blew his cover. As he opened the door, the rush of warm air felt welcome after the frigid air conditioning and his rapid heart rate. A man dressed in a linen suit stepped through as Aaron paused on the stoop.

"Dr. Graziano," Chloe said, stepping back from the doorway. "Funny meeting you here, sir."

The middle-aged man focused on Chloe through thick bifocal eyeglasses. "Good afternoon, Miss Galen. Is Kurt in?" he asked, but didn't wait for her answer. He pushed past her and headed toward the back room. Aaron noticed damp stains on his shirt collar and a flushed face, even though the temperature could hardly be described as stifling. Sweating under the lights is how detectives in the squad would describe his appearance.

"Must be in some big hurry," Chloe said after he disappeared into the back room. "He's my new professor at Leporte in the art department. Wonder what he's doing here."

Aaron scratched his stubbly jawline. Whiskers seemed to grow faster in the Big Easy than back home in Atlanta. Why indeed, he thought. Art professors don't usually shop at overpriced galleries. They decorated their walls with students' endeavors or their personal handiwork.

It was time for him to expand his own education. "I'm enrolling in Leporte," he announced.

"That's wonderful." She clamped a hand on his forearm, her enthusiasm heartbreakingly genuine.

Her touch ignited sparks that he didn't like one bit. "Let's go out tonight and celebrate my decision to go back to school."

She paused briefly to consider the invitation while he held his breath like an adolescent again.

"I've got a better idea. You should conserve cash if you're enrolling in Leporte. I'll cook for us instead. Sara will be working tonight." She winked and opened her palms. "What do you say? I . . . don't cook much, but I promise not to poison you."

Her face was earnest, her smile so cheery, her hair—so flaming red. He knew where this could possibly go and he didn't want to go there. He didn't want to get personally involved and didn't want her to get hurt.

He opened his mouth to decline, or at least insist they meet in a discreet public place, but instead blurted, "I'd love to. I'll bring the beer. Where do you live?"

Even though he already knew her address.

She grinned and jotted something on a La Bella business card. "Don't be scared by the neighborhood—hurricane restoration hasn't quite finished with us yet. I must get back to work, but I'll see you at seven." She tucked the card into his shirt pocket and disappeared into the aisles filled with beautiful antiquities.

Once back in his car and headed out of the Quarter, he called Detective Charles Rhodes on his cell. "Charlie?" he asked when his uncle picked up. "Do me a favor. Ask Joyce to start the paperwork. I need to enroll in Leporte. Have her register me as a freshman in the Fine Arts program."

Rhodes laughed from his ample belly. "I don't think you need any more background, son. You could probably teach freshman students."

"I've got a hunch on one of their professors. One just paid a social call on La Bella Gallery."

"Is that right? Is that where you are? How's that connection you were working on?"

"Good. I'm having dinner with her tonight, so please tell Aunt Sophie I'm eating out."

"With her? Why am I not surprised your connection is a woman? Probably a young, attractive woman, eh?"

Aaron didn't appreciate Charlie's innuendoes. He was a grown man, fully capable of keeping a professional distance, especially from an informant. At this point, he couldn't say if Chloe was somehow involved or not. He doubted it, since she and her roommate lived hand-to-mouth in a downwardly mobile neighborhood.

"Well?" Charlie demanded. "Is she young and attractive?"

"I suppose she is. She's certainly young and . . . attractive if you like the free-spirited, wild-child look."

"Hmm. You seem to have given her appearance some consideration." Again, the deep belly laugh. "You better watch yourself and not forget who's manipulating whom."

"I think I know how to do my job. And no woman, young and attractive or otherwise, will ever compromise an investigation." His tone conveyed irritation, if his words didn't get the point across. "This little bimbo will probably lead me nowhere. I'm just taking this route to see how far it gets me."

"An excellent plan. I'll talk to you in the morning and I'll tell Sophie to cook for five tonight, instead of fifteen."

His uncle clicked off. Aaron knew he had hurt Charlie's feelings with his attitude. This was the problem with running an investigation from your family's home. People's toes could get stepped on and that possibility made his gut tighten with remorse. His uncle had made him everything he was today.

Which was a damn good investigator.

What in the world had she been thinking? *I can't cook. I've never cooked in my entire life. And why did I invite him to Sara's?*

The apartment looked like someone had moved out and Sara adopted whatever had been left behind. And Chloe hadn't added much when she moved in. She liked living with Sara, enjoyed the austere lifestyle with no expectations from anyone due to family money. She just didn't relish the idea of entertaining Aaron here.

He would arrive in less than an hour and a half. After leaving the gallery, she'd stopped at the market to buy shrimp, fresh asparagus, tiny redskin potatoes, and salad in a plastic bag. How hard could cooking be? Jeanette, the family housekeeper living with Ethan and Cora at Grandmère's, was almost eighty and still threw dinner on the table without much effort. She thought of calling the sweet but cantankerous woman, but changed her mind. She was twenty years old—quite capable of fixing a simple meal for a dinner date.

A date. That's what this was. Despite what she had told Jason and Mr. Shaw, Aaron was no long-lost cousin. He was a big, powerful, gorgeous male specimen that made her feel even smaller than five feet tall and caused her armpits to sweat.

And nothing and no one ever made her armpits sweat.

Chloe threw the bag of shrimp into a pot of water and turned the burner on high. She'd seen her brothers boil shrimp and crawdads enough times to know how they were prepared. The potatoes were arranged in a ceramic bowl then placed in the microwave. Thirty minutes ought to do it. Still plenty of time to set the table and complete her personal toilette before the arrival of her gentleman caller. Another of Grandmère's endearing expressions. Chloe giggled, giddy with the thought of seeing Aaron. Although she couldn't stop the notion she was a child playing house, she was enjoying herself. It was the start of an independent, career-woman lifestyle.

Chloe found no placemats or linen napkins in Sara's drawers, so paper towels would have to suffice for both purposes. At least they sported a border of pink flowers and green vines instead of plain white. Sara's selection of dishes and flatware also proved disappointing. Martha Stewart would not be pleased. She hadn't expected bone china, delicate crystal and sterling silverware, but two matching dinner plates would've been nice. The apartment's only cups advertised the family restaurant where Sara worked.

Chloe set out the bizarre assortment then replaced the dead flowers with cut magnolia from a street vendor. The overall effect was rather pretty after she scattered flower petals across their plates on the window ledge and lit the sole candle.

Opening the shower taps, she let the water heat. A warm shower on her stiff back and shoulders would feel wonderful after standing on her feet all day. Just as she began peeling off her damp clothes, a sharp knock on her back door jarred her attention.

She re-buttoned her sweaty blouse and opened the door, praying Aaron hadn't arrived early. He hadn't. It was Jeanette Peteriere, Grandmère's housekeeper, whom Chloe had thought of three times during the last hour.

"Jeanette! How in the world did you find me?"

The birdlike elderly woman stared with a peevish glower.

"All these months without as much as a greeting card and that's all you have to say, Chloe?" Her tone took no prisoners, despite her tiny size.

"Sorry." Chloe sighed. "Come in, please. I am happy to see you." She pulled the woman into a crushing embrace. She was happy to see Jeanette, who'd been with the family since before Chloe was born. She loved her as much as Grandmère, but discovering her on the stoop had left Chloe feeling both nervous and somehow embarrassed.

"It was like pulling molars to get Miz Galen to tell me where you were," Jeanette said. She marched across the kitchen, setting her brocade pocketbook on the counter. Jeanette would always carry a pocketbook, never a purse or handbag. Chloe spotted her sniffing the air suspiciously.

"I can't believe Mama knows where I am," Chloe said, then remembered the tow truck. The driver had known exactly where to find the leased vehicle.

"Your mama can find out where the president hides his girly magazines if she wants. There's no stopping that woman when she's on a mission."

"*C'est vrai,*" Chloe mumbled her brother Ethan's favorite expression. "I just can't believe she's interested. She told me I could go live in a cardboard box, for all she cared."

Jeanette snorted. "Ma petite. You still know nothing even after your expensive college education." Jeanette sniffed again and wrinkled her nose. "Your mama loves you and your brothers very much, but doesn't show it how you would like." She walked to the window overlooking the alley then dragged a finger through the dust on the glass. Chloe saw her nose crinkle again.

"I just moved in, Jeanette. I haven't had time to clean." She felt annoyed defending the place, but compelled nevertheless. "Classes start next week, plus I'm working at an art gallery in the Quarter." She swiped at the dirty window with her dishtowel when Jeanette turned away. "Isn't that great?" she asked, desperate for the woman's approval. "I got a job." The dusty pane turned into a streaky mess.

Chloe's expectation of praise was short lived. Jeanette had already marched from the kitchen into the living room. Chloe found her clutching an Ole Miss sweatshirt up to her nose.

"Sweet Lord in heaven," Jeanette said in English, to make

sure Chloe understood. "Have you ever washed this thing?" She held the garment at arm's length.

"Not recently, but I will." Chloe reached for it, but Jeanette snapped it back and stuffed it into a black plastic bag that had materialized from nowhere.

"You brought your own garbage bag?" Chloe asked, utterly flabbergasted.

Jeanette narrowed her dark, almond eyes. "I've visited your dorm rooms in the past, remember?" She moved around the room efficiently, picking up clothes from the floor, bed and the backs of chairs. She performed her patented sniff-test and stuffed any offenders into her bag.

Chloe found it hard to get mad at someone who once changed her diapers, but was starting to. "Jeanette. What are you doing? You work for Grandmère, and she doesn't live here." She blocked Jeanette's path with hands fisted on her hips.

The older woman pushed past Chloe into the bathroom, using the bag as a battering ram. She snatched towels from the shower rod, the mat from the floor, even the tiny window curtain, leaving the room devoid of anything washable.

"Please, stop," Chloe demanded, placing her hands firmly on Jeanette's shoulders. "You probably took the streetcar here. I won't let you drag this heavy bag home on a crowded streetcar." The mental picture filled Chloe with shame.

"And I'll not have you wearing dirty clothes!" Jeanette snatched a sweater from the bathroom door hook, then held it to her nose." Her eyes rounded with extreme pique. "Did you take up smoking? This smells like an ashtray!"

"Of course not, but some places I go to still allow smoking." Chloe tried to wrestle the sweater away without any luck. Jeanette jammed the sweater in with the rest.

"You better not start, or I'll give you a kicking butt." Jeanette marched toward the front door, picking up more garments along the way. Most of which belonged to Sara.

"I think you mean a butt-kicking, Jeanette," Chloe said, trying to hide her laughter. "Who in the world taught you that expression? Ethan? He's a bad influence on you."

"Don't sass me. You understand my meaning. And you should call your brother since you still remember his name. He and Cora are worried sick about you. He's got that M'sieu Price watching out for you."

"What?" Chloe stopped laughing. "Ethan has a private detective spying on me?"

Whatever retort Jeanette had intended was lost as the ninety-pound dynamo swept open the door and rammed her laundry bag into a much larger person. "Oomph," she sputtered, staggering backward. She glared up at the man on the stoop. "Who are you?" she demanded.

Chloe glanced quickly into her date's amused face. "This is Aaron Porter, Jeanette."

"That tells me nothing," Jeanette scolded. "Who are you, Aaron Porter?" She clutched her pocketbook tighter to her chest.

Aaron stepped forward. "I am Miss Galen's guest for dinner, ma'am."

"Guest for dinner? The only thing Chloe can cook is instant oatmeal." Her eyes assessed him suspiciously.

"I love oatmeal. May I help you with that bag?"

"No," Jeanette snapped, tightening her grip on the laundry. "Who are you really?"

"He's a friend," Chloe said to Jeanette. Then added to Aaron, "This is Jeanette Peteriere. She's my . . . ahh . . . grandmother." Chloe didn't wish to explain that her family had on payroll a housekeeper, full cleaning staff, a gardener and a chauffeur for Grandmère. That didn't jive with her current digs.

Jeanette's mouth dropped open as she stared at Chloe.

Aaron looked from the diminutive, ebony-skinned woman to

the especially pale Chloe, noticing for the first time she wore only a big shirt. Her hair stood on end as though she'd put her finger into an electrical outlet. Suppressing a laugh, he extended his hand. "How do you do, ma'am. I'm pleased to meet you."

"Hello," Jeanette said, then turned on Chloe. "What are you talking about, ma petite? What's wrong with you? Have you been drinking?" She sniffed the air again, this time near Chloe's mouth.

"No," Chloe answered, then looked at Aaron. "I mean this is my grandmother's dearest friend, Mrs. Peteriere, who dotes on me so much, I forget which one is blood kin." Chloe wrestled the bag away from Jeanette, who didn't give it up without a fight. "I'll not have you dragging this heavy bag and that's final. If you insist on taking my laundry, send Ethan for the bag with his car. And only this once. I'll go to one of those laundrymatics after I get paid next Thursday."

Jeanette finally surrendered the laundry and focused on Chloe's outfit. "It's called a Laundromat, and if this man is only a friend, perhaps you should've finished getting dressed," she hissed.

For the first time, Chloe realized she was standing outdoors in nothing but a thin shirt, desperately in need of a shower and some makeup. Her expression and confidence plummeted.

Jeanette stretched up to kiss Chloe's forehead affectionately. "Go take a bath. You stink, m'amie." She turned and marched down the steps, her clunky orthopedic shoes raising a racket. "Enjoy your oatmeal, M'sieu," she called over her shoulder.

With the maelstrom of Jeanette gone, Chloe became painfully aware she had almost nothing on. And she did smell a little funny. "Sorry, Aaron. My unexpected visitor arrived as I was about to shower. Come in. Make yourself comfortable. I'll be quick about it."

Aaron looked from the top of Chloe's head to her bare toes,

trying not to linger on the interesting outline in between. "No problem. I'm in no hurry," he said, opening the door. He presented her with a grocery sack with a two-foot-long loaf of bread sticking out the top.

"What's all this? I got dinner perfectly handled."

"My aunt insisted that I not arrive empty-handed. I didn't know your menu, so I brought a bottle of red, one white and a six-pack. It's not all for tonight. Don't think I'm trying to get you drunk."

Chloe took the sack reluctantly and headed into the kitchen with Aaron on her heels. Billows of steam poured from beneath the lid on the clattering shrimp pot. "I think our shrimp are done," she announced, hurrying toward the stove.

"Whoa, Chloe. That baby's hot." In the nick of time, Aaron's hand grasped hers as she was about to lift the metal lid. "Where are your potholders?"

"I don't know. I just moved in," she said, aware of his close proximity in the small kitchen. His spicy aftershave smelled much better than the cooking aromas. She began opening cupboards, revealing a few canned goods and the art supplies she'd stashed to make the room look presentable.

Aaron scratched his chin. "Usually they're close to the stove." He pulled a ragged mitt from the first drawer. "Here we go," he said.

"I'll take that." Chloe reached for it, but he snapped it back.

"This is man's work. Where's your colander?"

"My what?" she asked, brushing damp hair from her forehead. The temperature in the kitchen must be over a hundred humid degrees.

"A colander, a strainer, a sieve, that round thing with a million holes. Come on, work with me here. These babies are ready to go." Aaron turned off the burner and pushed open the window. Stream poured out through the patched screen.

"Oh, that thing. Why didn't you say so?" Chloe said, flushing from the heat and embarrassment. She pulled the bent utensil from a lower cabinet. "I . . . just never called it that."

"Must be an Atlanta thing," Aaron said easily. He set the colander in the sink and deftly dumped in the shrimp.

Both peered through the steam at the grayish mass of shriveled crustaceans. "Good grief, you bought shrimp with their heads still on!" Aaron said. "They don't even sell them like that back home. I always buy peeled and deveined, ready to cook."

"Well, you ain't in Georgia anymore, boy. These are the real McCoy," Chloe said, but the real McCoys looked a little scary with limp antennae, dislodged shells and clinging bits of unidentified gray matter.

"Ahhuh. Why don't you finish getting ready, while I'll melt some butter for these babies."

"I don't have any . . ." Chloe paused, remembering she hadn't checked her potatoes. She pulled the bowl from the microwave and stared at six redskin potatoes the size and color of prunes. "Oh, dear. I guess thirty minutes was too long." Tears filled her eyes, but she blinked them back. Independent career women of the twenty-first century didn't cry over burned meals like women on old TV sitcoms.

"Nonsense. They're perfect. I'll just dice them up and mix with the crabmeat my aunt made me bring. Never show up empty-handed, she always says. Go on, Chloe. No reason why I can't put the finishing touches on dinner." He grinned at her.

"Well, if you insist. I'll just be a few minutes. She had no choice but to slink away since the hot kitchen made her shirt stick to her damp chest and accentuated the fact she wasn't wearing a bra. She didn't like feeling exposed to a man she barely knew.

Chloe stepped into the shower, anxious for the warm water to relieve the stiffness in her shoulders and wash away her anxiety over the meal.

Ice cold. Leaving the water run had been a mistake. How big was the hot water tank here? Five gallons? She shivered as she lathered up then washed her hair in record time. At least the cool water lowered her body temperature that seemed to rise around Aaron. She dressed in a mint green tank dress and sandals, allowing her hair to dry naturally. Without her gel and blow dryer, she would resemble Little Orphan Annie with a mass of tight curls, but she refused to keep Aaron waiting while she primped.

The look would be appropriate, considering her present financial situation.

When she reappeared fifteen minutes later, the kitchen felt cooler. The shrimp waited on a platter, her bag salad mounded in a bowl and the bread sliced into uniform pieces. Aaron sat by the window ledge, sipping something from a Zippy glass.

He gave her an appraising look when she entered. "You look very nice, Ms. Galen. Green becomes you." He lifted his glass in salute.

She laughed. "Becomes me? Nobody says that stuff anymore." She slipped into the chair at the other end of the ledge.

"They don't? What a shame. People should in situations like this." He poured some wine into the other Zippy glass. "I opened the white, since we're having seafood. That's what people still do, isn't it?" His left dimple deepened as he grinned.

"White is fine." Chloe peered at the shrimp. They didn't look too bad with their body armor and appendages removed. "Thanks for finishing dinner. Jeanette's visit caught me by surprise."

"Glad to help. I didn't find any butter so I used the extra virgin olive oil I brought for dipping the bread in. Sophie's idea. Don't give me any credit." He stretched his long legs out to the side. "I wonder what the difference is between regular virgin and extra virgin?" He winked with mischief.

She chose to ignore the innuendo. "I know nothing about olive oil, but if your Aunt Sophie is anything like Jeanette, you had no choice but to bring the stuff. Thanks."

"I'd say the two of them would make a formidable pair if they ever got together. Oh, I found your salad, but I didn't find any dressing," Aaron said, helping himself to a piece of bread.

"Dressing?" Chloe asked, sipping her wine. Things like butter or salad dressing hadn't occurred to her at the French Market.

"You know . . . French, Italian, blue cheese."

"I know what dressing is. I just don't think salad needs it." She plucked a leaf of romaine from the bowl and popped it into her mouth. "Delicious. Anything added would mask the delicate flavor."

"You're absolutely right," Aaron said, scooping a hefty quantity into his bowl and a smaller portion into hers. "We'll eat it naked as nature intended." A dimple on the right side of his face surfaced.

Chloe spooned the shrimp and the crabmeat-potato side dish onto their plates. She tentatively nibbled a shrimp. It was rather tough, but edible. The crab concoction tasted exquisite. "This stuff your aunt sent along is really quite good, but I'm curious about those little hard things she seasoned it with." She ate another forkful with relish.

"What little hard things?" Aaron studied his plate closely.

"Those right there." She pointed out a dark morsel with her knife tip then watched him suppress a smile.

"Those are your potatoes, Chloe."

"I didn't know you would cut them up so small." Her face flamed, her throat went dry. Her little redskins could be fired as buckshot. She took another sip of wine, wishing she'd ordered pizza and saved her culinary debut for a night at home with Sara.

"I think everything's delicious." He added another helping of shrimp to his plate.

"Oh, I forgot our asparagus. Excuse me a moment," she said softly. She walked to the fridge as though this were an elegant dinner party, instead of two people eating in a cramped kitchen with red rooster wallpaper and checkered linoleum.

She set the plate of spears on the table. At least, she had washed and trimmed the ends before Jeanette's interruption.

He studied them then slid half onto his plate. She watched aghast as he tried to saw through a spear with his bread knife to no avail.

"Let me try your knife, Chloe. It might be sharper." He endeavored again, but had no better luck.

"What's wrong?" she asked. The asparagus looked perfectly fine to her.

"I don't know how to ask this, but did you cook these before chilling?"

She arched her back and lifted her chin. "I'm serving them tonight like cauliflower or broccoli, you know, crudités."

"All righty then," he said, attacking the spear with renewed vigor. Finally, he severed the tough stalk into chewable pieces. Chewable, that is, if you took all evening, but Aaron persevered.

He was about to tackle his second spear, when Chloe pulled his plate from him. "Enough with the asparagus. Let's just eat the rest of the food." She felt her eyes tear up again, but this time couldn't stop them. "I didn't know they had to be cooked. I didn't know how long to nuke potatoes, and I've never boiled shrimp in my life," she sobbed, feeling very juvenile with her outbreak. "There you have it. This is the first dinner I ever made, and I really wanted it to be special."

If he'd laughed, even chuckled, she would've whacked him with the bread loaf, then showed him the door.

But he didn't. He reached across the makeshift table and

covered her hand with his. "It is special. I'm happy as a clam at this moment and very glad you invited me. Now if you don't mind, I'm going to polish off the rest of the shrimp. I love it."

She wiped her face with her pink-bordered paper towel then broke off another piece of bread. "Yeah, that came out pretty good, if I do say so myself."

"You may, and I agree."

But it wasn't his words that lifted her spirits and her heart. It was the fact he ate everything on his plate. Each overdone shrimp, all his undressed salad, even every spear of raw asparagus. A truer compliment had never been paid.

She glanced at him over the rim of her glass. This Aaron Porter from Atlanta, Georgia was a really nice man. Perhaps the last of a dying breed of perfect gentlemen. She'd run into few thus far.

Maybe he was too nice. What would he say if he knew she had beat the pledges in a sorority chugging contest? Or that she'd been arrested for disorderly conduct? Twice.

Nice boys only marry nice girls. The scornful words of Clotilde Galen echoed in her ears as she watched Aaron carry their plates to the sink. She had laughed at her mother during that particularly nasty fight. Marriage, a family, the whole hearth-and-home thing, wasn't something she ever wanted.

The world was a playground—she had her art, her friends and plenty of money for fun. Men were part of the fun, but nothing more. Aaron wasn't a man who would've interested her in the past. Too serious, too honest, too organized. For crying out loud, he was washing their dishes in the sink and they hadn't even crusted over yet.

He wouldn't have been interested in her either if they'd met at Henderson College or Ole Miss. For some reason, Chloe felt saddened by that realization. She felt like a liar or a cheat. This is who she was now. She had no desire to behave the old way again. And it was for her sake, not because Clotilde wanted it.

But if Aaron knew about her past, would he stick around? Probably not.

So for that reason and many others, she'd better not grow too attached to Mr. Atlanta's attentions.

She wanted nothing to miss when he was gone.

CHAPTER FOUR

Aaron studied his aunt over his first coffee of the morning as she bustled around the kitchen. Although the room looked like chaos, she moved with honed efficiency as pancakes, bacon, grits and sweet rolls all finished at the same time. Charlie loved a big breakfast before going to work, and nothing Aaron could say kept her from cooking for him, too. He ate some pancakes and bacon, remembering Chloe's dinner the previous night.

Not quite the same poetry-in-motion, but a relaxed and comfortable meal nevertheless. Probably the fact she was the most attractive woman he'd met in some time had improved the taste of the food. He'd been surprised to discover her ineptness in the kitchen. Serving asparagus raw? The girls he'd grown up with could at least put on a better act than that. Her waif-like figure suggested perhaps food wasn't high on her list of priorities.

Despite the rubbery shrimp, burned-beyond-recognition potatoes and unadorned lettuce, he couldn't remember a more enjoyable evening. Chloe laughed spontaneously and chatted with abandon, without artifice or pretense. It felt good to be around her. And it had nothing to do with her pretty face or figure. She was honest, down-to-earth, and sincere. There were more important things in life than eating, and Chloe Galen had the rest sown up tight.

In his beloved aunt and uncle's home, he often felt alien and stifled. Their middle-class domesticity didn't appeal to him. He had never longed for lawn mowers, swing sets in the backyard, or shopping for driveway patch on sale. Yet, Chloe's dinner on mismatched plates and advertisement glassware had wormed a place next to his heart. Maybe it reminded him of the tiny kitchen of his childhood, before they'd moved in with Uncle Charlie. They might have been poor, but his mother had done her best to provide a home for them. She had loved him.

And she'd been the last woman he had allowed to.

One thing bothered him about last night. When he'd hunted for salad dressing, he'd been shocked to discover their cupboard so bare. Old Mother Hubbard would've felt right at home at Chloe and Sara's. The refrigerator and pantry didn't contain enough food to keep mice alive. What did those women live on? Maybe Sara brought leftovers home from the restaurant where she worked, but considering the way Chloe devoured her beignets in the French Market, Sara didn't bring home much. He pondered how to improve their situation without insulting Chloe's dignity and strong will.

Hey Chloe, did you know they're running a two-for-one on canned goods at the salvage dock? Or perhaps, the food stamp office is open late on Thursdays . . . need a ride? Or maybe, aren't you taking this starving-artist thing a little too seriously? Here's fifty bucks. Buy some food.

"This case got you stumped, son? You're sucking on an empty cup." Uncle Charlie broke through Aaron's worries about Chloe.

"Among other things," he answered. "Good morning, Charlie." He rose to refill his cup at the carafe. He had time enough for one more before heading downtown.

"What've you found out? Anything new since your last briefing?" Charlie loaded his plate with everything his wife prepared, while she beamed as though she'd won the blue ribbon in a cooking competition.

"I've found no proof yet, but I'm certain La Bella is at the heart of this forgery ring. Maybe they're an innocent bystander duped into reselling fakes as originals, but I doubt it. And I saw a professor from Leporte the other day, paying a call on Shaw. An art professor. You think he was there to buy paintings on a teacher's salary?"

"Perhaps the man's independently wealthy, teaching young artists for altruistic reasons," Charlie said. He always loved to play devil's advocate, same as his nephew. "That's why I work as a cop in Orleans." He laughed his belly laugh, until Sophie smacked him with her spatula.

"Maybe so, but I'll look into his financial background. We'll know how altruistic he is then. He knows Chloe, too. He's one of her teachers. I don't like that."

"This Chloe, she your connection to La Bella? The one you had dinner with last night?"

"Yeah," Aaron said, wishing he hadn't brought her up. He carried his plate and cup to the sink.

"I packed your share of the crawfish étouffée up for your lunch. You can heat it in the precinct microwave," Sophie said with satisfaction.

"How did that dinner go? You came in pretty late last night, *n'est pas?*"

"No, I don't agree. And I'm not sure why you're keeping tabs on a nearly thirty-year-old man." Aaron tried his best to keep his tone non-confrontational, but he was unaccustomed to anyone keeping tabs on him.

Charlie smiled. "Easy, boy. You've got no curfew here. We were just curious about the young lady you had dinner with. Is she pretty like my Sophie?" He reached to pat his wife's arm.

Aaron looked from his uncle's weathered face to his aunt's blushing one, then smiled. "Not by half. Anyway, she's an informant, remember? You've a few on the New Orleans payroll yourself."

"Sure, son, whatever you say," Charlie said, eating hurriedly. "Can I ride with you to the station? Your aunt needs the car today. Unless you're on your way to see your unattractive informant, in which case I'll hop the streetcar."

Aaron flashed his uncle a warning, but the man was too busy filling a sack with sweet rolls for his coffee break. "Ride with me, Charlie. I haven't been badgered about my personal life in what . . . eight years?" He took the brown paper bag from Sophie. It had to weigh at least five pounds.

"Not because we haven't wanted to. You gotta come home more, boy. Your aunt and I grow bored and lonely in this big old house."

"Get another dog."

Charlie clucked his tongue. "It wouldn't be the same."

The research into Professor Sam Graziano's financial life proved inconclusive. He wasn't poor, yet the trail of deposits into investment and bank accounts wasn't out of line with his salary and benefits from the University. Which wasn't to say cash transactions hadn't been carried out of the country in duffel bags, secreted in Cayman or Bahamian accounts away from the reach of the IRS. An educated man like Graziano would know all about paper trails and wouldn't leave an unexplainable one behind.

The financial picture of Kurt Shaw, however, was far more complex. It would take a team of extraordinary forensic accountants to follow the maze of transactions, corporate trust arrangements and business deals he'd set up. Aaron knew this wasn't how he would catch this fish on the hook. The source had to be the professor, probably the mastermind of the operation, someone who knew exactly how art could be faked. Dr. Graziano, from the illustrious Leporte University, was at the heart of this.

He just hoped sweet Chloe Galen didn't get dragged into the mess. He didn't like the lecherous way Shaw looked at her, or the patronizing way Graziano treated her. Maybe he was imagining both things, since whenever Chloe came into the picture, he seemed to lose his objectivity.

That wouldn't help him get the job done one bit.

And that's why he came back to town.

Chloe had little time to ponder whether last night was a complete disaster or the most enjoyable six hours she'd ever spent. Aaron had buzzed a kiss across her head and left the apartment with a "Thanks for the great grub" over his shoulder. Then she'd fallen asleep within minutes of her head hitting the pillow.

Great grub. He'd been kidding, of course. The entire evening Aaron had amused and entertained her, but today, lugging her heavy backpack from the streetcar stop, all thoughts of a warm, attractive man were long gone. Did her last class have to be on the opposite end of campus from her advisor's office? After she'd completed the transfer paperwork and enrolled in sophomore classes, her advisor insisted she stop in today to pick up course requirements toward her degree. She hadn't walked this much in years and knew she'd better eat bigger lunches or start buying clothes in the children's department.

She banged her way into Dr. Graziano's office, almost upsetting a potted plant with her overstuffed pack.

"Jason!"

"Chloe! What are you doing here?" They both asked simultaneously then laughed. "You first," Jason said, looking cool and collected in a loose shirt tucked into his slim pants.

"Dr. Graziano is my advisor. He told me to stop by for my course selections for the next two years."

"Of course. So you really did enroll. I wasn't sure how much you told me was true the other night and how much was bullshit, like that guy being your cousin." His tone was icy, controlled.

Chloe felt his blue eyes bore holes into her torso. "He is my cousin. I just don't know him that well." She set her pack on the chair and wiped her forehead with her arm. "Now it's your turn."

He looked momentarily confused, then relaxed back in his chair. "I'm Dr. Graziano's graduate assistant. I work for him. My own class load is pretty light these days."

"Wow. You're his assistant?" Chloe's astonishment was apparent.

"That surprises you, Chlo? You don't think I'm talented enough to assist the department head?" His tone had turned soft, but deadly calm.

Who was this guy? "No," she drawled out the word. "I thought they only picked people who've actually graduated for the coveted position, that's all. What's with you, Jason? You got a bug up your butt?"

With that question, he laughed. "Yeah, I caught one in the Quarter the other night at Chaz's. Know a cure?"

"How 'bout a tequila suppository?"

"Only if you'll administer."

Dr. Graziano appeared in the doorway as Chloe erupted into a fit of giggles. "Miss Galen? I have your course selections done. Mr. Hightower will print off a copy for you."

Chloe tried her best to compose herself, but the professor looked dubiously from one of them to the other.

"Is something funny, Miss Galen? I can use a good laugh today myself."

"No sir, not really. Mr. Hightower and I have known each other from high school. We were just reminiscing."

Dr. Graziano looked from her to Jason with his tentative

smile fading. "Is that right? Well, you better not miss any class time or assignments this year, young lady. You know what they say, three strikes and you're out." He walked back into his office and closed the door.

Jason shook his head. "Don't worry about him. He's got some administrative problems. Are your classes over for the day? 'Cause I'm done here." He switched off his computer. His new, smooth mode had returned. "Why don't you come check out my new place? I'd love to show you some of my recent work, then you can judge for yourself if I'm worthy of the professor's high regard."

"Sure I'll come, if you lighten up. When did your skin get so thin?"

He grabbed her backpack from the chair then opened the door. "When this redheaded wench left town and broke my heart. Many years ago."

She glanced up to find him grinning, so she began to relax. She wouldn't mind renewing their friendship; she could use some pointers on performance and presentation expectations, but something about this new, sophisticated Jason made her nervous.

They drove to Metairie in his sleek Saab well over the speed limit. Chloe clung to the door handle as she studied Jason from the corner of her eye. Besides driving the expensive sedan, he wore a diamond-encrusted watch, and his silky pants and tailored shirt weren't knockoffs from the men's warehouse. No sweatshirts, jeans and sneakers on this college boy anymore. But it was his home that had Chloe scratching her head—a gorgeously restored loft in old Metairie—that should've been way out of his price range.

"I don't remember a graduate assistant to a department head making much money." She turned slowly around in the center of his living room, observing everything with an artist's eye.

Antiques had been mixed with contemporary pieces with a style only a professional decorator could pull off. "This is very nice," she said.

"Thanks," he called from the kitchen. "How 'bout some wine?"

"I prefer something non-alcoholic." She walked to a bank of windows overlooking the ornate crypts and lush gardens of Metairie Cemetery. The light in the room would be fantastic to work by, yet she spotted no easels or worktables.

Jason reappeared carrying two flutes, ignoring her request for something non-spirituous. "Champagne?" she asked, spotting the bubbles.

"A celebration. Chloe Galen has come back to town." He downed half his glass. "With her tail between her legs, but she's come back nonetheless."

She set her glass on a table. "If you'll notice, there's no tail between my legs. I've come back to town with my head held high, ready to start a new life."

"Hear, hear." He finished the contents of his glass. "Twenty years old and reinventing herself for the third time."

They used to spar in the past, tease each other mercilessly, yet now it didn't feel quite comfortable. "Tell me how you afford this place, Jason. I've got an inquiring mind."

"The academic world still pays nothing. I may want the credentials, but I'm not interested in being an art professor like Sam my whole life." He refilled his glass, then handed Chloe hers. "Taking a group of sophomores to Paris to view the Masters just to fund your own trip doesn't sound like fun to me," he said, cynicism sharpening his words. "I sold a couple paintings to department patrons to afford the place."

"I thought you would wait for your first one-man exhibition after graduation." She took a small sip from her flute.

"Hell with waiting. I'm not waiting for things anymore." He

walked back into the kitchen. "Let's eat. I'm starving. I've got cold pizza and leftover nachos."

At least some things about Jason Hightower hadn't changed. Chloe slipped onto a stool at his counter. "Me, too. Lay it out, buddy."

The two of them ate companionably with only small talk about Sara and other mutual friends between bites. Chloe felt herself relax as she sipped more champagne and studied him curiously. Jason looked more attractive than he had in high school. His freckles had faded into an even tan and he'd lightened his reddish hair into a streaky blond. He was still thin, but sinewy muscles had replaced his former scrawniness. She saw why Sara's mouth had dropped open when she'd seen him again. Sara had found the old Jason attractive for some inexplicable reason and the new irresistible.

With his pizza finished, Jason slanted her a sly gaze. "You look good, Chloe, better and better all the time." He trailed his fingers down her spine.

The compliment and his touch unnerved her. Not so much the words, but his inflection. She had no desire to go another round with his subtle, but relentless sexual overtures again. And they didn't seem as harmless coming from the new-and-improved version.

"Would you mind driving me to the Quarter?" she asked, moving out of reach.

"Why? I've got anything you need right here." His laugh rang hollow as he refilled both their glasses.

"No more for me. I need to get to work."

With eyebrows raised, he paused in mid-refill. "Work?"

"I took a job at La Bella Gallery."

"You're kidding, right?"

"I'm not. I must work. My delightful mother cut me off, remember?"

"I can't believe you're working there. So far from campus and all."

"What else can I do? Art is the only thing I know. I can't even get a job flipping burgers," she said, remembering her disaster of a dinner party last night.

"Take my advice, Chlo, patch things up with Clotilde. Having no money has nothing going for it—that much I know. Say whatever Mama-Bitch wants to hear to get restored to her good graces. What happens if she dies with you on her bad side? She could leave everything to your brothers."

Chloe stared at him. Even if her mother wasn't her favorite person at the moment, she resented him speaking so cavalierly of her death. "I'm not worried about my inheritance. And stop talking about my mom dying. I don't like it."

"You should worry about your inheritance. The oldest way to get money is still, by far, the best. Inherit it."

"What about earning it? What about my artistic talent?" She faced him defiantly, her temper flaring. "You used to say I had a real gift."

"Cool off. I think you have talent, plenty more than the trash I see come through the department these days. But good artists still line up downtown selling their plasma to pay the bills. Things haven't changed much in the last couple hundred years. Renoir, Monet, Manet—all would tell you the same thing if they could—poverty sucks. If you don't believe anything else I tell you, trust me on this one."

"My, you've grown skeptical since we last parted," she said softly, missing her old friend despite the fact he stood before her.

He set his glass down then tipped up her chin with one finger. "I'll give you a little time, sweet thing. You'll come round to my thinking soon enough, or more likely, go running back to Mommy Dearest."

She pulled her face away. "I don't think so."

He stared at her with an expression of pity as he picked up his keys. "I'll take you to work, Chlo. I've got business in the Quarter anyway."

Jason headed toward the door, leaving Chloe to trail after trying to figure out what happened to their pleasant lunch and how she managed to anger him. She didn't like the new Jason at the moment.

Halfway across town, she decided not to let the matter drop. "What happened to you, Jason, while I was away? Whatever happened to the guy who said, and I quote, 'Some people will sell their souls along with their art to make a dime, but not me.' "

He laughed with gusto. "I said that? Good God, what a jerk I was. No wonder you wouldn't let me in your pants." His laughter this time sounded brittle.

"You did say it, and I agreed with you. I still do, as a matter of fact."

"Then you're a jerk, plain and simple."

"Oh, yeah? Then you can forget about ever getting into my pants," she teased, growing again uncomfortable in the confining car.

He glanced over the top of his sunglasses. "I've lived without that particular taste-treat so far, I guess I can manage for the rest of my life." His focus returned to the heavy traffic on Airline Drive. "Your know, Chloe my girl, someday you'll come into your trust account or trust fund, or whatever they call those things. Then you won't worry about working in some tourist trap or even selling your precious watercolors. But the rest of your classmates will still be scraping together a down payment for some tacky three-bedroom dogtrot while trying to pay off student loans. When that happens, I want you to remember your haughty attitude right now and give me a call. In the meantime, shut the hell up."

Chloe did as instructed, mumbling only a quick "thanks" before she jumped out of his car in front of La Bella. She couldn't wait to get away from him. She knew part of what he said might be true, but when did he become so judgmental? She couldn't help being born into her particular family, any more than anyone else. Sara could keep Jason with her blessings, especially since intense conversation wasn't what Sara was after.

Chloe soon forgot her temperamental friend once inside La Bella. It was hopping with customers and many actually looked like they could afford what the shop offered. Mr. Shaw buzzed around like a hornet, explaining provenance, periods of style, and finance arrangements. A long-legged woman of around thirty hovered nearby, flashing a bright smile and tossing her blond hair. Chloe had seen her before, but Mr. Shaw had never bothered to introduce them. She apparently was his assistant, since her knowledge of early twentieth-century oils was far superior to Chloe's own.

Chloe had been relegated to holding coats and stashing wet umbrellas as customers entered the gallery. She knew very little about Fritzches other than she loved them, and they happened to be the hot topic lately with collectors. Two of Shaw's acquisitions had been reframed and hung under proper lightening on the gallery's feature wall. She wandered into the back room where the other two awaited the re-framer's handiwork. Picking up a magnifier lying nearby, Chloe examined the texture of the background for insight into Fritzche's masterful layering technique. Chloe spotted something in the cloudy sky of the landscape that astounded her. She held a light closer to confirm her suspicion—the painting had been recently repaired—and not very expertly. Brush strokes and a slightly different surface texture could be discerned upon close inspection. She examined the canvas from every angle, hoping to be wrong.

She peeked back into the gallery, anxious to alert Shaw, but not wishing to alarm customers about to purchase another piece from the collection. "Mr. Shaw," she whispered when she spotted him.

"Chloe, there you are. I'd wondered where you had disappeared. Heat up that other tray of canapés and open two more bottles of Cabernet." He turned on his heel like a dancer, eager to return to potential buyers.

"I need to talk to you, sir," she said, stepping into the doorway.

He glanced back with a frown. "Not now, Chloe. Can't you see the place is filled with customers? Get the wine," he snapped and returned to his clients with an artificial smile on his face.

Chloe did as she was told, doling out canapés and refilling wineglasses until she thought the crowd must be too drunk to write a check. At least two hours passed before the place cleared of well-dressed, expensive smelling senior citizens, leaving behind wadded napkins and empty glasses on every available antique surface.

Shaw disappeared into his office and Chloe followed close behind. She heard voices heated in argument—one female, one male—as she lifted her hand to knock. She decided instead to listen.

"They are in perfect condition, Alicia. And now, appropriately framed. I'm sure you'll verify my price of one-ten for the larger two and ninety-four for the two smaller works."

"You're dreaming, Kurt. Even if I sign off on these, what makes you think the buyers won't seek another appraisal once they get back home? They're from Connecticut. You know how those New York City suburbanites think they're superior to everyone else."

"If you had dropped your friends' names from the auction house they think so highly of, they wouldn't even consider paying for another appraisal."

"I've no intention of overusing my contacts and annoying high-placed acquaintances. I may want to move north if things here get too dull."

Her tone baited and teased. Chloe yearned to crack open the door.

"You think I'm getting dull, do you?"

The subsequent noises indicated the negative. What was going on in there?

"No," she said, "but I'm not burning any bridges. I made that mistake in Baton Rouge, and you know what they say about once burned."

Chloe pressed her ear firmly against the door and heard what could only be kissing. Oh, for heaven's sake. She rapped lightly on the door. "Mr. Shaw? Are you in there? I need to speak with you, sir."

A full minute passed before the door opened and her flushed boss appeared. "What is it, Chloe? New customers?" His gray hair was definitely mussed.

"Hello," Chloe said, addressing the woman patting down her own coiffure. "I'm Chloe Galen." She flashed her debutant smile.

"Ah, yes," Kurt said, stepping aside. "Chloe, this is Alicia Pierce, the gallery's appraiser. Alicia, this is Chloe Galen. She just started working part-time after class."

"Appraiser?" Chloe asked. "I thought she was your assistant."

"No," he drawled. "That's who you are supposed to be," Shaw said, his patience dwindling.

Alicia laughed, a low, throaty sound. "Well, I'll leave you two to hammer out job descriptions. Nice meeting you, Chloe." She tossed back her enviable hair and slipped from Shaw's office.

Shaw watched her go then exhaled an exaggerated sigh. "All right. You have my undivided attention. What did you want you ask me?" He looked down his patrician nose with forced composure.

"The Fritzches. They've been repaired, and not particularly well either." She looked up, expecting laurels for her astute observations. She gazed instead into a stony face.

"What are you talking about?" Shaw picked lint off his impeccable dark suit.

"The clouds and some of the sky have been retouched or whatever you call it. And I believe some of the waves in the foreground have been, too." She waited for his reaction since her discovery could save the gallery—and Shaw's reputation—much grief.

"Chloe, Chloe. You have much to learn." His thin smile didn't reach his eyes. "You might be a budding new artist, filled with love for the creative process, but this is the business end of the art world." His hand gesture took in the cluttered, but elegant, office. "This is how things are done. Minor repairs—enhancements as we prefer to call them—will make no difference to the collector who wishes to hang a Fritzche above his fireplace."

She started to interrupt, but he held up a hand. "But it makes a very big difference to a small gallery like ours, struggling to stay alive. I must compete with other galleries, the major auction houses, and now that damned online auction site." He plucked one last piece of lint from his sleeve. "If someone repaired the Fritzche before selling it to me, I have no choice but to resell it in the presumed condition. Or else, I would take a very substantial, potentially fatal, loss." He made eye contact with her at last. "Do you understand a little better how things work, my dear?"

She blinked while considering her options. She could tell him what she thought of selling repaired artwork as "perfect," as she heard him describe the piece.

Or she could storm out the front door, declaring she could

never work in a place with questionable ethics.

Or she could keep her mouth shut.

The memory of Sara's empty refrigerator without even leftovers from last night's supper crept back. Maybe Jason was right. Maybe she should grow up. Maybe she should start now to avoid looking for another job quite so soon.

She swallowed with a tight throat and dry mouth. "I think I understand, Mr. Shaw. I just wanted to make sure you were aware of it, that's all."

His eyes narrowed as he reached for the doorframe. "Why don't you confine your activities to those I specify? We can add appraisals to your job duties once you've learned the business a little better." He opened the door and ushered her out. "Clean up the mess left by that last group before someone sees it," he said as a final note on the subject.

Chloe, for the second time, did as she was told. She tidied up, then ran the feather duster over picture frames and porcelains. But something about her new boss, her dad's old friend, unsettled her. Maybe she was naïve, but she didn't like the idea of Shaw selling repaired paintings to unsuspecting collectors. Once he discovered he'd been sold an inaccurately described lot, he should've returned them to his source and demanded recompense. The art world needed to operate with integrity. Centuries of exquisite masterpieces, besides small fortunes, were at stake.

From the conversation she'd overheard with the appraiser, Shaw apparently was trying to pull the wool over Alicia's eyes, too. Chloe wondered if her father knew the tawdry side of Mr. Shaw. Her dad had been an honest man. He'd been someone to look up to, someone to respect. It wasn't until after his death that she started to go a little crazy. A shrink would make something out of that, and he would be right. But it finally occurred to Chloe that acting wild wasn't respecting her father or his memory. He didn't always make the right decision, didn't always have patience with those he loved—especially her brothers—but Etienne Galen was an honorable man.

And that's the kind of person she wanted to be.

What Mr. Shaw did to survive in his world wasn't her problem. She had her own demons to battle and her own past to live down. If she wanted to become a person others could respect, a person like Aaron Porter from Atlanta, she needed to devote all her time and energy. She liked Aaron, maybe a little too much considering the circumstances. She found herself thinking about him during the oddest moments. Like right now while vacuuming the Persian carpets of cracker crumbs, for instance.

Thinking about him and missing him and yearning to see him again—this wasn't typical Chloe Galen behavior. If they don't come beggin', there's plenty more dogs at the pound.

This might be something to worry about, not what mischief her boss was up to.

She better not be falling in love with this guy, because Aaron-from-Atlanta wouldn't like the old Chloe.

She could live with Clotilde being ashamed of her. She could tolerate the jabs and jokes from Sara or Jason. But she wouldn't like to disappoint Aaron. He wasn't the type to slap her on the back and encourage her to sing silly drinking songs on improv night. He wouldn't find her attractive waking up bleary-eyed, still wearing the same clothes from the night before.

Although she was fairly certain her old modis operandi was long gone, her less than pristine reputation could come back to haunt her any time. And a new reputation was something all the gold in Fort Knox couldn't buy.

CHAPTER FIVE

Aaron finished his weekly update with Charlie's department on new developments in the case. One detective turned up several other forgeries, one by the same artist, the others of the same style and period. Although the canvases hadn't been signed, they'd certainly been presumed to be Irving Blake's, an American painter associated with the Arts and Crafts movement.

Therein lay the legal dilemma. It wasn't a crime to emulate a style or even a particular artist. If you possessed the ability, you could paint copies of the Mona Lisa all day long, then sell them on the street corner to tourists for whatever you could get. As long as you didn't sign Leonardo da Vinci on the canvas or say they were his work. The problem arose when someone "discovered" one of your copies years later buried in the attic, assumed it to be real and sold it as such.

There wasn't much problem with da Vinci—few artists could pull off believable forgeries or possess the guts to try. It became trickier with early twentieth-century artists, whose works were only beginning to gain the fame and monetary worth they deserved. There were few experts in the field who could discern between an artist's early work and someone's emulation of period and style.

While at the NOPD, he'd tapped into Leporte's campus mainframe for registration information. FBI clearances came in handy in times like these. Hightower was already a five-year student. Something was keeping him tied to campus, and it wasn't the stipend he received as a graduate assistant. Hightower hadn't struck him as a living-on-a-shoestring professional student when they dined at Chaz's the other night. Aaron had become fairly adept at discerning bad guys, and something about this arrogant young man didn't feel right.

Aaron used his rusty charm to win a tour of the Fine Arts Building from the department secretary, which included a peek into the behind-the-scenes studios. His explanation of wishing to pursue an advanced degree in artistic techniques and mediums had been accepted without question. He had no trouble gaining the impressionable secretary's confidence.

Lying to Chloe Galen wouldn't be quite so easy. He didn't relish discovering another path that led back to her. She couldn't be involved in the forgeries since she'd only been on campus a couple of weeks. But that wasn't to say she wouldn't be drawn into the scheme later down the line. Aaron had seen the way her eyes lit up when she ran into Dr. Graziano at the gallery. Aaron didn't like it, and his irritation had little to do with the case. There was something about college professors and impressionable young women. Someone as gentle and naïve as Chloe could be easily manipulated by a persuasive teacher. He had to find a way to make sure that didn't happen without blowing his cover. He needed to keep her isolated until he discovered what Graziano was up to and gathered the necessary evidence to convict him.

But keeping himself distant from her wouldn't be easy. First, she was his only contact to Hightower and therefore, to Graziano's advanced placement class. And second, he couldn't seem to go ten minutes without thinking of her sweet face.

Aaron had no trouble finding Chloe on campus. With a copy of her schedule, he placed himself directly in her path as she traveled between classes. "Hello, Chloe," he said, trying to hide his pleasure upon seeing her. It proved more difficult than he would've thought.

"Aaron! How the heck are you? When I didn't hear from you, I feared you had died from my cooking." An impish smile lit her face, darkening her green eyes into shiny emeralds.

"The doctor says I'll make it."

"Super. I thought if I actually had poisoned you, the cops would've shown up by now."

"Have you rid yourself of unwanted attention from suitors before?"

She laughed until she clutched her midsection. "Unwanted attention from suitors? What's your major, by the way? The archaic dialects of Chaucer and Shakespeare?" She swung her backpack to the ground then shrugged out of her jacket. The spring morning had turned hot by midday. "I know they really don't talk like that in Atlanta."

"I'm bringing back a lost art," he said, trying not to focus on several inches of toned belly below her cropped top.

"What art would that be? Bullsh—I mean, wooing a woman with verbiage?"

"Exactly. I know the way to your heart isn't through your stomach, so I thought I'd charm you with words."

She lifted one brow in an exaggerated gesture. "Was that a jab at my dinner party?"

"Absolutely not, since I'm hoping for a second invitation." He picked her pack off the sidewalk as students surged past them.

"The next meal's on you. Sara and I don't cotton to food mooches."

"As you shouldn't," he said, remembering their empty fridge and pantry. "Dinner tonight? On me?"

She looked up through incredibly thick eyelashes. "As in a date?"

"Well, yeah. You know I have no friends here." He took her arm to steer her around a pair who'd paused on the walk to smooch. "If you don't date, you can think of it as two ships passing in the night. Two ships that happen to get hungry and stop to chow down."

"Ahhuh. You do have a knack for words, Atlanta, and I am hungry already . . ."

"Lunch then, right now. My next class isn't until three."

"How 'bout coffee, then I gotta go to work. You can buy me dinner later, only because I feel sorry for you—friendless and all." She drawled the words with southern belle charm. "Want me to pick the place? Something sloppy in the Quarter with loud music and plenty of spicy food? We can dance the night away to Zydecco. Maybe we'll get asked to play the washboard with spoons. Happens all the time. I'm pretty good at it."

He looked dubious. "We'll save that for another time. Let me pick the spot. I've got my heart set on something."

"Is it touristy?" she asked, crossing the grassy commons toward the coffee shop.

"Of course, I'm new to the Big Easy. Gotta see the sites."

"It's been more like the Big Difficult since Katrina, but let me guess—a haunted ghost walk, vampires, and the voodoo cemetery?"

"Not even close." He opened the door into a noisy crowded café.

Chloe ran her pink-nailed fingers through her hair, ruffling it into spiky curls. "A gambling cruise on Lake Pontchartrain with an all-you-can-eat buffet? We can wear sweaters with big pockets and bring food back for Sara."

Aaron laughed at the mental picture of an FBI agent loading up stolen food, then getting busted leaving the ship. "Excuse me, sir, we'll have to ask you to empty your pockets before disembarking."

"Let me surprise you. No more questions, but I've got a couple for you." They ordered coffee drinks, took a number, and slipped into a booth. "I was curious about your friend Hightower. Have you known him long?"

Chloe laughed with easy assurance. "Jason? I've known him forever. Since junior high, at least. Why do you want to know?"

"He seemed . . . protective of you. Like maybe he didn't like me hanging around."

She laughed again, a wonderful, spontaneous sound. "Don't worry 'bout him. That's just Jason. He used to think that he and I . . . Well, now he knows we're only friends and believe me, he's okay with that."

Two steaming mugs were set before them. Chloe pulled hers close and scooped whipped cream with a finger then licked it off.

The gesture momentarily transfixed him, and he felt his body stir despite their public surroundings. "I don't want to horn in on somebody's territory," Aaron said, taking a sip from his mug. The hot coffee burned his lips and tongue.

"Hone in? Good grief. I'd better have dinner with you. This must be your first date of the millennium with that kind of thinking." Chloe repeated the sensual gesture with the whipped cream, this time from the spoon instead of her finger. "I'm not anybody's territory, buster, and never have been."

Aaron felt himself flush. "Bad choice of words. Sorry." He wanted to divert conversation away from his dating history, which was rather sparse since his divorce, but a burned tongue made speaking difficult. "Is Jason an artist like yourself?"

"Yeah, but he's much better than me. You should see his work. Filled with passion and dark emotion, not light and spiritual like mine. Bleak, moody, but perfectly executed. He was selected to be assistant to the department head this year. That's quite an honor and I'd say well deserved." Chloe sipped from her mug. Some remaining froth stuck to her nose.

"What's his forte? Landscapes, seascapes, pastoral scenes like the French Impressionists?" Aaron thought he'd go mad until he reached out to wipe away the whipped milk.

Chloe swiped at her nose with the napkin, blushing slightly. "Oh, no. That's more my thing, not his. His favorites are the early twentieth century realists like Robert Henri."

"Who's the department head?" Aaron asked casually, already knowing the answer.

"Dr. Graziano. He's my advisor, too. I'm lucky to get him. I'd heard of his reputation at Henderson and at Ole Miss. He's a genius at inspiring students to their full potential." Chloe's face glowed with enthusiasm.

For the second time, he felt a stab of jealousy. He was just doing his job, but every time he turned around it felt personal. And the reason sat in front of him sipping a double mocha latte. "The talent lives within the student, not the teacher," he said.

"Untrained, untapped talent is worthless. Dr. Sam sets high expectations and expects results. You met him the other day, remember? Going into La Bella?"

"What was he doing there? Does he consign students' work for sale?"

Chloe grinned. "They wish. La Bella only takes the work of established artists, nobody unknown, no matter how talented."

"So where can I go to see some of your friend Hightower's work?" Aaron drained the remaining coffee in a long swallow.

She narrowed her gaze. "Why so interested, Atlanta? I told you, he's not my boyfriend."

"I enrolled in Secondary Education with an art history minor. I'd like to familiarize myself with all styles and time periods."

"You want to be a teacher?" She looked genuinely pleased. "That's great, so does Sara. I haven't seen any of Jason's recent work myself, so if I worm an invitation to a private showing, I'll bring you along. How's that? Sara, too, since she's . . . kind of interested in him."

"My social calendar is filling up. Now if I can just stop saying archaic things, I might be okay."

"I like your brand of anachronisms. They're rather entertaining." Her small hand shot out and clasped his arm. The touch—impetuous and electric—ended too soon. Chloe jumped up and hefted her backpack. "Gotta go. Pick me up at . . . what . . . seven? That should give me enough time to get ready."

Aaron scrambled to his feet. "Can I drive you to work? It would be no . . ."

He bit off his sentence since Chloe had already disappeared through the crowd milling at the counter. He smiled when he spotted her head of scarlet hair slip through the doorway without a backward glance.

He had much to learn about young college women.

Maybe about women in general.

But definitely about Chloe Galen. She wasn't like other women. She said whatever came to mind and did as she pleased with little thought to other people's perceptions.

A far cry from his ex-wife. A far cry . . . and an intriguing change. As much as he fought it, he found himself thinking about all one hundred pounds of her more and more.

And not in ways even remotely associated with his assignment.

Chloe walked home from the streetcar stop lugging four bags of groceries plus toiletries from the dollar store. No familiar, pricey name brands, but she'd paid cash for everything. Her feet hurt from walking between classes and standing at the gallery, her shirt stuck to her back, and her makeup had melted off her face long ago. Yet, she was happy. She'd just cashed the second paycheck of her life and bought enough food to keep her and

Sara from starving. The first check had gone toward the rent, leaving enough for streetcar fare and a cup of coffee on campus, although she'd given up her addiction to double Espresso mocha lattes unless someone else was buying.

She might not have much money, but she also had no bills to pay. Not having a credit card had advantages. Making it on her own seemed more feasible than it had two weeks ago in Clotilde's elegant living room.

Mama. She'd actually thought fondly of her today. A classmate had shared some oatmeal raisin cookies in between classes and they'd tasted like Clotilde's. Her mother used to make them just for her without the cook's help. And she would eat every single one, since Ethan and Hunter preferred chocolate chip.

A pang of nostalgia and regret gripped her heart. It had been her primary goal to be away from Mama's control, and now that she was, the victory tasted less sweet. Too bad her mother couldn't see her now. No living in a cardboard box under the freeway, no skipping school, and no partying till dawn with her sorority sisters. She went to class, worked on art projects and assignments, then worked at the gallery and went home. If Sara were out, Chloe would study or clean the apartment. Once she hopped the streetcar to the Garden District, not to visit her family but to walk the streets studying the antebellum architecture and landscaped gardens. The scent of magnolia and wisteria filled the air as she marveled over the symmetry and design, not as an envious have-not, but as an artist. Grace and style filled the rich old homes, a refined way of living almost gone in the fast-paced world.

Chloe lived a simple life now and didn't miss the old. For everything she'd given up, something worthy had been gained.

"Chloe! Don't you recognize me? I'm family now, remember?" A cheery voice broke through her day dreaming. She turned to see her sister-in-law, Cora, climbing down from her SUV parked in the alley. In a loose linen dress with her hair caught up in a chignon, she looked cool, comfortable and positively jubilant.

Chloe set down her bags. "Yeah, I remember you," she drawled. "Best damn wedding I've ever been to." She wrapped her arms around Ethan's wife, who hugged back with equal affection. "How is that rat brother of mine? I hope he's being nice to you," she teased, since Cora knew how much she adored her two brothers.

"He's been up to no good, as you can see." Cora patted her rounded tummy.

Chloe hugged her tightly again. "Super. I can't wait to be an aunt and spoil her rotten. Or him."

"So we can count on you for frequent babysitting?" Cora opened the SUV's hatch. "I've brought your laundry, all clean and pressed."

"Let me get that," Chloe insisted. "In your condition, you should take it easy." She stuck her head inside the car and spotted the beaming face of Jeanette Peteriere.

"Why is your hair all wet and stuck to your head, ma petite? It hasn't been raining."

"Good afternoon to you, too, Jeanette." Chloe looked dubiously at Cora, not sure she was up to a visit by two inquiring minds.

"She insisted on coming with me," Cora whispered. "Wouldn't take no for an answer." The elderly woman clambered out carrying a large bucket.

Chloe grew incensed when she noticed the bucket filled with sponges and cleaning products. "Absolutely not. I will not allow you to clean my apartment!"

"I have no intention of cleaning it," Jeanette said, heading toward the steps. "You are. I'm going to supervise to make sure you do a good job. Something smelled bad the last time I was here."

"Help me, please," she said to Cora, then ran to head off Jeanette.

Positioning herself a step higher, she blocked the passage up like a childhood game of Red Rover. "I appreciate the thought, but not tonight. I have a date. And I've only enough time to shower and dress." She parried to the right. "Leave the stuff and I'll do it. I'll call you if I have any questions." She shifted her weight from foot to foot in case the older woman had ideas of slipping past her.

Jeanette peered over her spectacles. "You got a date? With that Aaron Porter person?" Her brow furrowed into deep creases, while her thin hand reached higher on the railing.

Chloe pivoted left to block the opening. She wished, not for the first time, she was larger. "Yes, and I can't believe you remembered his name."

"I remember him. Nice boy, that Aaron Porter from Atlanta." Jeanette retreated down a step.

Chloe grew suspicious. "Is that right? You didn't seem to think so at the time. You practically knocked him out of your way with the laundry bag."

"It was just a little tap, nothing more, ma petite. I was . . . cranky from the streetcar."

Now Chloe knew something was wrong. Jeanette never admitted crankiness. Crankiness was her natural personality, not an occasional lapse due to external annoyances. "What's going on, Jeanette?"

"Nothing. Go up and get ready. Don't greet him naked like the last time." Jeanette thrust the bucket at Chloe. "Call me if you don't know what to do with this stuff. And scrub hard," she ordered, struggling down the steps.

Her arthritis must be flaring up. Chloe felt guilty all over again about the laundry, despite having had little choice. "Thanks for doing my clothes," she called.

"Naked like the last time?" Cora asked. "Ethan asked me to check up on you. He won't like hearing that little tidbit."

"Here's an idea for you, *cher*, don't tell him." Chloe hugged Cora's shoulder fiercely. "Thanks for bringing my laundry. Next time I'll come to your place so we can visit while I wash it." She shot Jeanette a glance, but the woman was busy trying to figure out how to get back into the SUV.

"Sundays and Wednesdays would work out best," Cora whispered. "They're Jeanette's days off. Now go get ready. No more showing up naked on dates or I will tell your brother."

Chloe was ready when Aaron knocked on the door an hour later with flowers in hand. "For me?" she asked, knowing that had to be the stupidest question in the universe. He looked like a tall cool drink in faded black jeans and white polo shirt. The sleeve bands cut into his upper arms, while the jeans hugged amazingly muscular thighs and narrow hips. He looked like a glossy designer magazine ad. Her female hormones spiked from all the lean, hard-bodied masculinity on her front stoop. As she glanced up from his Italian loafers to his suntanned face, she felt her breath catch in her throat. Perhaps she'd been hanging out with the artistic, sensitive types too long.

"I'll be right back," she said, leaving him outside as she put the flowers in water. She knew the apartment no longer smelled bad since she'd thrown out everything unidentifiable then scrubbed the fridge, but Jeanette still worried her. She didn't want Aaron inside until she used every cleaning product in the bucket.

"Ready?" he asked, crossing his arms over his chest. The gesture further accentuated his biceps.

"As I ever will be," she answered, glad she'd worn a long

dress instead of her usual jeans and cropped top.

"Wait," he said as they reached the alley. "Let's do things right." He opened the car door then waited while she settled herself comfortably. "You agreed to a second date, so I'm eager to impress you."

"I'm accustomed to men who don't even pick up the tab," she said, immediately wishing she hadn't. The last thing she wanted was to appear like a gold-digger. Her current level of duplicity was quite enough. "Not that I care," she stammered. "I don't mind splitting expenses, if that's what you had in mind." She felt her cheeks redden. "I think maybe I'll shut up now."

"Relax, Chloe. I have enough to pay for both of us. I've been saving all week." He gave her a wink as he accelerated into traffic then turned onto St. Charles.

Chloe took his advice and watched the progress of hurricane restoration while he made small talk about world news and the ubiquitous weather. His car was a conservative, late model sedan, not what you'd expect with a man returned from military service, ready to pursue higher education.

"Ah, we're headed back to the Quarter," she said as they passed Lafayette Square.

"We are. Where else would a bona fide tourist concentrate? I'll branch out after I master the basics." The car slowed to a crawl after crossing Canal since pedestrian traffic surged in on all sides.

Chloe stole surreptitious glances while they inched down Decatur, but his eyes were hidden behind sunglasses. Obscured, secretive like everything else about him. She realized she knew little about him, other than he obviously worked out and smelled like heaven. She decided to change that situation.

"Tell me, Aaron. How are your classes? Are you enrolled as a fresh . . ." Her question dangled in the air as he pulled into a parking space on Jackson Square, across from the queue of horse-drawn carriages. "We're not," she said with a giggle. "We're not taking a carriage ride . . . are we?"

He flashed a rakish smile. "We are. I read in a magazine that women find horses very romantic." His fingers slicked through his hair as he opened her door. "So I'm giving it a try." He offered his hand.

For some strange reason she clasped it, though she'd never needed help getting out of a car before. "This is the epitome of tourist traps! And pity the poor horse, except they're not really horses. They're mules. You think I'm falling for this schlock, an independent woman like me?" She sounded aghast, but inside she felt tiny seeds of excitement grow. She'd never taken a smaltzy carriage ride in her life, but part of her had always wanted to.

"Dear, sweet Chloe. I'm not trying to seduce, only entertain you. And myself in the process. What's wrong with that? Your virtue is safe tonight. I'll have the mule walk slow, so you can jump out if I get friskier than the beast."

She flushed up to her hairline. What was happening to her? She hadn't blushed this much since third grade. Luckily, Aaron had turned his back to speak to the carriage dispatcher and slip him what looked like a good deal of money. The liveried man checked his clipboard then disappeared into a small office. He returned with a wicker hamper, an ice bucket with a magnum of champagne and a checkered cloth and deposited everything behind the seat.

"Your carriage awaits, Miss," Aaron said, again offering his hand.

Chloe stepped up then settled herself on the tufted leather seat. "It seems like you've thought of everything." The carriage was open to the sights and sounds of the French Quarter but had a tasseled top to pull up in case of rain. She felt like Cinderella minus the wicked stepsisters.

Aaron spoke quietly to their driver and slipped in beside her. "We've got the carriage for four hours, so the mule will have an easy, slow-paced evening and an extra bucket of oats back at the stable. So don't worry about him."

"Then this whole shebang turns into a pumpkin?" Chloe bit the inside of her mouth. Much to her dismay, she usually turned into a stand-up comedienne whenever nervous.

"It better not. The magic carpet ride home was already booked for the evening." He unfolded a map of the Quarter from his pocket.

Chloe leaned over to peruse. "You won't start snapping pictures, will you? I don't like having my picture taken." She leaned back to peer at a clear sky filled with millions of stars.

Aaron slipped his arm around the seat and barely skimmed her head. He gazed upward, too. "Care to tell me why? I doubt that you're an American Indian. Not with those green eyes."

"No, your scalp is safe. It's a guillotine you should fear. I'm French on both sides of the family, all the way back to Bourgogne."

The clop, clopping of horseshoes on brick pavement soothed some of her anxiety. Music and laughter drifted from balconies and doorways, but the noise didn't intrude on the serenity in the carriage. She noticed their driver wore headphones, apparently listening to his own brand of entertainment.

"Ah, French. That explains the exquisite cuisine the other night," he said in a low, sexy voice. His hand drifted down to her shoulder.

Chloe laughed from her belly, not offended by his dig at her cooking. Anybody else would've received her formidable wrath.

"What about photographs? Care to share the story?" The mournful wail of a saxophone on Bourbon Street punctuated his question.

Chloe debated for a moment. Not because she didn't want to tell him the truth, but because she still couldn't tell the story without crying. She made up her mind this would be the first time with no waterworks.

"It's really no big thing." She drew in a deep breath. "Almost two years ago, we were at a family gathering—my parents, my two brothers, grandma, everybody. I took this picture of my parents at the table, then another of the whole family in front of the hearth. I posed people just so, like we were the Waltons or something. Everybody was smiling, everybody looked happy, especially my father." *Ma pere.*

She swallowed, fighting back her emotions. "When I printed the pictures, a white . . . blur covered my father's face. In both photos. You couldn't see his face. Like it was some kind of omen." Chloe's voice cracked as her words caught in her throat. "My dad . . . died two months later. A massive heart attack. The EMTs revived him, but they lost him on the operating table during triple bypass surgery. Doc said his heart was plain worn out." Despite her avowal that this recitation would be different, two salty tears ran down her cheeks, followed by a steady stream as the memory of that horrible night in the hospital flooded back.

Aaron's hand tightened on her shoulder, pulling her against him. The warmth and strength of his body comforted her.

But he didn't say anything. Somehow he knew—there wasn't one single thing anyone could say to make her feel better about her father's death.

"So, no photos, okay? No cameras, no video cams, no photo booths at the mall." Her voice sounded small and weak, irritating her greatly. Chloe Galen didn't show emotion—sarcasm, yes; temper, sometimes—but never maudlin emotion.

He reached into his pants pocket, extracted a disposable camera, then dropped it into the litterbag on the floor. "You got it," he murmured, running his fingers down her arm.

The touch made her tingle in places she'd all but forgotten about. A wave of heat shot through her as she became acutely aware of power emanating from the flex of his muscles and every other part of him. She didn't know if she should move closer or get away while she still could.

Chloe mimed as though talking into a microphone. "Hidden secrets revealed in back of horse-drawn carriage. More at eleven," she said. "I'm feeling rather tabloid. And not helping much on this tour." Chloe gestured toward the driver's back. "Isn't he supposed to be pointing out the highlights along the way?" she whispered.

"I paid him extra to say nothing and keep his eyes firmly on the road ahead." Aaron reached behind the seat for the champagne bottle and glasses.

"You dog. What are you up to?" She scooted away from him.

He carefully filled two glasses clutched between his knees. "I want a real tour by a born-and-bred, filled with personal vignettes and interesting anecdotes." He handed her a flute, but didn't close the distance between them. "Or else, no picnic dinner."

"Blackmail, that's what we call this in New Orleans."

"We call it that in Atlanta, too, but those are my terms." He took a long swallow and smiled.

She sipped hers. Very good stuff, not purchased at a local convenience store. "Let see. We just passed French Perfumes, where Grandmère orders her numbered fragrance, made in Paris especially for her. They won't sell her blend to anyone else." She glanced over her shoulder. "Back there, you can hop the ferry to Algiers for Mardi Gras World or board either of two paddlewheel boats that ply the Mississippi. You can imagine you're Huck Finn or Tom Sawyer on a raft. But you'll have to squint pretty hard to block out the refineries, chemical plants and hurricane damage."

"Where're the personal vignettes?" He topped off their glasses with the delicious bubbly while the mule slowed to a crawl.

"Let's see . . . We had our after-prom party in a warehouse in Algiers filled with old Mardi Gras floats. It was pretty eerie, actually. Macabre. I've never been into Goth, but most of the kids loved it. My date and I avoided each other the entire evening. We didn't much like each other anymore by prom time."

"And the paddlewheel boats? Any romantic interludes on board you wish to share? We've got cold salmon, julienne potato salad with artichokes, and raspberry cheesecake for dessert," he baited.

She met his eye then shook her head. "Next time we go out, I'm packing a lunch so I won't fall victim to extortion." But in truth, she didn't mind. Aaron was easy to talk to. Easy and somehow comforting.

"I've never been on a paddlewheel boat, but my brother Hunter and I once stowed-away on a freighter. We slipped aboard while it was in port on the Navigation Canal. We didn't get far, just a couple of miles, since Hunter insisted on exploring the ship. If we had stayed hidden, we could've made it to the Gulf of Mexico. Freedom from the oppression of our parents." She laughed, stretching her arms over her head.

Aaron studied her intently. "The truth?" he asked.

She nodded. "True story."

"What happened when you got caught?"

"The captain called the Coast Guard, who called our parents and the juvenile authorities. We had to appear in court. They charged us with criminal trespass and it went on our juvey records. Needless to say, mom and pop were a little pissed. They just about hired Pinkertons to keep an eye on us after that."

"I'd say so." Aaron laughed with that rich, throaty sound that made her heart ache.

"Have I said too much? Do you not wish to be seen with such a desperado?"

"Makes me want to be with you all the more." Without another word, he tipped up her chin and kissed her. Lightly, tenderly, but Chloe felt something click—like tumblers in a lock falling into sequence. Everything lined up and fell into place. But before she knew it, the kiss was over.

"Whoa," she breathed. "I guess you liked the story." Her nervous anxiety returned with a vengeance.

"I did. And I like you, Miss Huck Finn. We're here. You've earned your dinner." He opened the carriage door and helped her step down to the curb.

Chloe looked around, pulling her hand from his. "We're at the Ursulines Convent. What're you up to? I'm too old to take vows as a novice. Not that my parents didn't suggest it after the freighter incident."

Aaron lifted out the hamper, then the carriage clattered away down the street.

"Where's he going? How will we get back to the Square?" she demanded.

"Home to his own dinner, but he'll be back in an hour. Follow me." He hopped onto the stone wall then offered her his hand.

"No way. Criminal trespass is taken seriously as an adult, and I was only recently un-grounded."

"Relax. A generous contribution to their mission fund granted permission for a picnic under the crepe myrtle. But no littering and no funny stuff—the head nun might be watching." He hooked a thumb toward the leaded windows of the old stone convent that overlooked a garden that foretold of heaven itself.

"You bribed the Catholic Church for our picnic? Why?"

"Because it's incredibly beautiful here, and I don't like being locked on the wrong side of the fence." He shook out a blanket under a low-hanging live oak, dripping with Spanish moss.

Chloe plopped down in the center as he began digging containers from the hamper. "That bothers you, Aaron? Being shut out of something or some place?" she asked in a soft voice.

He studied her for a moment. "Yeah, it does. My mom and I grew up in a tin can mobile home on the edge of town. Everyday I would walk to school past this . . . mansion with the most incredible yard. Every kind of tree and shrub and flower grew there. Something was always blooming year round."

He set out two plates then began spooning salad and fish onto each. "But a ten-foot fence surrounded the property, and they had a security gate. You had to punch in a code to open the gate. My mom told me a very old woman lived there alone. All that beauty and no one to enjoy it. I never once saw her outdoors."

Chloe took the plate and fork he offered. The food looked and smelled delicious. "I sense this personal vignette is about to take a nasty turn."

"It is," he said, after tasting the cold salmon. He refilled both glasses, then exhaled a deep sigh. "One Saturday morning I hid in the bushes until this delivery truck arrived and punched in the code. I slipped in behind the truck to pick flowers for Mother's Day. She had so many, I knew she wouldn't miss a handful." He took another bite then set his fork down with a clatter. Chloe held her breath.

"Just as I finished picking, this woman appeared out of nowhere and yelled at me to get off her property. I tried to apologize, to explain about Mother's Day, but she wouldn't listen. She told me to leave the flowers since she didn't allow trailer trash to help themselves in her yard." Aaron met her eye. Chloe saw very old, well-buried pain welling to the surface.

"She said it might be different if I came from decent people, but I didn't, so I should just drop them in the dirt." He picked up his glass and downed half the contents. "So I did."

"Wow, what a witch. By now, she's roasting where all witches go when they die." Chloe reached for him, but he settled back against the tree trunk with his plate.

"I was eight years old. I didn't think people who lived in trailers were inherently inferior to those who live behind brick walls." He ate some potato salad then noticed her untouched plate. "Eat your dinner, Chloe. I didn't mean to upset you with my woeful tale." He grinned and winked. "Really, I'm all better now. But if any rich people step in front of the carriage, you'll understand if I suddenly yell 'giddy-up.' "

Chloe smiled back at him, but something big lodged in her throat, something she would have a hard time swallowing. She sipped her drink then whispered, "If any rich people step in front of our carriage, I'll smack the mule's rump, and you know what an animal lover I am."

He clinked wineglasses with her, then leaned in for a kiss. Not quite so short and sweet as the last kiss. This one settled in the pit of her belly and sent ripples of heat up her spine.

She set the plate aside and wrapped her arms around him, kissing him with every ounce of passion she could muster. Deep, sweet, toe-curling, mind-boggling. She felt the earth move and heard trumpets and cymbals in the background, instead of the cacophony of tree frogs and crickets. The scent of jasmine and magnolia wafted on the night breeze, electrifying all five senses at once.

When they finally broke the exquisite contact and pulled back, she found him staring with his mouth slightly agape. "I would've told you that story sooner if I'd known it would spark such a reaction," he said in a husky voice. A bead of sweat had formed on his upper lip.

"Who knew?" She picked up her plate and began to eat, not

from hunger but because he'd made such an effort with the picnic.

And because she wanted to put some space between them. A vision of them stretched out on the plaid blanket, making passionate love for the rest of the night had flitted through her mind during the kiss. On the grounds of a convent, no less.

This couldn't be happening. She wouldn't allow it. Chloe Galen never felt desire for anyone—too much vulnerability and weakness for her taste buds. Besides, motto number three: Never start something you cannot finish.

Aaron wouldn't like her much if he knew the real truth.

She'd be the person pushed in front of the stampeding animal and carriage.

Aaron snaked his arm around her waist and tried to pull her close, but Chloe swatted him away like a bug. "I forgot myself for a moment," she said. "Remember Mother Superior? She might be watching." She pointed at the windows overlooking the garden. "My place in heaven is already shaky. I don't wish to further jeopardize it."

Aaron laughed and began cleaning up the remains of their dinner. "You're right. It's getting late. I'd better get you back, Cinderella, before the clock chimes midnight."

The perfect moment had been lost for him, too. He helped her to her feet and they walked back to the stone wall in silence. Only a mockingbird could be heard in the misty enchanted garden. His sorrowful cry silenced the other night creatures.

An appropriate bird, all things considered.

Their carriage awaited, the driver roused from a nap as they returned. They talked of nothing-subjects on the ride back, as people do when they've already said or done too much. In his car, Aaron sped across town once they'd left the throng of tourists behind.

"Have you had enough of the Quarter yet, Atlanta?" she asked when they reached the freeway.

"Not by a long shot. I want to walk every street and look in every window, since I've got the best tour guide in the city." His hand skimmed her knee then returned to the steering wheel.

"Peeping in windows in Louisiana is illegal, buddy. My life of crime is long past."

"Mine, too. But as Stacey used to say, it's good to reinvent yourself every few years."

That snapped Chloe back from replaying the events of the convent garden in her mind. She turned on the seat to face him. "Who is Stacey?"

His features hardened, his focus on the road narrowed to a glare. "My ex-wife."

CHAPTER SIX

Stacey. What in the world had he been thinking of, to bring up that sorry name from his past? Everything had been perfect up until then—the carriage ride, dinner in the secret garden, spending time with Chloe. Then that kiss . . . more than perfect . . . everything a kiss should be and what future kisses would be judged by. A meeting of souls, of hearts, of minds, besides rocking every carnal fiber in his body right down to his toenails.

Not that he deserved such a kiss. Everything about Chloe was young, fresh and unsullied. In her company, he felt like the man he once was, before going undercover with FBI Anticrime.

Before lying and subterfuge became a way of life.

And long before marrying the woman who destroyed his trust in womankind forever—a woman who'd married him without bothering to divorce her first husband. Stacey—an honest-to-goodness bigamist who thought she could buy a bus ticket to another town, dye her hair, and start over like a character in a Faulkner novel.

He shouldn't have mentioned her name, but not because he still harbored a soft spot. He was long over her, but he didn't want Chloe dredging up history. Nothing from the past affected who he was now. Not anymore.

Stacey had been young like Chloe, but that's where similarities stopped. Stacey wrote her name at the top of every agenda. All her decisions were based on how much would be brought to the table, what advantage could she gain. When she realized his graduation from Quantico promised a regular, ample paycheck, she readily accepted his proposal. The fact she'd already married someone else, someone who didn't want a divorce, didn't matter to her. After all, husband number one couldn't hold down a job, and a wife could only put up with so much. She didn't think anybody would look at the court records of tiny Camellia, Georgia. And maybe no one would have if Aaron hadn't sought high-level security clearance.

With his thick skin, he could handle the locker room jokes from other agents.

He could handle drunken late night calls from the scorned husband accusing him of everything in the book.

But what he couldn't handle was a woman who had looked him in the eye every day and told one lie after another. With his heart wrapped firmly around her finger, he had believed all her fabrications. After their annulment, he vowed never to make that mistake again.

Now his whole life involved deception. His career demanded he slip into a situation to gain information unnoticed, then disappear before anyone figured him out. And the duplicity never bothered him one jot.

Kissing Chloe last night had been a mistake. He needed to maintain a profession distance. She was his only connection to both La Bella gallery and the art professor at Leporte. If Graziano was up to his overeducated neck in this, involving Chloe could endanger her safety besides threaten his cover. There was no telling what people would do to cover their tracks or protect their investment with this much money involved—and plenty was at stake with these forgeries.

But now that he'd kissed her and allowed himself to feel something for the first time since Stacey, staying away wouldn't be easy. He felt like an addict who wished he'd never sampled the initial taste. He was drawn to her, attracted to her infectious spirit and vitality. It wouldn't last; it couldn't last. This wildfire would burn itself out, but until it did, avoiding Chloe would be like planning not to breathe again.

Pointless to even try.

Aaron arrived at the precinct earlier than usual. Uncle Charlie had gone to Baton Rouge to examine evidence in another case. The squad detectives either hadn't arrived yet or were out on assignment. He had a few hours to tie into the FBI mainframe and track things leading into or out of the Fine Arts Department of Leporte University. After four cups of bad coffee and three hours at a computer monitor, Aaron learned that the department was fiscally sound as far as he could see. No mysterious transfers of wealth, no programs funded without legitimate sources or clandestine midnight transfers of artwork. Everything seemed upright and legitimate.

Except for one small detail that might prove to be nothing. However, his gut instincts told him otherwise.

In 1979, an associate professor stumbled upon a stack of signed canvases stored in a studio backroom and reported it to his department head. Blank canvases, but signed by the early twentieth century master Irving Blake. Such a finding would be unlikely and highly suspicious if the signature was real. Apparently, his report received little attention and was written off as some sort of prank, like signing Vincent Van Gogh to your least favorite work as a bitter joke. According to the report, the associate professor didn't believe it to be a joke, since the canvases were decades old and not made of currently used materials. When the department head investigated, however, the stack of canvases had mysteriously disappeared. Unfounded allegations of this sort could damage the college's reputation. The associate professor was threatened with dismissal, and he shortly thereafter lost his job due to budgetary cutbacks.

Aaron discovered this little mystery quite by serendipity. In

1979, such reports weren't scanned into the university's hard drive as they were now. They would have languished in some file cabinet until finally pitched out during an office cleaning. But this particular associate professor filed an unfair dismissal complaint against the college years after the incident, blaming his subsequent career failures on this one turning point. The unfair dismissal complaint was thrown out of court for lack of evidence, but reference to the original report became part of the record. No further information on the professor could be found.

Aaron had discovered something he desperately needed in the case. The department head at the time was Dr. Sam Graziano, same as now. And Aaron might have something concrete to connect him to the frauds. In 1939, Blake reportedly signed dozens of blank canvases right before his death. When he'd discovered he was dying of tuberculosis, he wanted to financially provide for his wife and children. He'd planned to allow his protégées to create the works, then sell them as his, splitting the proceeds with his family. Only six forgeries were ever discovered by experts at the Metropolitan Museum of Art. The remaining signed, blank canvases never had been accounted for.

Although the story of Blake's tragic and untimely death wouldn't interest the masses, anyone in the academic art world would have heard the rumors. If those canvases still existed, someone in a position like Graziano would have the money and connections to find them.

Now all he had to do was prove his tidy little theory.

Aaron stretched out his tight back muscles. He yearned for hard physical exercise, a good cup of coffee, and Chloe Galen. Not necessarily in that order. For the past three hours, he'd thought of her only twice. That was a new record, considering his past two weeks.

After changing into sweats and a t-shirt, he ran five miles

along the Riverwalk, his favorite spot to wind up his body and unwind his mind. Past the Spanish Plaza, he caught a whiff of diesel exhaust from the freighters carrying endless loads of hurricane debris to reclamation sites downriver. Despite the fact it would never be the same as before the Big One, Aaron loved this city with its shortcomings and idiosyncrasies. And he'd gained a new appreciation since checking out the tourist haunts. Everyone should spend a weekend as a sightseer in his hometown, especially with a gorgeous tour guide like Chloe.

He grabbed a sandwich and coffee from a French Quarter bakery then parked just far enough away from La Bella to watch its front door. His Braves ball cap pulled low and torn Saints jersey might allow him to blend in with the street crowd, but not with those entering and exiting the gallery. He saw nothing out of the ordinary in the well-heeled clientele. Most patrons left empty handed, only a few carrying wrapped parcels. Shaw's car never left the reserved spot in back, and the car parked next to it was registered to Alicia Pierce of Baton Rouge. No criminal record, not even a parking ticket came up on the routine DMV. In keeping with routine surveillance, he gained nothing after four hours except stiff legs and a sour stomach from too much caffeine.

Tomorrow he would call Chloe. Not to hear her sexy drawl or be charmed by her effervescent laughter, but to pump her for whatever she knew about Dr. Graziano. She had spent time in his office and might have heard something that could help.

But tonight he'd promised to spend the evening with Charlie and Sophie. He'd been avoiding them lately without knowing why. All their friendly sparring, their cat-and-mouse-ing once had annoyed him. Now he saw it for what it was—their personal expression of love. Maybe he was being sucked into their parental trap. Maybe he was growing complacent. But maybe something in him recognized the rarity of their relationship.

Uncle Charlie was without question a happy man.

His aunt had planned an old-fashioned family barbeque to celebrate the Rhodes' thirtieth wedding anniversary. Cousins he hadn't seen in years would be there. He bought roses for his aunt and a box of Dominican cigars for Charlie. Nothing particularly Cajun or Creole tonight. They would feast on ribs, fried chicken, hot dogs, potato salad, and corn on the cob. It would be an all-American cookout, like anywhere across the country, but he seldom attended family events.

Sophie had suggested he bring a date. Once he saw the backyard festooned with tiny lights in the trees, Japanese lanterns lining the walkway and checkered cloths on the picnic tables, he wished he had. Something in him wanted Chloe to share the occasion with him, to lick barbeque sauce from her fingers and drink cold sweet tea, to meet his extended family and laugh at bad jokes.

Despite being the only guest over fifteen and not married or at least engaged, Aaron enjoyed himself. He ate too much, sparred with his cousins, and loved seeing his aunt and uncle so happy. They opened each gift and reacted as though presented with the Hope diamond. Once, his aunt met his gaze and whispered that she wished his mom could've been there.

"How goes it, boy? What's new on the case?" Charlie asked as they cleaned up the soda cans and paper plates after everyone left.

"You can't get through one evening without thinking of work, can you?" Aaron teased, yet filled him in on what he'd learned about the blank canvases and their connection to the professor.

"You think a distinguished professor would be part of a swindle?" Charlie asked, skepticism shading his words.

"He's got to be. Who better than him would know how to create fakes that would fool most experts in the field? Who knows how long he's been at this shell game?" Aaron opened the beer his uncle offered, his first of the evening. His aunt didn't allow alcohol to be served if kids were present. And nobody argued with Sophie on that matter or any other.

"Is the man living beyond his means?" Charlie asked, sinking down on a metal chaise.

"Not that I could discover. He's too clever to leave a trail. Probably squirrels away money abroad, preparing for the day he leaves the academic life behind. He's a P-H-D, you know." Aaron chuckled, knowing Charlie's intrinsic distrust of highly educated people.

"Is that so? Better set an intelligent trap to catch this fly." Charlie massaged his arthritic knees below his Bermuda shorts.

"Tomorrow I'll question Chloe Galen about what she knows about her campus advisor."

"Who?" Charlie stopped rubbing his kneecaps.

"Chloe Galen, the young woman I met with contacts to both La Bella and the Leporte Art Department. I told you about her."

To Aaron's profound confusion, Charlie laughed for two minutes, spilling his beer in the process. "You never told me her last name, son." He clutched his stomach in hysterical parody. "That's the girl you've been going on and on about?"

"I haven't been going on and on about anybody," he said defensively. "Could you fill me in on what's so funny, Charlie? I can use a joke right about now." Aaron's patience with his uncle was wearing thin.

"You're in for a run for your money, if this is the same Chloe I think it is. Wild purple-red hair, big green eyes, and stands no bigger than a palmetto bug? Great smile, like a snake-charmer with that smile."

Aaron stared in disbelief, then slumped into the other lawn chair.

Charlie settled back in the chaise to study his nephew. "From the look on your face I believe we're talking about the same woman."

"How do you know Chloe?" he asked, not sure he wanted to hear the answer.

"Worked with her big brother on an interesting case out in the bayou last year. Pair of con artists tried to rip off her brother's insurance company, one of the many corporations the Galen family owns. The family is old money, all the way back to their French provincial roots."

"Can't be the same Galens. Chloe is dirt poor. Hell, she and her roommate don't even get enough to eat they're so tapped out after paying for school." He scrambled to his feet and started to pace the shadowy patio.

"Her grandmère is one classy lady—a true philanthropist and community activist, especially after Katrina. And at an age when most have resigned themselves to playing bridge on the terrace."

Chloe's words during the ride down Decatur filtered back. *There's the shop where Grandmère orders her perfume. It's a numbered fragrance that they won't sell to anyone else.* He should have caught it. Most other grandmothers order perfume from the Avon™ lady, not a personal concoction from Paris.

"All right, Charlie. I think you've made your point." He kicked over one of Sophie's paper lanterns, spilling the tea light.

"What're you getting so mad about, son? Just because I'm acquainted with the girl's family?"

Aaron sucked in a deep breath, not wanting to take his anger out on Charlie. He heard traffic noise, the streetcar bells, and the infernal TV set of the neighbors, but nothing drowned out the buzzing in his head. He gritted his teeth and turned to face his uncle.

"If you just found out the woman you thought you were falling in love with has told you nothing but a pack of lies from the git-go, wouldn't you be a tad upset?"

Charlie met his gaze as he struggled to his feet, his jovial demeanor vanishing in a heartbeat. "I think I'll go help your aunt with the dishes, son. You need some time to yourself. Have another beer from the cooler."

Aaron didn't want another beer. He wanted some answers, but if he went over to Chloe's apartment now, he would tip his hand and probably a good deal more. He needed to think, to get his head straight. He was a trained professional on assignment, not some lovesick kid home on spring break.

But one thing was certain. He was glad he found out what a phony she was before he made himself into a first class fool.

Stacey. Stacey Porter. Chloe played the name over in her mind so much she almost missed her streetcar stop. After the most perfect evening in her life, the day had been nothing but aggravation. Her classes were proving tougher than those at State. The professors' demands in technique and style challenged her to new levels. Leporte compared favorably with Henderson College if her classmates' work was any indication.

Work at the gallery involved constant running back and forth, interspersed with "yes, ma'am" and "no, ma'am" all afternoon. The stunning Alicia Pierce even started giving orders by midshift. Not fun being low woman on the totem pole. Mr. Shaw wore a pinched, worried expression despite the cash register ringing up several good sales.

Then the memory that Aaron—the only interesting man she'd met since her Sunday School days—had a wife added to her wounded spirit and sore feet. At least, he'd said ex-wife. At least she wasn't dating a married man, something she'd never do.

Probably tall, blond, and pale skinned.

He'd picked her so as not to be reminded of his ex-wife.

Hopefully, not to be reminded how much he still loved Stacey.

At that moment, trudging home from the streetcar, hot, tired, and cranky, it occurred to her she might be in love. The idea struck her like a two-by-four applied to her head. Why else would she care about some phantom ex-wife or what the woman looked like?

Chloe climbed the metal steps to their apartment, hoping Sara would bring dinner home from work. Their fridge once again looked like they had moved out. Two distinct voices carried from the other room when Chloe dropped her backpack and sank into the couch. Sara emerged from her bedroom with Jason Hightower right behind. At least both were fully dressed and didn't look as though they'd been up to mischief.

"Yo, Chlo," Jason said. "You look like you walked all the way from the Quarter." He settled himself next to her, his aftershave strong and citrusy.

"That's pretty much how I feel."

"Poor baby," Sara cooed from the kitchen. When she returned she lifted Chloe's feet onto the coffee table, then handed her a diet soda. "Put your feet up."

"Diet?" Chloe asked. "My weight isn't even into triple digits." She took a long swallow.

"Sorry girl, that's all we got left. I brought home some lasagna for supper that they were throwing out. It still smells pretty good." Sara snuggled onto the couch, too.

"I'll wear nose plugs if I have to," Chloe said. "I'm starving. Could we have some now?"

This apparently was too much for Jason's sophisticated sensibilities. "Listen to yourselves. It's pathetic. You're eating food headed for the dumpster." He rose to his feet to glare down his nose at them.

"So?" They chimed in unison, their favored retort stretched

into two syllables.

"Chloe, Chloe. You have talent. Even Graziano has taken notice. Why are you living like this?" He gestured around the apartment, now spotlessly clean but still tacky. "Move in with me, baby, and I'll help you with technique. You're almost there. Only a few sophomoric tendencies to lose and you can start making money."

Chloe caught Sara's hurt expression with Jason's invitation, whether in jest or not. "You're such a silver-tongued devil, Hightower, how can I resist such an offer?" She scrambled to her feet, not comfortable looking up at him. "If you mentor me, will I become a total jackass, too?"

Sara laughed. Jason did not.

"You're halfway there already. Look, Chloe. Sara knows what she wants out of life. She's only living like this till she graduates and becomes a schoolteacher. Then she'll make the big bucks and move into a two-bedroom dump." Derision dripped from his words.

Chloe's opinion of him sank to a new low when she saw tears fill Sara's eyes. "When did you turn into such a jerk?" she snapped.

"At least I know what I want. I've got a plan. But you? What do you want? If you don't want to suck up to Clotilde to get your credit cards back, you better make some plans. Or you'll be living like this for the rest of your life."

"I'll tell you what I want, Jason. I want to stand on my own two feet. Not be under Mama's control, or anyone else's for that matter. I want to finish college and earn a living. I'll live on whatever I make, no matter how paltry. You and Sara don't know what it's like to have everything handed to you. It doesn't do much for your self-esteem."

They both stared at her as though she'd grown a second head, then Sara burst into laughter. "If you launch into some movie theme song or give that soliloquy about never eating radishes again, I'm outta here."

Chloe forced a smile for her friend. "I know how stupid that sounds. And I'm not saying I had it rough. But now that the gravy-train's over, I want to make it on my own. I want to prove to myself I can."

"That's all I'm offering, Chlo," Jason said. "What'd ya think? I was proposing or something?" He opened the fridge then snorted in disgust. "You weren't kidding about diet soda is all that's left." He slammed the door shut. "Come over to my place. See how I live. I've got both food and beverages on hand. I'm making it on my own and living pretty well, I might add. You could, too." He walked toward the front door. "I can help you."

"Help me what?" Chloe asked.

"Show you how to start creating artwork that'll sell right now. Earn some dough. Maybe nothing big-time to start, but better than the chump-change the gallery pays. Then you'll never have to run back to Mama since that's so damn important to you."

"I don't think so, Jason, but thanks just the same."

"Sure, kid. I'm a patient guy. But eventually you'll get tired of living like a panhandler. The novelty will wear off, and you'll be anxious for a little help from your friends."

He walked out, slamming the door behind him.

Sara and Chloe stared for a long moment, utterly speechless. Then they looked at each other and breathed a sigh of relief. They heard his car squeal from the parking lot, spinning gravel in its wake.

"When did he get so pushy?" Chloe asked. "He was starting to make me nervous."

"He's always had strong opinions how others should live. You just never paid much attention before." Then Sara added with a giggle, "but he's so darn cute."

"Nobody's that cute," Chloe said. "Let's eat, then I have a call to make."

As soon as they finished the vintage lasagna, Chloe dialed Aaron's number. "Helloooo," she drawled. "This is Cinderella from the previous evening. I believe I left my shoe in your carriage and I'd like it back."

Dead silence.

"It's me, Chloe," she said with normal intonation. "I got paid, and it's burning a hole in my pocket. If you're drivin', I'm buyin'."

After another long moment, Aaron spoke, dispelling the notion she'd dialed the wrong number. "All right, Chloe. I'll pick you up in half an hour. We've got to talk."

"Sure . . . talk, drink, neck . . . whatever you're into."

No laughter ensued. No snappy retort. "See you in thirty," he said and hung up. Chloe stared at the phone. *Hmmmm. I thought only women PMS'ed.*

She had little time to think about his chilly attitude since, true to his word, he pulled in front of her building in less than half an hour. Chloe attempted chitchat ranging from the humid weather to how the Saints looked in the draft, but Aaron's responses gave nothing away. They drove to Haiku Bar in relative silence then found a small booth far away from the dance floor.

Chloe pulled out her wallet. "Tonight is on me, so don't even try to argue. I'm an independent woman, with a right to throw a little money around on a man who's caught my eye." She punctuated her declaration with an exaggerated wink. "Just don't order a magnum of champagne like the other night. I've got a powerful thirst for some of those one dollar draughts." She gave the order to the waitress.

This time he smiled, although it didn't quite reach his dark eyes. They remained fathomless and unreadable.

"So, Miss Galen," he said. "Miss Chloe Galen, daughter of Etienne and Clotilde Galen, society debutante and heiress to shipping fortune of granddaddy Etienne Galen, Sr.—who will also buy her perfume from Paris someday—you wish to buy a round of beers? Sure, why not. I'm thirsty." His voice had dropped to a deadly whisper.

Chloe felt the blood drain from her face as though someone had pulled a plug. "You make it sound like I've committed murder and gotten away with it."

"If you had, I'm sure you would get away with it."

"Well, I haven't killed anybody. What are you so mad about, Atlanta?" She cocked her chin defiantly, not liking the way he made her feel guilty. "I didn't think it was a crime to have parents with money."

The beers arrived and they both took hearty swallows. "It's not," he said, setting down the mug. "I just can't figure out why you didn't tell me. What's the big secret?"

"So I didn't tell you everything in my past history before we met. You just told me about your ex-wife last night, and I didn't go off the deep end."

"The opportunity to mention my previous marriage hadn't come up. What was I supposed to say? Hi, I'm Aaron Porter. I was once briefly married to a lady in Atlanta but that's all over with now. Can I buy you ladies a drink?" He inhaled a deep breath. "But you've had plenty of chances you didn't take. What were you worried about?"

"There was no master plot. I wanted to get to know you better," she said softly.

He seemed to consider this, but his expression didn't change. "Why are you and Sara living in that apartment in that neighborhood, since you come from one of the richest families in Orleans? It's not safe for either of you." His tone had mellowed a hair.

"Who told you . . . about my family?" She had trouble meeting his eye.

"My uncle, whom I'm staying with right now. He's . . . heard of your family."

She nodded, contemplating how much to tell. She decided to come clean. "I'm living on lovely Avalon Lane because it's what I can afford. I had a falling out with my mother. She threw me out and cut me off financially. I haven't spoken to her since. The only member of the family I've seen has been Cora, my sister-in-law. She even called yesterday. And, of course, Jeanette."

"Your grandmother's friend."

"Yeah, her friend and . . . housekeeper."

He whistled through his teeth. "Gee whiz. I've never met anyone with a real, live maid before." His snide tone cut through her skin.

"She's not a maid. They have a cook, cleaning staff and a laundry service. Jeanette just sort of . . . runs things."

"You see, Chloe, most of us wouldn't know about distinctions like that." He drained his mug.

"I realize that, but I don't understand why you're holding it against me. It's all over with. I don't live like that anymore."

He laughed then met her eye. "I don't hold your family's wealth against you. You can't help being rich anymore than I can help being poor. But get one thing straight—it'll never be over. Even if you don't reconcile with your family—which is highly unlikely—growing up wealthy will define every thought you have and every action you take. Trust me. Even if you have the same bank balance as a bum sleeping on the levee, you will never be poor. You've had enormous advantages that you'll continue to benefit from for the rest of your life."

Chloe stared at him, wanting to argue, but somehow she knew he was right. "Well . . . shoot. See why I didn't tell you? I liked it better when I was just Chloe. I can't change how I grew

up, but I shouldn't be judged by those circumstances forever."
Her voice raised a notch; people were starting to stare. She
lowered it back to a whisper. "When I met you, I liked you. I
wanted you to get to know . . . just plain me. Without the family
baggage."

Aaron stretched his long legs under the opposite bench and
slicked a hand through his hair. "There's nothing plain about
you." The start of a smile turned up a corner of his mouth.
"What did you do to get ex-communicated?"

She exhaled a pent-up breath. "If I tell you, you might think
me an awful person. If I don't, I remain a big fat liar."

"A small, skinny liar, but try me." His tiny grin broadened.
"Did you kill somebody?"

"Nobody that didn't have it comin'."

They both laughed, and she could feel herself relax for the
first time since calling him. But with his eyes intently on her,
she knew she had more to explain. She opted for the mini-
version.

"I was expelled from Ole Miss for drunk-and-disorderly at a
sorority party. This sorry episode after I'd already been expelled
from Henderson College . . . for similar crimes. My mother
didn't think this becoming behavior for a young lady, so she
clipped my wings. She said she would pay my tuition at Leporte
until graduation, but I wasn't getting a dime more. I'm on my
own for room and board. She cancelled my credit cards, closed
my debit account, even had my leased car repossessed."

If she thought he would be disgusted by her disclosure, she
was wrong. He broke into peals of laughter and actually slapped
his thigh. "She had your car repo-ed? I would've loved to see
your face when they hooked your car and drove off."

She wasn't sure how to react. "I'll check with Sara if she
snapped any digital pics. It wasn't my happiest moment."

"Do that," he said, then ordered another round. They both

studied each other cautiously while waiting for the beers.

Chloe decided this had to be a good thing. She felt relieved Aaron knew her past. He was the first man she'd ever wanted to be honest with. "I'm glad you found out. I only regret I didn't tell you myself. You probably won't believe this, but I'm also glad this happened with my mother. I didn't realize how . . . spoiled I was or how easy I had life. I'm learning to do things for myself. I'm surviving. And I kinda like myself better now." She wiped her damp palms on her jeans then looked into his face. "I'm sorry I wasn't upfront with you." A load had been lifted; one she hadn't realized she'd been carrying.

"This sure explains a few things."

"Like what?" Chloe picked up the icy mug and took a swallow. The stuff was starting to grow on her.

"Like why you'd never filled out a W-4 form before and didn't know how to cook, or shop, or do much of anything."

"I know how to shop," she said, lifting one eyebrow.

"I mean for necessities like food and toilet paper and salad dressing, not haute couture. Speaking of food, have you eaten? Do you want to split a dessert or something? Let's order something to take back to Sara."

"Sure," she said, but felt little relief with the change of subject. The temperature in the booth seemed to have dropped twenty degrees. Something had changed between them. Some imperceptible curtain had fallen. She could feel it, but hadn't a clue what to do. He was no longer the same man who'd eaten every bite of her atrocious dinner or kissed her in the Ursulines' convent garden.

Funny how things worked out.

Right after she realized she might be in love with him, he started looking at her like a stranger.

CHAPTER SEVEN

Aaron awoke to a splitting headache and a sour taste in his mouth. Part could be attributed to the mint mango cheesecake they'd split at the Haiku bar, but mostly it was due to his hot-headed exasperation with Chloe. Much as it irked him to discover she came from very rich, very old blood in New Orleans, he remembered telling a few lies of his own regarding personal history: *Could you show me around the French Quarter? I'm new to town and would love to see some tourist attractions.* Or how about: *I'm thinking of enrolling at Leporte for art education. I plan to become an art teacher using the GI bill.*

What right did he have to condemn her for not being honest about her past when he was working undercover, using every possible false pretense? That's why they tell you in the Academy never to get involved with anyone during an investigation, especially an informant. Nothing good could ever come from it.

Nothing good will come from his relationship with Ms. Chloe Galen of New Orleans. They were from different worlds, too unlike to find common ground on which to base a relationship. But that didn't mean he didn't regret his double standard in the honesty department. He was sorry he came down so hard on her. She had her own reasons for living a lie, same as he. Too bad their reasons couldn't have been more diverse. He lived subterfuge as a career choice. Now it didn't feel quite so noble, but there was no way he could come clean. He could only wield some damage control and hope for the best.

Chloe Galen wasn't a survivor like Sara or himself. She might last awhile—working, going to school, juggling homework projects with mundane everyday tasks. But eventually, she'd crash from the pressure of managing too many things at once. Or worse, she'd put herself into a precarious or dangerous situation. Even with her spunk and energy, Chloe wasn't cut out to take care of herself. Some women just weren't. With all their talk of independence and liberation, they would graduate from their parents' care to their husband's without realizing it.

He would never be the man to take care of Chloe Galen and he wasn't about to fool himself. The best thing he could do was to help restore her to her family's good graces. Then at the end of his assignment, he could return to his own life without worrying about the green-eyed hellcat with hair the color of fire.

He'd be left with only a few regrets. So the sooner he got her off his mind, the faster he could concentrate on the job he was paid to do.

Aaron telephoned her on the way to his morning History of American Art class. A sleepy-sounding Chloe answered on the fourth ring.

"Chloe, it's me. I'm not exactly Prince Charming after last night, but I've still got that shoe you were looking for."

"Hang onto it for awhile. Right now, what I need is coffee and lots of it."

He heard things banging around in her kitchen as she attempted to get the pot brewing. "Would you like me to bring you a double Espresso latte?" he asked.

"Absolutely not. I'm not dressed, and I no longer engage in unbecoming behavior for a lady, remember?" Something crashed to the floor in the background.

"I was hoping for one last exception in the name of caffeine."

"Nice try. Now tell me what you really want at eight-oh-five in the morning."

"I was wondering why your sister-in-law called you two days ago," he said.

"You woke me from a perfectly fine dream to ask me what Cora wanted?"

"Yeah," he said, hoping she wouldn't hang up. This thin limb he'd climbed onto was the only one he had to get Chloe into a safer environment.

"There . . . the machine is dripping. Won't be long now." He heard the sound of the coffeemaker hissing. "Why in the world do you want to know?" she asked.

"Just humor me for a moment. What did she want?"

Chloe paused before answering. "She asked me again to come to dinner. My brother is worried about me. And she wants me to bring my laundry, so I don't have to go to the laundry-matic. I told her I was too busy this week."

Aaron considered correcting her terminology, but decided against it. "I think you should call her back and accept the invitation. And invite me along."

He heard a gulp of coffee being swallowed. "You want to meet my family? Why? After last night, I sure didn't think you would want to."

"Never mind last night. I said some things I wish I hadn't. I might've been a jerk. Just maybe. I'm not saying for sure."

"Ahhuh," Chloe said suspiciously. "What are you up to, Atlanta?"

"Nothing. I just think you should see your brother and sister-in-law, that's all."

"It's not quite so easy as all that, as I tried to explain." A hint of impatience had crept into her voice. "Going to Ethan and Cora's would be like waving the white flag, giving up the ship, admitting defeat. I'm not ready for that."

"I believe your analogies might be a little extreme. I'm just suggesting dinner with them. Not throwing yourself on their Italian leather shoes and groveling. You don't have to relinquish any ground."

"What's in this for you?" He heard her take a long gulp. "I'm fully awake now and I smell a fox."

He smiled into the phone. "I'm anxious for someone's cooking other than my own, curious to see where rich people live, and would like you to communicate with at least part of your family. I don't have much family myself, Chloe. And I know firsthand the price you pay when too much time goes by without contact."

"That's three reasons. You've been giving this some serious consideration."

"Don't give up your independence. Just tell your sister-in-law you'll come for dinner, no strings attached. They're probably worried about you. You can reassure them you're doing fine on your own."

"I don't know. You don't know my brother, Ethan. He can be a little overbearing. Not like my mother, but in his own inimitable way. And what if they call Mama? There's no way I'm ready to face Clotilde yet. Not until I've cured cancer or walked on Mars or at least sold a few paintings."

"Tell Cora not to invite her or you won't come."

"You really want to come with me, Atlanta?" She sounded like a little girl.

"I do. I want to meet your family, Chloe. I said things last night that I probably shouldn't have. To make up for it, I want to help you get on solid ground, at least with your brother."

"I'll call her. That's all I can promise. And if this turns out to be a bad idea, I'll come looking for you, Atlanta. And I won't be smiling when I get done with you."

Aaron felt his headache begin to abate as he arrived on campus. He was pretty sure he'd made the right decision.

But since meeting Chloe, he wasn't positive about anything.

His American Art History class helped little with the investigation, since it centered mainly on the early primitive period of the late eighteenth century and early nineteenth. His call to Rose, the secretary in the Fine Arts Department, proved more useful. She agreed to give him a behind-the-scenes tour of the studios and storage areas, under the pretense of observing student work in progress. He'd explained he wasn't sure which professor to approach regarding placement in the program and wished to save embarrassment by first viewing his competition.

She'd looked dubious since this wasn't standard procedure, but finally agreed to meet him during her lunch hour. An offer of coffee and burgers afterward made up her mind. Aaron met her promptly at 12:30, feeling sorry about his ploy.

If these guilty feelings continued, he'd have to consider a career change to forensics or maybe traffic control. The last thing an undercover investigator needed was an overly developed conscience.

Luckily, few people milled the hallways or worked in the studios. Either they'd decided to grab lunch or take advantage of the lovely spring day outdoors. During Rose's thorough tour, he spotted no cache of signed blank canvases leaning against a wall that would crack his case wide open.

However, the artwork he viewed drying on easels or waiting to be matted proved rather interesting. He recognized the distinct styles of three famous artists—one a European old master and two American painters, Charles Davis and George Inness, who specialized in dreamy landscapes. Since the works were obviously in progress and both artists deceased, Aaron was taken aback.

He stopped in front of one stylistically superb example of a dark brooding storm front approaching landfall. "This is an interesting work. Looks just like an Inness I saw hanging in a museum back East."

Rose peered around his shoulder. "It should. That was the artist's intent."

"He or she planned to copy someone else's painting? Whatever happened to creative originality and all that?"

Rose laughed. "That'll come later, once they've mastered technique within their chosen style. Right now, they need to learn the basics before they make their creative mark in the world."

"Their teacher encourages them to copy other artists' work?"

She looked a little surprised by the question. "Of course. As I said, you must become adept working with your materials. Artists are no different from any other craftsmen. The student selects a medium—oil, watercolors or acrylics—studies a work by an established artist he appreciates, then mimics the style and process from plain canvas to finished painting. Creating true art will come later."

Aaron moved closer to study the fine detail. "Imitation is the highest form of flattery, I suppose."

"I'm surprised you haven't run into this in previous classes. It's no different than learning scuba diving before embarking on a career of underwater treasure recovery," Rose said, moving closer to peer at the work.

Aaron thought that correlation interesting. "So what happens to these copies when they're finished?"

"They're graded by the professor, like assignments in any other field, then they're destroyed." She stole a surreptitious glance at her watch. "You're looking at one of the best in the department, done by a grad student. Most are no way near this accomplished," she whispered. "Come into the next studio."

He followed her into the next work area where watercolors in various stages of completion dried on racks. They couldn't be confused with great works of art by even an untrained eye. "These are from an undergraduate class," she said quietly.

"And the graduate placement class in oils—are there any examples from them?"

"Yes, the one you were just admiring in the last studio. It was done by Dr. Graziano's assistant, Jason." She beamed upon mentioning his name.

What's with these women? Were they all charmed by the temperamental sensitive types? Aaron ground his teeth and tried to remain polite. "That would be Jason Hightower?"

"Yes, do you know him?"

"I met him once through a mutual acquaintance. This advanced class, how many are enrolled this semester?"

"Right now, seventeen. All hand picked by the class instructor." Rose moved with purpose from the studio, closing the door behind them.

"And who would that be?"

"Why, Dr. Graziano, of course, the department head."

Lunch with the helpful Rose—mushroom burgers and coffee—turned up little else useful to his case. He deftly circumvented subtle invitations to concerts and gallery showings with the excuse he needed time to prepare a portfolio. By one-fifteen, she headed back to her office, while he prowled the campus, mulling over the new information.

The advanced placement class in oils had him worried. All of the forgeries discovered up till now had been oils. Interesting, too, was the fact Dr. Sam Graziano taught the class. Even more interesting, Chloe's old buddy from high school, Jason Hightower, was his most talented protégé.

The idea that her friend might be involved in Dr. Graziano's little scheme to fund a happy retirement bothered him. The possibility that Jason might try to include Chloe bothered him even more.

The customers through an art gallery were always feast or famine. Either you twiddled your thumbs watching dust rise from the street cobbles or you had a crowd on your hands, all demanding their questions be answered at once. Today was the latter. Chloe, Mr. Shaw and Ms. Pierce worked without break for three hours straight. Finally, Chloe's last customer placed the vase back on the pedestal, then declared she'd return tomorrow after she slept on it. Chloe stood alone in an empty, but blissfully quiet showroom. She drained the remains of her cold coffee and went looking for Shaw. A few customers had asked questions she needed answers for.

She was about to knock on his office door when she heard two voices from inside. Glancing around, she pressed her ear close to listen.

"You don't mess with a major auction house or museum. We need their expertise and support—another gallery, fine, a collector, but not a museum. You'll be cutting your own throat." Alicia's voice floated through the ether.

Since business was being discussed, this seemed a good time for her questions. But to her dismay, he wasn't in a question-answering position when she opened the office door. He stood with his back to her with Ms. Pierce's legs wrapped around his thighs. They were kissing in a manner not consistent with a normal employer/appraiser relationship. Luckily, Chloe interrupted early in their consultation so both were still dressed.

"Excuse me, Mr. Shaw, I didn't know you were indisposed," she said then laughed at the inanity of her comment.

"Yes, well, that's why people usually knock first, Miss Galen." He straightened quickly, patting down first his hair then his impeccable suit. Simultaneously, Alicia scooted off the desk and tugged down her short skirt discreetly.

"I am sorry, sir," Chloe said. "I have a few questions to ask."

"I'll leave you two to your questions and start closing up shop," Alicia said, seeming not embarrassed by what just happened.

Shaw waited until Alicia left, then pointed to a chair by his desk. "Come in and have a seat. I wanted to talk to you, too." His demeanor changed a hundred and eighty degrees as he resumed his usual paternal air.

Chloe sat down, deciding to hear him out first.

"I overheard you steering customers to the Edward Hopper. You were great with your presentation. And I appreciated that you came to me about the repairs done to the Fritzche." He sat down behind his desk. "I'm so busy all the time. Sometimes little things like that slip past me, and not disclosing a work has been repaired can ruin a gallery's reputation. My integrity and financial future is always on the line. Too many dealers and auctioneers try to pass things off these days." He brushed some dust from his palms. "You're very bright, Chloe, and industrious. I've decided to give you a small raise, plus teach you more about the business when I have a chance."

"I appreciate your confidence in me." She'd expected to get fired for barging in on him with Miss Pierce, rather than offered a raise.

"I know you aspire to be a great artist," he murmured, "and I have every faith you will be, but it doesn't hurt to know the business end of the art world. Who knows? You might own a gallery someday as a write-off against the enormous income from your paintings."

"I don't know what to say. Thank you, sir."

"Not at all. You were the apple of your father's eye. And he was my friend. I'd be remiss if I didn't take you under my wing, so to speak. I'll have Alicia work with you, too. She's the finest art appraiser in the city and also an art authenticator. She evaluates whatever the gallery purchases or accepts on consignment. She knows her stuff. La Bella stakes its future on her appraisals—her seal of approval get us top dollar at resale." He rose to his feet. "We'll speak more again. Let's close up now. You must be tired."

Chloe scrambled to her feet and headed for the door, her customers' questions long forgotten. She had only one more thing to do—call Aaron. Considering her busy afternoon, she had gone a full twenty minutes without thinking about his rippling muscles, tight stomach or wonderfully large hands. A new personal record since much of her workday was spent daydreaming about the guy. Her call to Cora had garnered a dinner invitation for them for the following evening. Now that that particular bridge had been crossed, she was looking forward to it . . . and looking forward to seeing Aaron again. She loved her brother and his wife, plus maybe Hunter would come, too. Then it would be complete. Other than Sara and Grandmère, everyone she cared about would be in the same room. She just had to make sure fur didn't fly and all weapons remained inside locked cabinets.

Aaron would meet her at Ethan's home instead of picking her up, because she had a few things to get straight with her brother first.

Chloe walked from the streetcar stop carrying an industrial-sized garbage bag filled with her and Sara's laundry. Since Sara's classes had begun, she was busier than a pickpocket at Mardi Gras. Cora had offered to pick her up, but Chloe insisted on arriving on her own. Might as well let them know right away that she would maintain her autonomy and independence from the family. This was dinner and nothing more.

She received more than one curious glance as she lugged the

heavy bag down the street. Few residents in this National Historic Landmark neighborhood carried their entire wardrobes over their shoulders when invited to supper. Chloe paid no attention. No one knew her here and she didn't care if someone did. Grandmère's house on Chestnut Street was one of the largest and oldest structures in the area. The architecture was West Indian style with iron galleries cast in New Orleans and elegant side gardens. It was rumored that the artist, Edgar Degas, attended parties in the mansion. Now an eighty-year-old woman lived there alone with her seventy-five-year-old housekeeper and best friend. Chloe's brother Ethan and his wife were house-sitting until granny returned from Europe, then they would move either back to his apartment in the Quarter or another of his residences. Ethan refused to let Jeanette stay in the house alone at her age, and she refused to stay with her family in Baltimore during Grandmère's absence.

Chloe's breath caught in her throat when she arrived at the locked gate, necessary to keep exuberant tourists at bay. Once Grandmère looked out to find a family dining on fried chicken under her shady Live Oak tree. Another time, a daycare group wandered her flagstone paths singing camp songs while their teacher pointed out various plants. Chloe dug for her key and let herself in, feeling tightness in her belly and throat. Many happy childhood memories danced with her along the walkway and were waiting on the porch. She loved her grandmother in some ways more than her mother, since the elder woman always accepted her exactly as she was. No expectations, no requirements. Just plain love.

Suddenly the door flew open and an exuberant Cora greeted her, hugging her tightly and reaching for the laundry bag. "I can't believe you carried his heavy thing all the way. Why didn't you let Aaron drive you? We're dyin' to meet him." She dragged Chloe through the doorway then cocked an appraising eye.

"Have you lost more weight? I'm getting big as a house while you dwindle down to size zero."

Chloe smiled at her sister-in-law and hugged her again. Despite the fact they'd only known each other for a year, the two women had bonded instantly. "Calm down," Chloe said. "I haven't lost weight, and all other mysteries regarding the wayward sibling will be answered in due time. And give me back that bag. You're not lifting it in your delicate condition." Chloe marched toward the laundry room off the kitchen with Cora on her heels.

"Remember," Cora said, "Ethan doesn't know I already spilled the beans about the baby. He wanted to be the one to tell you our good news, so act surprised."

"Don't worry. I'm getting very good at acting. I'll look appropriately flabbergasted."

"Why are you here so early, not that I mind. To start your laundry?"

"Yes, and also to talk to Ethan. I don't want him rehashing all my . . . activities of the past few years. That's all behind me. I'm not that person anymore." She shoved her first load of delicates into the washer, fully comprehending why you didn't wash lingerie along with bath towels.

"You must really like this guy. Don't want to scare him off, huh?"

Chloe frowned. "Am I that transparent?"

"Only to another woman who's been there and done that." Cora dumped the garbage bag onto the floor. Something small, black and evil started to scurry away from the clothes. Both women gasped, then stomped around like flamenco dancers until they finally squashed the bug.

"Good grief, don't tell Ethan about that! He'll make me move from Avalon Lane, and it's so quaint there."

Cora looked paler than before, while her brow furrowed into

creases. "Okay, I guess, but I could call an exterminator for you. Ethan doesn't have to know."

"No, no, no. Isolated incident. Never saw one of those before." It was a lie, but she didn't want Cora to worry. "Where is Ethan?" she asked, changing the subject from the nasty insect.

"Still at the office. He's usually not home this early."

"Call him. He and I need to talk before Aaron gets here. I want to dole things out to Aaron in teaspoons."

After the call, Ethan arrived in twenty minutes. Chloe followed him up the double flying staircases to the guest suite. The walls on either side were covered with nineteenth century pastorals that Grandmère favored, each lit with an accent light. She watched her brother's rigid back, stiff shoulders and hooded eyes and knew this conversation would not be easy. Since their father's death, Ethan had placed himself in the paternal role with her. Add that to his already haughty, commanding manner and you got a man difficult to deal with.

"I'm pleased beyond words you decided to dine with your family," Ethan said, entering the palatial bedroom. "Cora and I have been concerned about you." He turned to face her as he stripped off his tie.

"Here I am, fine and dandy. No worse for the wear since Mama's banishment."

"You look skinnier and haggard. Don't you get enough to eat or time to sleep?"

"Stop. You'll turn my head with all your compliments." She followed him into the bathroom. It was the size of Chloe and Sara's entire apartment. A soaking tub had been added during the last renovation that could hold six people. A skylight let in natural illumination from the ten-foot ceilings for the pots of blooming hibiscus and bougainvillea. The room had the feel of an enchanted garden pool.

Ethan turned on his heel with a scowl. A silver-streaked

strand of hair hung in his eye as he pulled off his shirt. "Do you mind, Chloe? I'm going to take a shower."

"Oh, sorry. I'll talk from out here." She retreated into the bedroom, closing the bathroom door behind her.

"Why don't we just talk during dinner," he said over the running water.

"Because I need to talk to you now, before Aaron gets here." She listened but heard nothing but the sound of water.

"I'm waiting," he snapped. "What is it you don't want me to bring up in front of him? I could think of a whole list of things."

"I don't want you airing our family's dirty laundry in front of someone I just met."

"Not our family's, Chloe, just yours. What's the matter? Afraid he'll go running back to Atlanta if he knew what you were really like?"

"How did you know . . . oh, never mind." Now was not the time to get sidetracked. "Look, Ethan, all things will be made known to him if and when things turn serious. Which they probably won't. Which they definitely won't if you make me sound like a wild child from a David Lynch movie."

He must have liked that one. She heard his laughter over the shower.

"He just found out I haven't always been . . . poor. I'd like to break some of the other news regarding my background slowly, over time. Is there anything wrong with that idea? Couldn't you trust my judgment on this one?"

Chloe heard him mutter several long sentences in French and, unfortunately, she'd never mastered the language as he had. "In English, if you don't mind," she called.

The water shut off abruptly, then Ethan spoke in a soft voice. "All right, *ma petite soeur*, I have no desire to ruin your chance of capturing this hapless man in your net. But I won't sit there while you paint a picture of yourself as an angel sent from heaven. I have the male brotherhood to consider."

The door swung open and he loomed over her wrapped in a terry robe. "And I'm only going along with this because I'm worried about you. I can't have my wife and Jeanette checking up on you all the time." He walked past her and pulled open the door. "Come home more often. I've missed you, *ma petite* pain-in-the-ass."

"You could've left that one in French."

"I wanted to make sure you understood me. Now let me get dressed. I can't wait to meet the man who has my sister worried about her reputation." He backed her out of the room and shut the door.

Aaron arrived an hour later as Chloe put in her last load of laundry. She made introductions in the three-story foyer. Cora greeted him graciously, while Ethan sized Aaron up in his not-too-subtle manner then asked, "How about a beer?" He apparently determined Aaron posed no immediate threat.

With beers in hand, Chloe led Aaron on a tour while the newlyweds finished dinner preparations. "I've never been in a house this large without paying admission," he said, once upstairs. He grinned at her, without an ounce of envy or spite in his voice.

"Well, you know what they say. They don't build them like this anymore. It takes a lot to maintain the place, especially when a hurricane comes to town, but I guess it's worth it."

"It's a beautiful house. Did you ever live here with your grandmother?"

"Until I left for college. I grew up here. My parents always lived with my grandparents when they weren't traveling. Kind of a European thing. Right up until my father died. Then my mother bought a house on Lake Pontchartrain and spends most of her time there. I hate that place. So modern, so sterile, it should be in a Manhattan loft." She gazed through the spotless leaded panes to the manicured garden below.

Aaron joined her at the window, resting his hand lightly on her waist. "So, you're really an old-fashioned girl at heart," he said, picking up a delicate crystal figurine whose eyes seem to follow them around the room.

"Who would have guessed that by her choice of hair color?" Ethan interrupted from the top of the stairs. They both turned with a start. "Dinner is served on the lower verandah," he drawled in a voice from a classic movie.

Chloe made a face at him. Aaron laughed.

"Hey, Cora told me to say that," Ethan said, winking at his sister. "Let's eat. I'm starved."

Aaron took her hand and led her downstairs. His grip felt strong and comforting, but this dinner had been a mistake. She wasn't ready to face her family, especially not Ethan with his acerbic humor.

As promised, Cora served on the back porch overlooking the garden. She'd set out their best silver, crystal and china. A dozen votives surrounded by rose petals lined the center, adding their scent to the heavy magnolia and wisteria from the trellis. For once, Chloe wished she'd brought out the everyday dishes, but Cora had no way of knowing. Luckily her menu of baked ham, cold potato salad and green bean casserole wasn't over-the-top. This was not the time for French haute cuisine.

Aaron pulled out her chair then took the one on her left. At least her brother seated himself and Cora across from them, instead of taking his usual head-of-the-table position.

"Everything looks and smells wonderful. Thanks for the invitation," Aaron said.

"It's our pleasure," Cora said graciously.

"Cora and Ethan are newlyweds, although you'd never know it by the way they've settled in here," Chloe said to Aaron. It was an attempt at polite dinner table conversation.

Ethan took it as a gauntlet thrown down. "We're glad you can join us, Porter, and ecstatic that Chloe decided to spend time with her family. Especially since she doesn't bother to return my phone calls."

Chloe steeled her gaze on him, hopeful to bore a small hole between his eyes. "I've been very busy between working at the gallery and classes at Leporte. I simply don't have time on my hands like I used to."

"That's right. You're working at Shaw's place. How's that going? Putting your education to good use, are you?" He took two slices of ham then passed the platter to her.

She stabbed a slice with more force than necessary and passed the platter to Aaron. "It's going just fine. I'm learning a lot about the business end of art. That might come in handy some day."

"You need to concentrate on your classes to keep your grades up. You're running out of colleges this side of the Mississippi." His voice had risen a notch.

"Potatoes, anyone?" Cora asked.

"Yes, please," Aaron said, accepting the bowl.

Chloe and Ethan glared at each other like two junkyard dogs separated by a fence. "I haven't missed a single class yet, and I think my grades will reflect that. But then, you probably already know my grades with your ace-detective Nathan Price checking up on me."

Aaron straightened in his chair, his interest apparently piqued. "You have a detective watching Chloe?"

Ethan accepted the bowl of potatoes from Aaron with a smile. "No, that's ridiculous. She's a bit delusional, but I wasn't supposed to tell you that."

"Ha, ha, very funny. My brother loves to think himself a standup comic when not at work. It relieves stress."

"I just had a friend find out where she's living," Ethan said to Aaron, "since my sister has no idea how dangerous the world is, especially that neighborhood she lives in."

Cora leaned forward to capture Aaron's attention. "I understand you're from Atlanta. How do the Braves look this year? Whom did they pick up in the off-season?"

Aaron looked from Chloe to Ethan to Cora and grinned. "They look good. I think we're headed for another pennant, but I sure could use a scorecard right now."

"Don't pay any attention to them," Cora whispered. "This is how they show affection for one another."

Chloe pointed her fork at her brother. "I can and will make decisions for myself. I knew I had something to prove to Mama before coming back into the fold, but I didn't know I had something to prove to you, too."

"You have nothing to prove to me, but why are you making your life difficult and dangerous to show the world how grown up you are? An adult would use the advantages she was blessed with."

"Oh, really? Before when I sat back on my advantages, I was accused of being a spoiled brat."

"That's because you used them for your folly, not your benefit." Ethan glanced at Aaron, then back to Chloe. "Oh, never mind. I see I'm not getting through your purple-haired head."

"Chloe's hair isn't purple, big brother. It's a lovely shade of Bordeaux, like the wine of our ancestors." A disembodied voice floated from the kitchen. Hunter Galen, Chloe's brother and middle sibling, stepped from the doorway onto the porch. "Good evening everyone."

"It's about time," Ethan said, "I could use some backup."

"Sorry I'm late, Cora." He bent to kiss his sister-in-law's cheek. "A crisis at the office . . . and I see another one develop-

149

ing on the patio." He turned his attention to Aaron who watched him with amusement. "Hi. Hunter Galen," he said, extending his hand. "The quiet one in the family."

Aaron shook his hand heartily. "You probably had no other choice growing up. Chloe has kept her second brother a secret."

Chloe inhaled to keep from exploding. If Aaron turned on her, too, she'd go mad. "Oh, I have not. I just wanted you to know me better before I exposed you to the entire Munster clan."

"Does that make me a Munster?" Cora asked, passing Hunter the food.

"I'm afraid so, dear. You're a Munster-by-marriage," Ethan said, leaning over to kiss his wife. "Chloe has a spat with Mother and she pitches us all in the recycle bin."

"Is that little tiff still going on?" Hunter asked, scraping the remaining ham onto his plate. "I'll send her flowers tomorrow, sign your name to the card, and the whole silly thing will be over."

"You'll do no such thing!" Chloe had been enjoying her dinner, but now dropped her fork with a clatter. "This is between me and Clotilde, and I'll thank you to butt out."

"Uhoh. You really must be mad if you're calling her that," Hunter said, finishing off the bowl of potatoes.

"It's her badge of independence from the family," Ethan said, never one to remain silent for long.

Chloe pushed her chair back from the table, but Hunter held up his hand. "Settle down," he commanded then turned to Ethan. "You can't blame her for rebelling. Mama has always tried to mold Chloe in her image. She has a right to find her own path in the world."

Ethan snarled. "Check out her path down Avalon Lane and then talk to me. You haven't seen where she lives."

"It's not that bad," Chloe insisted. "Anyway, I live with Sara

Klein from high school. Remember her?"

"That only means two helpless women are endangering their lives. But that's what gives you the thrill, isn't it? A grand adventure?" Ethan sipped his wine before turning to Aaron. "The last time Chloe kept running away, we tried to get her into a convent, but she escaped from there. Finally the nuns started returning our Sunday contributions until we agreed to keep her at home." He glanced at Chloe's face, then added, "But I probably wasn't supposed to tell you that."

"Aaron, will you help me clear the table and bring in dessert?" Cora asked.

Dear sweet Cora. Chloe knew she was trying to keep Aaron from joining in on her side—and incurring Ethan's wrath at their first meeting.

"Of course," Aaron said, scrambling to his feet, "but I hope I don't miss anything. Salvos are lobbing in all directions. No quarter offered or accepted."

"A military man, eh? You might be good for Chloe. Instill some discipline into her life," Hunter said, wiggling his eyebrows in jest.

"I'll help you, Cora. It'll keep me from doing twenty-five-to-life for murder." Chloe followed her into the kitchen. "I knew this would be a mistake," she muttered under her breath.

Cora faced her with a patient smile. "You really think so? I thought the evening has gone smashingly well so far."

Apparently Aaron thought so, too, since he laughed all the way back to her apartment. He rehashed one choice morsel of conversation after another with relish.

"See, I told you my family was awful." Chloe leaned her head against the car window.

"Are you kidding? I loved them. I mean, I didn't like how Ethan bullied you, but he's just concerned about your welfare. I was hoping Jeanette—you know, your grandmother—would have popped in to add her two cents."

"It was her day off or she would have." Chloe glared at him. "You're really enjoying this, aren't you? Dinner on the verandah with the deranged Galens. I was totally embarrassed while you were entertained."

Aaron wrapped his arm around her shoulder and drew her close. "Don't be mad because I liked your family. Believe me, you could have done far worse." He squeezed her tightly and she felt the tension and anger drain away.

Aaron had that special ability—to take away whatever worried her, to reduce things to their simplest denominators and lessen the impact.

He had the magic touch. She nestled into the crook of his shoulder and put her domineering brothers out of mind. She breathed in his warm, heady aftershave and the scent of something raw, powerful and infinitely male. And felt completely safe.

He was her magic man. She just hoped she wouldn't regret falling under his spell.

CHAPTER EIGHT

Aaron turned off the AC and rolled down the windows on the slow drive back from the Galen ancestral home in the Garden District. He breathed in the warm spring air, without the oppressive humidity of summer, wanting to savor their pleasant camaraderie as long as possible.

Chloe still stewed over her oldest brother's domination, but Aaron had liked the man. A person knew where he stood with Ethan Galen. He said what was on his mind, and didn't waste time with pretense. Ethan simply loved his sister and wished the best for her. His wife, Cora, seemed to be an ephemeral angel who had drifted down to earth to soothe wounded bodies and souls. Hunter acted as the family mediator and probably also played devil's advocate when the spirit moved him. Aaron liked the whole clan especially since they all adored Chloe, despite her protests to the contrary.

Wishing to protect and insulate Chloe appeared to be natural instinct, since he too found himself wanting to shield her from murderers, muggers, and any persistent telemarketers. And Ethan was sure right about her neighborhood. Aaron had spotted prostitutes, panhandlers, and teenager gang members on the drive back to Avalon Ave. Chloe remained oblivious to evil, pointing out instead a lovely garden here or some intricate ironwork on a fence there.

Everything during the evening had gone better than he'd expected. Cora and Ethan shared an easy, relaxed kind of relationship. Hard to imagine they were newlyweds. They communicated with gestures, eye contact and the subtle nuances of lovers, besides the not-so-subtle kissing and handholding. Once you witnessed their mutual respect and deep affection for each other, it was normal to want the same for yourself.

But he'd put away such fantasies after Stacey had packed up and returned to her first husband. Ethan and Cora numbered among the chosen lucky ones. And Aaron knew with certainty he would never have what they enjoyed.

Not with Chloe . . . or any other woman. He must lack something in his character—some necessary attribute in his personality was missing. Or Stacey never would've left him with nothing more than a sink full of dirty dishes and a pile of credit card bills. Aaron shut out the memories of his first wife as he pulled in front of Chloe's apartment.

"Why don't you come up, Atlanta?" she drawled then winked. "Neither of us has an early class tomorrow, and the night is young." A strand of shiny hair fell into her cat eyes, completing the seductive pose.

"How could a red-blooded man resist an invite like that?" He parked the car and came around to her side. She stepped into his arms as soon as her door swung open.

"You really don't think my family's a pack of well-dressed psychos?" she asked, locking her arms around his neck.

He kissed her lightly on the forehead, then her nose. "No. Psychos don't serve ham and potato salad for Thursday supper with ice cream for dessert. They eat only expired TV dinners." His mouth found her lips and he kissed her tentatively.

"Better not mention that theory to Sara," she said, kissing him back without any tentativeness whatsoever. "She eats those all the time."

Her lips were soft and delicate. She smelled like gardenias and tasted like the peaches topping their dessert. He longed to pick her up and carry her far away from noxious trashcans and loud music blaring from open windows.

"Let's go up," she whispered in his ear. "It's Sara's night to work late, so while the cat's away . . ." She dangled the adage like a sultry temptation as she skipped across the parking lot.

"Just what does this feline have him mind?" he asked, following her up the steps into the dark apartment. At that moment he would've followed her barefoot across the Sahara Desert.

"Don't turn on the lights," she whispered, foregoing the stark bulb hanging from a cord. She began lighting candles around the room, each one adding more illumination to her elfin activity. The effect of light and shadows playing off the wall and ceiling was almost as erotic as her kiss. Almost, but not quite.

"I wouldn't dream of it." He wrapped his arms around her tiny waist as she lit the last votive on the fake mantel. The austere living room was a fairyland of twinkling glow.

"What are you up to?" He nuzzled his lips into her hair.

"I think you know." She escaped from his embrace and headed for the boom box on the windowsill. "We need music for atmosphere—something sultry and bluesy, but not sad. I'm feelin' a little frisky. I think Stevie Ray Vaughan will do nicely." Soon the soft wail of a lead guitar with the rhythmic strumming of a bass all but undid him. Candlelight reflected off her too-innocent, too-young face, while her eyes sparkled with more than their usual mischief. He recognized desire in her eyes. Age old, yet new as the rain at dawn on the delta.

"I find you sexy as hell. There's no reason we can't get to know each other a little better," she said, swaying to the music with perfect rhythm.

Nothing was as provocative, nothing as compelling as someone wanting you. More than anything, he yearned to carry her into her room and make passionate love until morning. But if he kissed her now, if he even touched her, their platonic friendship would be over. And what exactly did he have to offer in return? He stepped back—from her intoxicating fragrance, her mesmerizing eyes, from something he wanted more than to wake up tomorrow.

"What's the matter, Atlanta? You scared?" she baited, moving closer. Her smile hypnotized him.

"Like never before in my life. Where's my string of garlic cloves?" He walked backward till he bumped into the door to Sara's room.

"Do I look like a vampire to you? I promise I won't hurt you," she said then closed the space between them in two strides. "At least, it won't hurt for long." She turned her sweet face up to him, expecting to be kissed and made love to and cherished as she deserved.

And he was only human, right?

Wrong. He was far less than human. He was the man who'd condemned her for not being honest, yet he'd told one lie after another. She would hardly want to make love to him if she knew the truth—that he had used her from the beginning.

And was still using her to get his job done.

Not that he didn't care about her. He cared very deeply. He might even be in love, whatever that was. But the fact remained. Chloe was offering herself to a fake, to a phony. He might be a liar, but he wasn't a cad, and guilt was the quickest killer of passion. He brushed a kiss across her nose then walked toward the kitchen.

She sighed with exasperation. "What's wrong? Bad breath? Sloppy kisses? Was it something I said? Where are you going?" she demanded.

He glanced over his shoulder. "None of the above. I just want to go slow, Chloe. Not rush things. I don't want to mess up." He reached for her hand. "Let's make some coffee and talk."

"Okay. I'm good with that. But gosh, the one time I become

femme fatale, it turns disastrous. I thought men liked aggressive females."

"I can't speak for other men, but I like you coming on like gangbusters or standing around for a bus. That's not the problem."

"Well, that's nice to know." She rummaged in the cupboard for the coffee things.

That gave him the time it took to brew a pot of coffee to decide what to say. The truth? Tell her he's undercover for the FBI investigating an art fraud ring in which her favorite teacher and old boyfriend might be up to their necks in? Admit the uncle who'd raised him happens to be New Orleans Chief of Detectives? Mention that he grew up here and that his tourist act was simply part of the ruse? He wanted to come clean more than anything, yet he couldn't risk the operation. He was close to catching someone proffering fakes as valuable works of art. If he blew his cover now, he risked alerting the thieves. All evidence of fraud would suddenly evaporate into thin air. He'd be left with nothing and return to Atlanta after a substantial loss of taxpayer money. He needed more time.

But he hoped it wouldn't cost him something more precious than his career.

"You allowed me a peek into your old family life," he said over the final sputters from the coffeemaker. "I think I owe you the same courtesy." He poured two mugs and carried them to the window ledge.

A soft breeze fluttered the new lace curtains as Chloe slipped into the opposite chair and picked up her mug. "You're going to tell me you come from a family of ax murderers?" She took a sip. "It's okay, Aaron, I can handle it. All Sara's knives are too dull to do much damage."

"Nothing quite that dramatic." He sucked in a deep breath. "We were very poor. My dad worked at the shoe factory when he bothered to work at all. He cashed his check on Friday nights at the local bar. Whatever he managed to bring home was what we used for food and rent. He drank up most of his take-home pay, like they say." He forced a brittle laugh. "Funny how that doesn't sound so grim in a song as in real life." He glanced to gauge her reaction. She waited wide-eyed and alert for whatever was coming.

"My mom worked for a maid service, cleaning mansions along Mobile Bay from eight in the morning till six at night. Those rich women would act really noble, sending home boxes of food and bags of clothes. But the food was usually stale and the clothes out-of-style. I know I should've appreciated whatever was thrown our way, but it's tough growing up, tougher still when someone recognizes your shirt as the one they threw out."

"That's what gave you your strength of character today," Chloe said in a soft voice.

Aaron tried not to think about his strength of character. He didn't feel like he had much at the moment. "My mother would call Dad at the local watering hole and beg him to come home, before he spent all the rent money. One day he'd had enough of her badgering and took off. Left us, just like that, while she was at work and I was in school. I never saw him again. My aunt and uncle took us in since mom wasn't very good at money management either. Her weakness was instant lottery tickets. She set aside part of her pay for them, convinced that the winning ticket that would change our lives was just one scratch away. She always made sure we had enough to eat though, not like my poor excuse for a father."

He took a long drink, wishing for something stronger than black coffee. "Then to finish this sorry tale . . . my mother got sick and died, leaving me with her sister and husband to raise. It wasn't the best time of my life. At first I took my anger at being orphaned out on them. But if they hadn't stepped up, I would've ended in foster care, even more hardened and embittered by the cruel hand I'd been dealt."

At least, that much was true. If he couldn't tell Chloe everything, he wanted to tell her as much truth as possible. He looked into her eyes, but didn't see the pity he anticipated. Compassion, tenderness, maybe even respect—respect he didn't deserve.

"Sounds like you lucked out in the aunt-and-uncle department."

He nodded. "They were more than kind. Once I settled down, I grew to love them as much as my mom. They were so normal, like people on TV. They paid their bills on time, collection agencies never hounded them, the phone didn't get disconnected, and they had plenty of food in the house all month long. It was nice bringing friends home after school and not feeling ashamed."

He had no idea why he'd said that; it'd just slipped out. "You must think I'm a jerk for saying something like that." He felt himself blush for the first time in years.

As usual, Chloe's reaction was unexpected. She laughed with abandon. "Are you kidding, Aaron? Every kid is ashamed of his parents at some time or another. Not just poor kids." She walked to the fridge and peered inside, then muttered, "I sure wish I'd eaten more of Cora's dinner instead of letting Ethan get under my skin. It tasted so good and now I'm hungry again." She returned to the table with a jar of peanut butter and a spoon. "Know what Clotilde did to make me want to crawl under a rock?"

"I can't even guess." He walked to the drawer for his own spoon.

"She would get real dolled up for everything. If I invited friends over, Clotilde would make an appearance in full battle makeup, high heels and couture clothes. She once wore a fur coat to a parent-teacher conference. Fur in New Orleans in September. And my teacher was president of a local animal rights' group. It was a disaster. I thought the two of them would resort to face slapping and hair pulling before the session ended. And I would spend the rest of my life in the seventh grade." Chloe laughed again. "Just once I wished she would wear sweat pants and a t-shirt like everybody else's mom."

"I'm anxious to meet your legendary mother."

"Don't be. She chews up my potential boyfriends and spits out the seeds. But at least I solved the rich-girl conundrum."

Aaron narrowed his gaze. "How's that?"

She straightened her back against the chair. "I intend to never be rich again, unless it's due to my own hard work. I want to make sure I don't inherit any wealth passed from my grandfather to my father, then to my mom. I plan to make an appointment with the family lawyer to cut myself out. Let the pie be divided between the other heirs named in his estate." She held her chin high with pride.

Aaron thought carefully about what to say. No perfect answer was handy. Few people have experience in these matters. "I understand and respect why you want to do it, but think about what you witnessed in the aftermath of Katrina. A great deal of money could go far funding reconstruction projects on individual and community levels."

Chloe cocked her head to the side then passed him the jar of peanut butter. "I'll give that some thought, Aaron, but believe me, every kid, rich or poor, wishes they had any parent but their own at one point or another. Don't worry. We'll end up being the mortal humiliation of our children someday. It's part of the cycle."

"Our children?" he asked, lifting an eyebrow.

It was her turn to blush. "I didn't mean necessarily yours and mine being one and the same. I was speaking categorically."

"Just checking. But I can't imagine any child being embarrassed by you, Chloe. Other than maybe your hair color. You are perfection."

She pulled the jar of peanut butter away from him. "I don't like hedged compliments, Atlanta. You should have said 'You are perfection,' period." She wrinkled her nose at him. "Tell me more about this aunt and uncle who put up with you during your rebellious youth. They're probably up for sainthood."

He settled back in his chair. "That tells the story right there. I owe them everything. They not only took me in, but had me tutored, put me in Cub Scouts, sent me to summer camp, got me involved with sports. In short, kept me too busy to get into trouble. Then they paid for college, which was no small sacrifice on their budget."

"Hmmm. I bet you were cute in your Cub Scout uniform," she said, licking peanut butter from the spoon in a lascivious fashion.

"I had a feeling I would regret that particular disclosure."

"Hey, I thought you went into the service after high school. And just started college right here, right now." She tossed the empty peanut butter jar into the trash.

Aaron's gut tightened. True confessions were over.

"I enrolled for a couple quarters then dropped out. I'm not sure if any credits will transfer." He hated all this covering tracks, layering fabrications that would only trip him up later.

He stood slowly, straightening the kinks in his back. "It's getting late, Chloe. You better get some sleep." He reached for her, tangling his fingers through her hair. It was so soft, so inviting, like all the rest of her.

"Okay, go home if you want. But I want you to know you're passing up the opportunity of a lifetime."

Helplessly he bent down to brush his lips across hers before heading toward the door. He caught the scent of her perfume and the smell of raspberries in her hair and felt his heart would break. "Of that, I have no doubt whatsoever."

Aaron left the apartment without a backward glance. Chloe watched from her window until his taillights turned onto St. Charles Street. Like the scorned heroine in a melodrama, it felt like she'd never see the love-of-her-life again. She laughed at the absurd notion since she would see him tomorrow on campus. But something bothered her just the same. His tender, honest portrayal of his upbringing underscored a huge difference in their backgrounds. Her only taste of going-without before now was when Clotilde decided she was too young for Armani at seventeen and made her return purchases to the mall. And she had carried on as though a major injustice had been done. Shame and regret filled her at the memory of that particular fight with her mother.

You're nothing but a selfish, spoiled brat, Chloe.

Her father's words, uttered after overhearing their argument, stung as much today as they had years ago. She had apologized to her mother then returned the Armani to restore herself to Papa's good graces, but felt like a misunderstood martyr. She shook her head to dispel the mind-picture, still painful after all this time. She was no longer that silly, vapid girl, but that didn't change the chasm her upbringing created between herself and Aaron.

The fact that her family was wealthy might be something Aaron couldn't get past. She understood his contempt for rich people, especially rich women, considering how his mother had been treated. Yet the fact remained, no matter how poor she was now, no matter how she and Sara scrimped and scrounged to pay their bills, one day she would become a very rich woman. Grandpère's estate had included a trust, naming her as beneficiary to the bulk of his wealth. Plenty was left over to support Grandmère in her antebellum mansion for the rest of her life, while her brothers had inherited the family's business holdings. She possessed no interest in business, so Grandpère had determined this solution would be the best. In a little over a year, she and Sara could move anywhere they wished and never clip a two-for-one coupon again.

But where would that leave her and Aaron?

The front door banged against the wall as Sara stomped in, carrying two brown bags of cast-off food. "Honey, I'm home," she crowed. "And I've brought provisions to share with the pilgrims."

Chloe laughed as Sara dumped everything onto the kitchen table. "I was just thinking about you, and here you are." She pulled several long baguettes and a bag of torn lettuce and sliced veggies from one sack.

"They were going to throw that salad out. Can you believe it? It was just chopped up this morning! I'll get the dressing." She walked toward the fridge. "Hey, how was dinner at your brother's? Did he interrogate Aaron? Give him the third degree for daring to date his little sister?" Her laugh echoed in the empty refrigerator.

"No, he was too busy berating me for not making up with Clotilde. He seemed to like Aaron, believe it or not."

"That's fabulous. If Aaron turns out to be a keeper—and I think he just might—you don't want Ethan Galen against the idea. Your brother still scares me a little."

"That's because he caught you sneaking a beer and chased you all the way home."

"Yeah, and I lived twelve blocks away. That guy is temperamental."

"The man I'm worried about is Aaron." Chloe divided the salad between two large bowls. "He hates rich women. I'm afraid when I come into my trust fund, he might decide to hate me, too."

"Really? That's what you're worried about?" Sara pulled one bowl over and covered it with Ranch dressing. "The solution's simple—sign it all over to me. Then we'll both be happy." She popped a grape tomato into her mouth and grinned. "You do make mountains out of molehills."

"I would hate to ruin your practical nature with an influx of cash, but I'll put your name in." She straightened in her chair and assumed a serious air. "I've decided to refuse my inheritance. Renounce it, or whatever they call it. I'll contact the family lawyer tomorrow. Grandpère must've named a secondary beneficiary in case I choked on a chicken bone, so it could just go to them."

"I think you can only renounce a throne, Princess Chloe, so don't get all carried away."

"And I want to make sure I don't inherit anything when my mother dies either." Her voice had grown strangled and weak; she hated talking about her mother's mortality, especially since they were more often estranged than not.

"You're serious, aren't you?" Sara asked, staring at her with disbelief.

"I am. Aaron told me . . . a rather personal story about his childhood. He can't trust people with money. He finds them arrogant, self-centered, corrupt, and manipulative. We won't have any future if he thinks I might be those things." Chloe set down her fork, her appetite evaporating.

"Well, you're not those things anymore." Sara took another huge forkful of salad.

"Thanks, Sara. I know I'll never be conceited with you around."

"You know what I mean. You may have been born with a silver spoon, but you've made real progress since you moved in with me. Why just yesterday I saw you make your own bed, gather all our change to take to the coin-a-matic and not even flinch when you lifted the garbage can lid. You've come a long way, girl."

Chloe screwed up her face at her roommate. Sara wasn't taking this seriously, and nothing was more important to her right now.

"Relax! You're probably overreacting to his story. Why don't you ask him what he thinks before you give away your money like some stupid reality show?"

"Oh, sure, Sara. I'll just draw more attention to our disparity by making a big deal out of this. I want to keep everything low-key. He knows about my family, but not about the trust fund. I told him I'm committed to making it on my own with my paintings and that was no lie. I'll just keep myself honest by getting rid of my one distraction to serious artwork. That's the only way our relationship will have a chance. I don't want to lose him."

Sara shook her head. "Six million dollars described as a 'little distraction.' What is the world coming to?"

"You don't—"

Sara held up her hands. "I get it. I'm just messing with you. You know I stand by you, no matter what lame-brain idea . . ."

She didn't get to finish her sentence. Chloe sprang from the table and onto Sara, mimicking women's professional wrestling. The chair fell over backward, sprawling both girls onto the kitchen floor. Chloe playfully punched Sara's ribs while Sara tried to defend herself in between hysterical giggles. Lettuce and bits of purple cabbage clung to both women while dressing streaked through their hair. Sara managed to whap Chloe's head several times with a baguette until it broke in half. Chloe scored the final lick by squishing a tomato slice against Sara's forehead before both women collapsed against the linoleum in laughter.

When she finally caught her breath, Sara taunted, "You're cleaning this pigsty up, Missy, or I'll know the reason why." Shredded carrot added its own particular highlights to her bangs.

Chloe struggled to her feet on the slippery floor, then reached down for Sara's hand in truce. "You know, maybe Ethan's right. Maybe reconciling with Mama is the lesser of two evils."

Sara took the offered hand with an innocent smile then pulled Chloe back down into the mess.

That night Chloe slept like a baby. After they'd cleaned up the kitchen, she fell asleep as soon as her head hit the pillow and dreamed of a shining knight with strong arms and long fingers. The man in the dream looked mighty familiar. The next morning she whistled a tune during the streetcar ride, and practically skipped along the walkway to her first class. For the first time since coming home, she felt a weight had been lifted from her shoulders. She didn't mind the heat, her heavy backpack, or her excruciatingly boring literature class. Nothing could dampen her spirits today.

Finally, with her morning classes behind her, she headed to the studio to work on projects with three blissful hours to spend on what she loved best—her art.

Other than Aaron from Atlanta, that is.

Love—a simple enough concept for most women, but for her the idea had seemed as elusive as the Grail. Now she knew what those poets and blues singers were talking about. The sensation was emotional, psychological and physical; she could no more stop her feelings than a hurricane force wind.

Settling into her art gave her a few hours without man-on-the-mind, Sara's pet expression. Chloe's current work in progress was oil on canvas, about half-finished. Impressionistic in style, it featured a snowy mountain town at early dawn, soft candlelight glowing from a shop window, a child trudging down the lane, with a scrap of a farmer tending his sheep in the distance. Perhaps a bit of tribute to the English Impressionist Alfred Sisley, but mainly just Chloe Galen's imagination since she'd only seen snow twice in her life, both times while skiing in Aspen. She liked the painting thus far. She wasn't sure the world would, but an artist must strive to please herself.

"Not bad, Miss Galen."

The voice over her shoulder nearly made her leap from her sandals. "You startled me, Professor," she said, turning to see Dr. Graziano. He peered at her work with hands clasped behind his back and glasses perched on the end of his nose.

"Excuse me for interrupting your concentration," he murmured, still studying the canvas.

Chloe stood stock-still and waited anxiously while he leaned and bobbed and gazed some more. His head moved sideways, then in and out, as light caught the texture of the oils.

"Yes, this is not bad at all," he finally declared.

"Thank you, sir. I'll take that as high compliment."

He chuckled. "You may indeed. Your background is more extensive than most juniors. Your layering and abstraction of light is far more advanced than your peers. Your technique still needs work—brush strokes too coarse, colors a bit garish for the style you're attempting—but all in all, you have true potential." He straightened his back, then pushed his glasses up his nose.

Chloe stared up at her tall, balding, middle-aged professor as though he were Zeus from Mount Olympus himself. She swallowed before trying to speak. "Thank you, sir. I appreciate your encouragement," she said, smiling like a pageant contestant.

"Thanks aren't necessary, Miss Galen. Art is the combination of truth and beauty. Your work contains truth—it's an honest reflection of your soul at this stage of your life. And beauty? Well, we know the old saw about that, but I find your work more than proficient in conveying your message in the piece."

Chloe wasn't sure which message he referred to—she'd wanted to create the perfect idyllic village of a by-gone era. Sort of her personal dream-town where she could steal away with her dashing, handsome hero and live out a serene, but sensual life.

But she'd take Graziano's compliment and any others he wished to dole out. "This is my favorite piece so far," she said, striving to sound modest yet confident.

"I see real potential here and in the portfolio you submitted for admission placement. It's my job to see your potential realized." He stepped away from the easel. "I'm considering allowing you into advance placement oils. Not for credit, of course, not with your undergraduate status, but you may audit the class for valuable experience in technique and style. We've got a powerful group in the class this year. If you watch and listen, I think you'll benefit immensely." He paused to gauge her reaction.

Her mouth had locked into fly-catching mode. She couldn't speak.

"I don't usually allow anyone into the class not already accepted into the graduate program, but since I'm department head, I'm granted a little latitude regarding audits." He again clasped his hands behind his back, looking every bit the scholarly professor seen in movies.

Chloe swallowed hard. "I don't know what to say. Thank you, sir. I'll be quiet as a church mouse. I'll just watch and learn and dabble at my own humble work." She arched up on her tiptoes as some self-assurance returned.

"You have Mr. Hightower to thank, Chloe. He speaks highly of your work and your dedication. He's brought your name up so often I felt I had to take a look for myself. I'm glad I did. Your abilities will not only benefit, but I think you might just have something to offer the class in return as Jason insisted." With that, he turned and strode from the room.

Chloe stood in the sunlit room beaming like a giddy child. Her good day had grown infinitely better. The head of the art department had seen promise in her painting. She was about to be admitted into the most coveted advanced class the college offered. Her old friend, Jason Hightower, who'd become more unreadable than a Sanskrit newspaper, had sung her praises and opened doors others would kill for.

Add this to yesterday's decision to refuse her trust fund, therefore all but assuring smooth sailing with Aaron from Atlanta, and life looked rosy indeed. Chloe did levitate from her sandals this time and glided toward the studio door with feet not touching the floor.

She couldn't wait to find him. She couldn't wait to find the love of her life and tell him the career of her dreams got one step closer.

CHAPTER NINE

Chloe called the family lawyer and scheduled an appointment the moment she got home. She then straightened the apartment, did the dishes and washed the kitchen floor with spray cleaner and an old t-shirt. She invited Aaron for dinner, anxious to share her good news, but opted for delivery pizza. This wasn't the time for a repeat performance of her culinary abilities. She showered, dressed in her favorite jeans and tank top, then dried her hair into soft curls. No harried, scary wild woman tonight. She couldn't help remembering the tender, poignant story of his childhood as she applied some lip gloss and blush. This was a man unafraid to show emotion, secure in who he was and what he wanted. And what she wanted was to make him proud of her.

Aaron arrived ten minutes after the pizza, carrying a six-pack of Coke and a bottle of burgundy wine. "Always be prepared," he drawled, stowing them in the refrigerator. "That's what my scout leader taught us." He winked with exaggeration then leaned against the counter, crossing his arms over his chest.

He seemed to take up all the space in the small kitchen. And not just because he was six-two and close to two hundred solid pounds. His male aura filled and dominated a room. She didn't feel intimidated or overwhelmed, yet nonetheless slipped on her four-inch platform sandals to prevent a strained neck.

"Coke will be perfect with the pizza. Thanks," she said, opening two cans and handing him one. Clinking her can with his, she blurted her news with uncontrollable zeal. "I've been invited to audit a graduate placement course in oils. I know I usually work with watercolors, but working with another medium will expand my abilities. Nobody gets into this class unless they're already accepted into grad school. It won't be for credit, but the experience will be invaluable." She sucked in air like a deep-sea diver then continued. "I can't believe my good luck. While I was working in the studio today, Dr. Graziano came in to observe my work. He said that I showed real potential." She pronounced each word as though a declaration of highest praise, then glanced at Aaron for his reaction to the news.

He was leaning against the counter drinking his beverage, his face unreadable.

Chloe continued, trying to temper her enthusiasm. "He said my current work-in-progress was his favorite and that he would make an exception and allow me into the class. He's the department head, you know," she added inanely, wondering why Aaron's expression was so strange.

"That's wonderful. I can't wait to see your work, Chloe," he finally said in a soft voice.

"Thanks. Now I'll have the confidence to show you and anybody else who wants to see it. I've never had confirmation of my ability except by Sara, Mom and Dad—and Jason, of course. You know, people who have to say nice things," she said, laughing.

Aaron walked to the window and settled into a chair, his eyes assessing her. "Any clue as to why Graziano showed up in the studio? Does he usually take such personal interest in a student's work? Especially those he doesn't have in class?" His tone sounded doubtful, almost suspicious. Chloe didn't like it.

"Not usually, but Jason—you remember him from Chaz's—is his assistant and asked him to take a look." She drew another deep breath, wanting, willing Aaron to support her, to recognize the great opportunity she'd been handed. "I'm kind of surprised Jason went out on the limb."

Aaron rose to get another Coke so his face turned unreadable again. "So why do you think your good-old-friend Jason went out on this limb?" Aaron's voice floated out from inside the refrigerator.

Chloe's back stiffened and she fought to control her temper. "I don't know, but I'm glad he did. What's wrong with you, Atlanta? Why aren't you happy for me? This could be my big break." Unable to help herself, she stamped her foot.

Aaron straightened to his full height then gazed down at her feet with comic amusement. "Simmer down, Chloe. I don't want to hurt your feelings. I believe your well-deserved break will come without Graziano or Hightower's help. I think Hightower might have some . . . ulterior motive for promoting you."

Chloe saw him wince as though he didn't like his choice of words. And she liked them even less. "You're jealous, Aaron. And there's no reason for it. Jason knows he and I will never be anything but friends. Believe me, he can live with that." She forced a laugh, although it sounded as hollow as it felt.

"I'm not jealous, Chloe," Aaron said, slicking a hand through his hair.

She was distracted for a moment by how shiny his hair was. Why were they having this ridiculous discussion when they could eat their pizza then go on to more enjoyable pursuits? "If you're not jealous, then what is it?"

His expression registered utter sorrow—similar to Papa's right before he grounded her for the entire summer. "I don't know, Chloe. I don't trust Hightower. He's up to something; I can feel it. I'd prefer you stay away from him. Graziano, too."

Chloe set her soda can on the counter before she launched it like a missile. "Are you out of your mind? There's no reason to stay away from Jason. We're friends—that's all. Do you not understand the concept?" She took two steps toward Aaron who'd settled back into the chair.

She assumed a familiar hip-shot pose, one she hadn't resorted to in awhile. "And stay away from Dr. Graziano? Have you lost your mind? He's my campus advisor—the one who decides if I get into grad school or not—whether or not I get the training needed to really be an artist, not just a dabbler in the spare room after work. I'm running out of colleges. I can't afford to blow this chance!" She immediately regretted the last part of her diatribe, not wishing to trot out details of her previous art school enrollments.

Aaron rose to his feet with smooth assuredness and towered over her despite the four-inch heels. His hands gently gripped her shoulders as he spoke. "Chloe. Sweet Chloe. You're young. You'll get lots of chances. And anyway, I didn't say you shouldn't audit the class, only be wary of those two." His long fingers rubbed her shoulder blades soothingly.

His patronizing tone was too much. He was too much, so very like . . . Mama! Chloe stumbled back from his touch. "You're granting me permission to audit the class? Do I have the story right? Maybe this controlling routine works with the ladies from Atlanta, but I don't appreciate it one bit."

She saw his pained look and knew she'd hit a nerve, but Chloe didn't care. She'd just crawled out from under her mother's dominance and wasn't about to get under someone else's. "I don't need your permission to take a class, Aaron. And I don't like your possessiveness." She crossed her arms over her tank top and wondered how her plans for the enjoyable evening had gone so wrong.

Aaron walked to the lidded trash bin and tossed in his coke can. When he met her gaze, his eyes were bleak and his mouth set in a hard line. "I don't want to control you, Chloe. I just want to keep you from something you might not be able to handle."

"Can't handle?" Chloe spat. "I can handle anything that graduate class throws at me. Or at least I'll give it an honest try." She picked up the pizza box from the counter and shoved it at him, jabbing mercilessly in his solar plexus. "I'll tell you what I can't handle! A man who thinks he can dictate what I do with my life after three dates!" She punctuated each word with a prod from the box, effectively moving Aaron through the kitchen and out of the apartment.

"Chloe. Chloe!" Aaron said, wrestling the box from her grip. "I didn't mean—"

"No, Aaron. I know exactly what you meant. Now take this pizza and go. I've lost my appetite for both of you." She stepped back inside and slammed the door.

But that wasn't exactly true. Her stomach tumbled and churned, complaining about the aromatic pizza getting away. And she hadn't lost her taste for the man heading down the steps either. Not by a long shot. She stepped onto the balcony and watched Aaron offer one final plea from inside his truck.

So was this it? Three dates and kaput? The only man she could imagine spending her life with started the engine, drove down the alley, and turned the corner. For a moment she visualized herself chasing his taillights down the block.

Wait! I've changed my mind. I'll forget about Graziano's placement class for now. Just don't go.

But instead she remained where she was. She couldn't allow herself to surrender her hard-fought dignity. Not over a man. What was her and Sara's mantra? If they don't come begging, throw 'em back. There's plenty more dogs at the pound.

But that no longer felt right either.

She'd wanted Aaron to be happy for her, to be proud. He had no way of knowing her artistic education hadn't quite been stellar, nor had she set the art world on fire with her paintings. Chloe walked back into the tiny apartment that felt lonelier and more forlorn than usual.

She wished she hadn't lost her temper.

She wished Sara were home. She needed to talk to someone before she messed up the first relationship that had ever meant anything to her. Exhaling a pent-up breath, she punched in Jason's number. He was her friend after all. And right about now, a friend was what she needed, especially one with a male point of view. Of course, she couldn't tell Jason that Aaron's jealousy was at the heart of the matter. But Jason was smart. He would suggest a logical conclusion to her crisis without the emotional free-fall she'd been on.

Jason picked up on the second ring. He was not only home, but anxious to see her, too. It felt good to have a course of action. So good, in fact, she splurged and called a cab to take her to Old Metairie. A fresh perspective would straighten out the mess her temper had caused.

Jason met her at the door wearing tight jeans and a white silky shirt, open at the neck and un-tucked. His feet were bare and his hair slicked back with gel, showing off great cheekbones. He looked like an ad for expensive cognac.

"Look at you," she said, tossing her purse on a chair. "Were you expecting a supermodel, and instead got a call from your old high school class-skippin' pal?"

"You're as good as any supermodel, just not as tall."

"Thanks . . . I think." Chloe walked through the living room toward the back windows that overlooked a neighborhood under reconstruction. The opulence of the apartment still surprised her. This guy used to think upended milk crates were chairs and stacked beer cans the perfect decorative touch. The walls had suede wallpaper, the carpets were hand woven and the furniture was expensive. "And look at this place. I'd ask for the name of your decorator but I don't think he works in our neighborhood."

"Only hookers and dealers work your area, Chlo." He joined her at the window and gazed down on the renovations below. "Your neighborhood should've been washed away in the Great Flood. It's not worth saving."

"That's not very nice. I see lots of people working hard on their homes and yards. And I saw a poster promoting a neighborhood Block Watch."

He exhaled a snort. "Watch what? Nobody's got anything worth stealing where you live."

"Why are you being so mean?" She took a step back. He was standing too close for comfort and had on too much cologne. The scent overpowered her empty stomach. She should've swallowed her pride and eaten a piece of pizza.

"And when did you become the consummate humanitarian?" He issued a wicked laugh. "The queen of conspicuous consumption has developed a social conscience?" He tipped up her chin and smiled. His teeth looked unnaturally white. "Oh, I get it. You still haven't patched things up with your mother. That's why you have this affinity for the downtrodden."

Chloe jerked her face from his grip. "No, I haven't patched things up, but that's got nothing to do with it." She walked across the room to the leather sofa and plopped down. Why was she arguing with Jason? Couldn't she get along with anyone?

"Okay. Fine. Don't get your lacy ones in a twist." He walked into the kitchen. "How 'bout something to drink. Wine? Champagne? Whiskey? Tequila, with worm or without?"

"How about a Coke or Pepsi? I don't drink much."

"Yeah, right." His voice floated from the other room. "That's not the story I heard."

"Rumors of my capacity for inebriation have been greatly

exaggerated." She thumbed through a copy of *Wine Connoisseur* magazine. What happened to his subscription to *Sports Illustrated?*

True to his new interest in reading matter, Jason walked back carrying two wine glasses, up to the rim with something dark red.

"That doesn't look like a soft drink to me." She straightened her back against the couch.

"Relax. One glass, Chloe. You're so uptight, I can't even talk to you." He set down the glasses and settled into the couch.

He was sure right about that. The knot between her shoulder blades had spread and tightened up her entire back. She sipped the wine. It tasted very dry and well aged.

"That's a good girl," he soothed. "For a second there, I was afraid Chloe Galen had lost her sense of humor. And that would be a cryin' shame." His long fingers gently rubbed the base of her neck.

The touch felt so soothing she sighed. "I have lost my sense of humor. I need to mend my ways." She took another sip of wine and scooted a bit closer on the couch. "And I need some friendly advice—a male viewpoint. I'm afraid I've made a mess of my life."

"Just call me Dr. Therapy." Jason's hand kneaded her tight shoulder and neck muscles.

Chloe leaned forward, swinging her head down to her knees. "That feels so good. My neck's been killing me. Sara tries to give neck rubs but she's too wimpy."

"Nobody's ever accused me of that." Jason paused in his ministrations to drink half his glass. "There's something I want to talk to you about, too."

"You go first. I need to work up my courage." She started to relax from his comforting touch and from the wine on an empty stomach.

"I talked to Sam right before you called—"

"Sam?" Chloe interrupted from her head-between-the-knees position. "You're on first-name basis with the department head?" A cloud of curls hid her face.

"Yeah, we're old buddies. Anyway, he agrees with my assessment of your work. He thinks you have real talent, sweet thing. I thought he would." His fingers worked down her spine plying each vertebra with firm pressure.

"I really appreciate you sticking your neck out. Every undergrad wants him to take a serious look at their work. I know he's a busy man."

"You have no idea how busy. Getting into the oils class is just a beginning for you. You'll learn things you can't imagine. The path to riches lies straight ahead. Just stick with your old pal Jason."

His strong hand moved down her lower back where her t-shirt had ridden up from the waistband of her jeans. His fingers on her bare flesh didn't quite feel right, but she had no desire to insult him. Her list of friends was already short enough. "I don't know about any path to riches. I'd just like to have a good portfolio to present for graduate admissions. It'll be awhile before anyone spends good money to buy a Galen original."

"That's where your thinking has gone astray. Most of the world's great artists died broke. Their paintings weren't worth squat until they were cold in the grave. I'm talking real money right now, while we're still young." He finished off his wine.

Chloe raised her head and shook the hair from her face. "Hello, Jason? It's me, Chloe Galen. Not one of the world's great artists. Not yet anyway."

Using both hands, Jason pressed Chloe down into a doubled-over position. "You're good enough, or at least you'll be good enough after you take this class." His hands worked up and down her back with increasing boldness, grazing the sides of her breasts. When he ventured under the waistband of her jeans, she fell off the couch into a heap on the floor.

"Hey, watch it, buddy. Private territory." Scrambling to her feet, she picked up her wineglass and put some distance between them. He was acting strangely. "What are you talking about— real money right now?" She took another sip as her stomach growled.

"Let me show you. Actions speak louder than words." Jason walked into his bedroom then returned before she had a chance to assess his behavior. He held out a small rectangular box of gold foil. The name of a prominent New Orleans jeweler was emblazoned across the top. "I didn't have time to wrap it. Your call was an . . . unexpected surprise. I was waiting for the right moment to give this to you."

Chloe accepted the box. Jason's gifts were always beautifully wrapped, heightening one's expectations, but usually contained a t-shirt proclaiming "World's Biggest Loser". "I love presents," she exclaimed then pried off the lid. "It's not even my birthday."

And she certainly should have loved this one. Inside was a drop pendant on a wide gold chain. The slide contained five diamonds and none were chips, increasing in size to the bottom gem of at least a full carat. She gasped while her uneasy feeling returned with a vengeance.

"It's gorgeous, Jason, but I can't accept this. It had to cost a fortune."

He closed the distance between them in three strides then settled his hands on her hips. "It did. And you'd be a fool not to accept it. It's just a token of my . . . esteem and a taste of what's to come. For you and for me." He kissed her forehead chastely.

Chloe gazed again at the necklace. She'd seen nothing nicer even in her mother's and Grandmère's jewelry boxes. "Don't think I don't like your gift. I do. But it's way over the top." She handed the box back to him.

He shook his head in denial. "Don't overreact, Chloe. If I couldn't afford the thing, I wouldn't have bought it. It's no big deal. At least try it on."

Before she could think of an excuse, he lifted the diamonds from the box and wrapped the chain around her neck. His fingertips felt soft on her skin as he snapped the closure, not roughened like Aaron's. Aaron. Just thinking about him filled her with pangs of regret for losing her temper. She missed his laugh, his touch, and his kiss—kisses too few and spaced too far apart. She needed to get this mission for lovelorn advice back on track.

"Just wear it today. I've got thirty days to return it. It's no big deal."

Chloe gazed at her reflection in his beveled mirror. The necklace looked silly with her shorts and t-shirt. "What do you mean . . . a taste of what's to come?"

"It's very simple, my naïve little artist. Only after you're dead is your work worth anything. Tourists will come into a gallery and haggle down a price so far that the artist barely recovers the cost of materials. Then they trot home to Chicago and tell their friends what a steal they found. Steal being the operative and accurate word. They probably pray every night for you to get hit by a bus so they can resell the thing online and make a fortune."

Chloe couldn't help herself—she laughed at his little scenario. "Come on, Jason. Isn't the joy in the creative process anyway?"

He stared at her with cool detachment. "You haven't had enough poverty yet, Chlo? You're starting to look like a poster child for anorexia. Want to know the real joy in life? It's in fine things. Let's not be stupid." He picked up the wine bottle and walked slowly to where she stood. He refilled her empty glass then set down the bottle. "I thought you had something to prove to your mother, that you didn't need her money with all the strings attached. I'm offering you a chance to stand on your own two feet. To more than support yourself while you finish your precious degree. Get out of the slums and live like you should. And take pathetic Sara with you. She'll never get out on her abilities." He ran his finger up her bare forearm.

An innocent gesture, but it didn't feel innocent. She gulped her wine. "How, Jason? You're not making any sense." He seemed to loom over her with a threatening familiarity.

"When you're ready, when you're good enough, you can join me in my effort to get more Blakes out in the world. His missing canvases are turning up," he said, a grin suffusing his face. "Too bad the guy's dead and won't be able to enjoy the fruits of his labor." Without warning, Jason took the glass from Chloe's hand then pulled her into an embrace that left no doubt about his non-platonic intentions.

"What are you doing," she sputtered, but his mouth choked off her words. He kissed her long and hard with frightening intensity. She struggled against him but he was too strong.

"You know what I'm doing. Something I should've done a long time ago. I'm not waiting around while you play your little two-step with me. I want you, Chloe, and I'm offering you everything you could possibly want. That necklace is just the beginning."

"Have you lost your mind?" It was not a rhetorical question.

He tightened his grip on her forearms when she tried to squirm away. "Don't fight me. I know what's best for both of us, even if you're too immature to see how the world works. You'll have plenty of time for principles when we're old and gray."

His chest crushed her breasts as he pushed her against the wall. For the first time in her life, Chloe felt scared. This wasn't a frisky boy trying to cop a feel in the backseat of Daddy's car. Jason was hurting her, and he didn't seem to care. From the glint in his eye, her pain appeared to be part of his pleasure.

"Stop it, Jason!" she demanded, but his mouth choked off her protests. Chloe inexplicably felt she was betraying both Aaron and Sara. Aaron, since that's where her heart lay, and Sara because she fancied herself in love with the creep breaking her wrists. Her mind juggled the scenarios for escape she'd seen on TV over the years: A swift knee kick to the groin? No, she was too short to be effective.

Smash a vase over his head? Nothing in view could be lifted with one hand.

Only one lame possibility came to mind. Chloe forced herself to stop struggling against his hold on her. She relaxed against his body and felt his full male power almost crush her. She stopped fighting his kisses, too. He paused briefly in attacking her to meet her eye.

"Just don't hurt me. Okay?" Her eyes filled with tears as though on command.

"Sure, baby." The glint had turned his eyes to black obsidian, but he released one wrist and trailed his hand down her shirt to her breast. His teeth nipped at the skin of her throat.

Chloe held her breath, willing herself to be patient, to wait for the right moment. When his mouth returned to hers, she opened her lips and accepted his kiss fully. His tongue explored the recesses of her mouth as he practically devoured her. She could feel his carnal response and fought a wave of revulsion, but still continued to kiss him back.

His small moan of pleasure signaled her opportunity. Chloe bit down on his tongue with every ounce of strength she could muster. She remembered her dentist's instructions to crunch down hard on a new filling to align the proper bite and she gave no less effort.

Jason howled like a dog with his tail caught in a car door. He immediately released his grip on her arm and stumbled backward in pain and shock.

Chloe made her move. His surprise and anguish would soon change to hatred and revenge. She ran for the door like an Olympic sprinter. Yanking it open she caught a glimpse of Jason from the corner of her eye. He was holding his hand to a mouth covered with pink foamy blood. Their eyes met for an instant as Chloe fled the apartment and she saw him form the words "You, bitch." Speech appeared to be difficult at the moment.

She joined a couple entering the elevator on his floor and held her breath until the doors closed. For several seconds, she pictured Jason forcing the doors open like Jack Nicholson in *The Shining,* foaming like a rabid dog, then killing all three of them in a bloody frenzy. But the doors remained closed until the elevator opened onto the airy lobby.

The doorman called "Have a good day, miss," as Chloe ran through the doorway to the street. She had reached the next block before she turned to look. Jason wasn't following her.

Leaning against a telephone pole, she struggled to catch her breath. Traffic crisscrossed the intersection unaware that a dreadful crime had just been averted. Chloe forced herself to slow her breathing and heart rate and think logically about her next move.

She remembered her purse on Jason's hall chair, but decided not to return for it. *Say, Jason. Did I leave my purse here when I left in a hurry? How's that mouth doin'?* She had no cell phone, no change for a pay phone, nothing on her but rubber flip-flops.

When no other options came to mind, Chloe stood at the Metairie intersection and assessed car occupants waiting for the light to change. She selected the minivan of a middle-aged woman with soccer field stickers plastered across the back window and knocked timidly on the glass.

"Excuse me, ma'am," she pleaded when the woman lowered her window. "I just had a horrible fight with my boyfriend and had to get outta there. I left without my purse and I'm afraid to go back. I've got no way home. Could you please take me uptown? Please?"

Maybe it was the sincerity in her eyes.

Maybe it was her bedraggled look.

Or perhaps it was Jason's blood dotting her white shirt, but the woman unlocked the door and drove to her neighborhood. She asked few questions—mainly kept her eyes focused on traffic. And Chloe said little to her rescuer, just cried and sniffled and wiped her nose with a fast food napkin.

But when the woman dropped her on the corner of Avalon Avenue, she gave Chloe a long curious stare. Maybe she wondered why a girl without cab fare was wearing a diamond necklace worth at least ten grand.

Luckily Chloe found the superintendent to let her into the apartment. She took off the necklace, dropped it into her sock drawer then stood under the shower stream until her skin puckered like a raisin. Her t-shirt went into the trashcan. She made a cup of lemon tea and stared out of the window, trying to make sense of what just happened. Violence never had been Jason's forte before. He had changed. Something had changed the sweet, mischievous kid she'd thought she knew so well. And it had something to do with his scheme to pass off fakes as the works of a long-dead artist.

Money is the root of all evil. Grandmère's favorite expression when Chloe had begged for more allowance came to mind. An odd maxim for a woman who wore Parisian suits and carried designer luggage, but Grandmère possessed a practical side, too, one that insisted the cook use leftovers in the next pot of gumbo.

Money had corrupted Jason. She had no idea how deep he'd gotten himself and didn't want to know, pledging to keep far away from him in the future. Aaron had been right. He'd recognized something in Jason not quite aboveboard and had tried to warn her. She'd dismissed his misgivings as typical male jealousy, as though they were still in junior high. She longed to talk to Aaron—to patch up their misunderstanding and admit he was right to be suspicious about Jason. But no way could she tell him she went to his house tonight. How could she explain why she went to her old boyfriend for advice on how to handle her new boyfriend?

If only Sara would come home. Sara. What exactly would she say to her best friend about the man Sara thought herself in love with? Oh, by the way. I asked Jason for advice and he offered me an interesting business proposition then proceeded to rape me. How's that for the man of your dreams?

Chloe rubbed her wrists, already purpling with bruises. The less she said to Sara about tonight, the better. Sara had once accused her of dangling Jason—not wanting him, but not wanting to let go of his affection either. And she might've been guilty of that in the past. The old Chloe, the immature Chloe, who didn't have a clue what she wanted in life, might have behaved in that fashion.

She curled into a fetal position on the couch and tried to block out the memory of Jason's mouth, his hands, his hard body pressed against her. Tears streamed down her face when she remembered why she went to his apartment in the first place. Her argument with Aaron seemed petty now. Apparently things were happening on campus she wasn't aware of. Jason was into some kind of get-rich-quick scheme. But if she told Aaron about it, he would jump to the conclusion Dr. Graziano was in on it, too. Dr. Graziano was the first art professional to take her work seriously. She needed this chance to prove herself in his class.

She stared at the door, willing Sara to come home as tears

streamed down her face. She desperately needed advice before she squashed her chances with Aaron. Chloe cried for messing up again—and this time, the best thing to ever come her way.

"Chloe. Chloe," Sara's voiced broke through her bad dream and Chloe bolted upright on the couch. Her neck hurt due to her sleeping position but Sara's expression shifted the concern to her. The girl's pale face was streaked with mascara and her eyes were red-rimmed and watery.

"Sara, what happened? Are you all right?" Chloe's arm snaked around Sara's waist as she sat down shakily.

"No, I'm not all right," Sara wailed. She alternately sobbed and hiccupped like a child. Chloe patiently waited for the crying jag to diminish before pressing her roommate for details.

"What happened? Did something happen at work?" Chloe gently rubbed Sara's back between the shoulder blades.

"Not at work," Sara sobbed. "Afterwards. Jason called me."

Chloe gulped. She couldn't breathe; she couldn't think.

Sara continued without noticing Chloe had turned paper white. "He asked me to come over after my shift. He sounded . . . upset. I have no idea why. But he said he had a full bottle of tequila and needed a little help with it." Sara blew her nose then cast a glance at Chloe. "I know you think he uses women, but tonight I didn't care. I needed a tequila night after the week I had at school." She sucked in deep gulps of air, as though she'd forgotten to breathe. "I planned to use him as much as he used me, if you catch my drift." She tried to inject humor into her tone, but a fresh wave of tears ruined the jocular attempt. Her nose began to run.

Chloe handed her the tissue box from the coffee table. "Go on," she murmured. "What happened when you got there?" She struggled to suck air into her own lungs. "Did he . . . get out of line while you were there?"

"No," she sobbed, dragging the word out into two syllables. "He didn't get out of line because . . . because . . ." She hiccoughed and spluttered, but couldn't seem to talk. "Because he was dead," she finally blurted.

Chloe went silent. She stared at her roommate hoping, praying this was some kind of sick joke—a way to get back at her if Jason told about the earlier visit. But no laughter, no snide guffaw ensued, only relentless tears.

Sara continued. "He had left the door unlocked. When he didn't answer my knock, I went inside." Sara dabbed her eyes with a fresh tissue, finally reining in her emotions. "I found him lying on the kitchen floor still holding the bottle of tequila." Sara met Chloe's eyes, her lower lip trembling. "He'd been shot. There was a big hole in the back of his head, and blood spattered everywhere. On the wall, the cabinets, all over the floor." She dissolved into fresh tears and collapsed onto Chloe's shoulder, her body wracked with pain and emotion.

Chloe wrapped her arms around her friend while a dozen thoughts flooded her mind.

Such as her purse lying on the hall chair.

The expensive diamond necklace sitting in her sock drawer.

And the likely possibility she was the last person to see him alive.

Aaron finished the last of his bitter coffee and waited for cars to crawl around a load of drywall that had spilled from a flatbed truck. At least the traffic snarl would give him a chance to figure out what to say to Chloe when he got there. With any luck the highway mess would tie up all exit routes for the rest of his life and he'd never have to tell the only woman he cared about since Stacey that she was wanted by Homicide.

The FBI had no jurisdiction in the murder of a local college student, but Aaron had been asked to bring Chloe Galen downtown for questioning first thing this morning. Cop courtesy would only extend so far. He was being kept in the loop because of Uncle Charlie and the off-chance the two cases were somehow related.

Aaron knew in his gut that they were. Despite the bag of cocaine in Hightower's apartment, his murder wasn't drug related. The diamond watch he'd been wearing when shot could easily bring a thousand dollars from a fence. Not too many crack-heads or irate dealers would leave something like that behind. His death had something to do with his involvement with the fraud ring, but proving the connection wouldn't be easy. And trying to keep Chloe out of jail on suspicion of murder would be harder still.

Her purse had been found in his apartment. What woman left without her purse?

The doorman had described her to a T as the woman leaving the apartment in an all-fired hurry.

According to the Coroner's timeline, Chloe most likely had been the last person to see Hightower alive. The only thing keeping her from being charged with murder was a lack of motive. Even still, it wouldn't be easy for Chloe in the interrogation room. His heart ached as he thought about what lay ahead for her. If she requested a lawyer, she would look guilty. If she didn't, they would browbeat her for hours for any possible reason she had to shoot Hightower in the back of the head at close range.

Chloe opened the door wearing red shorts and a black tank top. Dark smudges beneath her eyes betrayed she hadn't slept any better than he had. Her hair was damp and tousled from the shower; her feet were bare. Without any makeup she looked far younger than her twenty-one years.

"Hey, Atlanta," she said, a shy smile spreading across her face. "I'm glad you're still speaking to me. You want coffee? I just made a pot." She shifted her weight from one leg to the other, swaying slightly.

She had no clue why he was there. His self-loathing ratcheted up a notch.

"Coffee sounds good." He spilled the dregs from his mug into the bushes below and followed her into the kitchen.

She held her forefinger to her lips. "Let's be very quiet so Sara can sleep. She had a rough night."

He watched her pour two mugs and pondered how to break the news that he'd been lying to her from the start. Chloe made it easy for him.

"Wow, look at you. You're all dressed up. What's the occasion?"

He stupidly looked down at his sport coat and creased chinos. Business-as-usual attire for his Atlanta office, but Chloe had only seen him in jeans, to fit in with college couture. He took a gulp of the black coffee then spoke. "I know about Jason Hightower. I'm sorry about your friend, Chloe."

Her dark eyes flooded with tears, making them look huge in her pale face. "How could you know? You mean the story already hit *The Times*? That was fast." She slumped against the counter, her coffee sloshing over the rim. "Oh, Aaron. I've made a mess of things. I went to talk to him last night."

"Chloe, wait, stop. You shouldn't—"

"No, let me talk. I wanted a man's perspective after our little spat." She glanced up at him through wet, spiky lashes, while his heart plummeted lower in his chest. He yearned to take her into his arms, to kiss her, to make her pain go away. And tell her Hightower wasn't worthy of her friendship or respect.

"But he wasn't interested in dispensing friendly advice," she continued.

Aaron noticed the ugly purple bruises on the wrists of both hands. Something sharp twisted in his gut. Hightower had hurt her. It was a good thing the guy was already dead.

"What happened, Chloe? Did he hurt you?" he asked, dreading the obvious answer.

"Almost, but I'm okay. Really." She attempted a half-smile then lowered her voice to a whisper. "He started talking crazy. I think he might have been on something." She looked up in anguish. "He wanted us to get together on a business venture."

Aaron knew he was walking a tightrope. He needed to identify himself as law enforcement. What would he do if she blurted out something incriminating? Damn it. He'd taken an oath to uphold the law. Not bend it around a tiny, red-haired fireball with a turned-up nose and eyes a man could get lost in.

But his all male alter ego needed to hear what happened in Hightower's apartment. And if necessary, pull him off the slab in the coroner's office and kill him a second time.

The veteran cop won out. "Stop, Chloe! Don't say anything more until you hear me out." The look on her innocent face made him feel very old and very tired. "I didn't read about Jason's murder in *The Times*." Her brow furrowed with uncertainty. "Orleans Homicide detectives called me. They thought this might be related to the case I'm working on and I'm certain it is."

She stared at him, growing paler by the moment. "I don't understand," she murmured.

He held up a hand. "I know you don't. I wish I'd been upfront with you from the beginning, but I couldn't be. That's the nature of my job." He sighed and let the rest of the truth spill out. "I'm an agent with the Atlanta FBI office, working undercover to investigate an art fraud ring, potentially out of Leporte."

Her mouth dropped open and she stared as though he were a stranger. "Wow, honesty certainly isn't your best policy." Her tone carried little venom, only sad resignation.

The sharp blade he had apparently swallowed twisted deeper. "How can it be? This is what I do—ingratiate myself with people, hoping they'll divulge information to break my case and put the bad guys in jail." He swiped a hand through his tangled hair, a gesture of abject frustration. "Trust me. I've never hated my career choice before this assignment. I know what a hypocrite I've been—getting angry because you weren't upfront about your family, while I was investigating your old boyfriend." He set his mug in the sink then turned to face her. "You've got no reason to believe me now, but I never thought this would . . . get close to you. I thought I could do my job and still get to know you better."

"So I was just part of your charade?" Her plaintive plea cut him in half.

"No, Chloe. I liked you from the moment I laid eyes on you in Haiku Bar. And yeah, I realized you'd be useful, but I never thought . . ."

"Useful? My, wouldn't Mama be proud of me now. She never thought I'd ever be useful in the world."

"Bad choice of words. I thought I could choose my time to tell you the truth once I collected enough evidence for the prosecutor."

She stared up at him defiantly. "Well, you sure picked a fine time to let the cat out of the bag!"

"I thought I could keep you out of it."

"I told you I was rich. Why couldn't you just tell me you were a cop?"

"It's not that simple, Chloe."

She nudged him aside at the sink and began washing the dirty mugs. He tried to put his arms around her but she wouldn't have it. "Back off," she demanded. "I'm still mulling over what to believe and what not."

Aaron stepped back and dug his hands in his pockets. "Can't

blame you there, Orleans." He added the third syllable like she did. "There's more, Chloe. I need to take you downtown for questioning."

"Ask me whatever you want right now."

"Not by me, by homicide detectives. Your purse was found in Hightower's apartment. You were seen leaving his building in a hurry."

She turned off the water; her shoulders were shaking but her voice remained level. "And if you check the trash, you'll find my shirt with Jason's blood on it."

He held up both palms now. "Stop, Chloe! This isn't a game. Don't say anything more to me." He pulled his phone from his jacket pocket. "I'm calling your brother to have his lawyer meet you at the station."

She pulled the phone from his grasp and snapped it shut. "You'll do no such thing. The last thing I want is Ethan and Hunter down there. I'll end up in prison for sure." She walked out of the kitchen. "If I haven't done anything wrong, I don't need a lawyer. Isn't that what they say on TV?"

He caught her arm as she headed for her bedroom. "This isn't TV. You might say something incriminating without realizing it. A lawyer is in your best interest."

She shrugged from his light grip with a fierce glare. "I told you, Aaron. I had a fight with Jason and I bit his tongue. That's where his blood came from. But I didn't kill him. He was still alive when I left his apartment. I don't need a lawyer, and I don't need my overbearing brothers."

"What is so wrong with calling your family?" Aaron felt his temper flaring at her stubbornness. "I've met them. They love you and only want what's best for you."

This apparently was the wrong thing to say. He watched the color flush up Chloe's neck while her hands knotted into fists. "You just don't get it, Mister Big FBI Man. I've spent my entire life with my family deciding what's best for me. I've been dragged around like a rag doll and spied on when not in plain site. Part of that was my own fault." She drew in a breath. "But I'm a grown woman now, on my own. If Ethan or Hunter shows up, I'm once again the family goof-up needing to be bailed out. Frankly, Atlanta, I'd rather rot in jail." She stamped her foot for emphasis, bringing the sound of Sara stirring in the second bedroom.

"Now let's go," she whispered. "I'm not ready to explain to Sara. I'd rather face some New Orleans' trained inquisitors." She picked up her phone and headed out the door. "And you can choose to believe whatever you like."

Chapter Ten

Aaron dropped Chloe off in front of the imposing downtown precinct. She wouldn't allow him to go in with her or call anyone, and if she suspected he was peeping through one-way glass, she'd confess to the whole shebang. His heart ached in every hidden cranny as he watched her climb the steps and pull open the heavy glass door. She was so small. It was part of the reason people clambered around her to protect her. Tall people just looked stronger, more resilient, even though he knew how wrong that prejudice could be.

Lieutenant Rhodes had ordered him to keep his distance after he delivered Chloe to the detectives working Hightower's murder. He was too close, too personally involved.

And Uncle Charlie had no idea just how personally involved he was. He drove around the French Quarter, then the Warehouse District, thinking about nothing other than a hundred pounds of the most desirable woman he'd ever met. Maybe too long since being with a woman might be part of the problem, but just a small part. He wanted Chloe Galen—not just her full luscious lips or gentle caressing hands, but her heart, mind and soul. He yearned to possess her, cherish her and keep anything bad from getting close to her.

Charlie was right. He couldn't be present during her questioning. If things turned sour and it looked like they might charge her with murder, he'd be tempted to pull his thirty-eight, yell "Everybody back," grab Chloe and run for it. What she didn't need was a reenactment of a bad Hollywood movie.

He wasn't sure if she needed him at all. What could he offer a woman struggling to stand on her own two feet? A woman who once had everything, but now only wanted autonomy— something no one can help with.

Aaron narrowly missed rear-ending a car parked in front of Haiku Bar. Nostalgia had drawn him to the old neighborhood where he'd met the two irrepressible women. Lonesomeness kept him from going inside for a cold one, but he might accidentally kill somebody if he kept aimlessly driving around. Aaron called in to dispatch then headed home. He'd be worthless until Chloe's interrogation was over and they ruled her out as a suspect. Fortunately, Aunt Sophie was busy packing for a weekend trip to Lafayette to visit her sister, giving him the solitude he needed.

His uncle arrived home by four p.m. Charlie changed out of his rumpled suit into rumpled Bermuda shorts and a plaid shirt. Aaron had spotted his aunt ironing several times since he'd moved back, yet everything his uncle wore was wrinkled. He reminded Aaron of Chloe's description of the consummate tourist except for the lack of sandals with socks. Charlie's final words before heading to the bayou was an admonition to stay away from Miss Galen until this whole mess blew over.

Right. Absolutely. No problem. Why not ask him to stop a hurricane over the Gulf from heading toward shore? Aaron gritted out a hundred sit-ups, another hundred push-ups, then showered until the water ran cold. He contemplated raiding Charlie's meager hard liquor cabinet—a very rare indulgence— when he heard a knock on the door.

Something very sweet, something very wild waited on the other side.

Aaron opened the door to a whirlwind carrying grocery bags.

"What took you? This stuff is heavy," Chloe said, pushing

past him into the living room. "Which way to the kitchen?" She glanced around, hefting her bags higher.

"Can I help you with those?" Aaron shook off the shock of seeing her and tried to take the groceries.

"Stand back," she ordered. "Just point me in the right direction."

Aaron gestured with his thumb then followed her through the swinging door. "What's all this? I made dinner reservations at Bernard's. I thought you could use a good meal after your ordeal."

"Call and cancel." She dropped the bags on the counter just as one tore open, spilling an array of fresh vegetables. "It wasn't so bad, Atlanta. No thumb screws, no molar extractions." Chloe turned to face him. Since he'd dropped her off at the station, she'd changed into a long pink tank dress with pink high-heeled sandals. With her burgundy hair color, she was a sugarplum confection. He felt every male hormone shift into overdrive.

"They didn't even shine a spotlight in my eyes. I think the tide turned when I told them about my t-shirt with Jason's blood in the trash. No guilty person would leave evidence around, then tell the cops where to find it."

Aaron scratched his head, not agreeing with her assessment but not anxious to argue either. "Charlie said they were releasing you, that you wouldn't be charged."

"Yeah, I met your uncle, Atlanta. He was leaning against the back wall while they questioned me. Kept whispering things to Bad Cop when the guy got a little pushy." She pulled a mini carrot from the bag and began to nibble. "Looks like I'm not the only one with meddling relatives."

"That is the truth, sweet thing." He stepped closer and brushed a kiss across her suntanned nose.

She shoved a carrot into his mouth. "Not so fast. Food first."

Aaron remembered her disastrous cooking attempt and how

much it had upset her. "This looks like a lot of work. We could just go for pizza if you're not in the mood for Bernard's."

She lifted one delicately arched eyebrow. "Your Uncle Charlie walked me to the streetcar stop. He shared a few colorful vignettes about how Ethan and Cora met. He also mentioned he and your *tante* were headed to Lafayette Parish. They'll be gone for the whole weekend." The brow wiggled wickedly. "We have the house to ourselves. No Sara, no Ethan, no Hunter, no Grandmère and no Jeanette." She placed both hands on his shoulders and stretched up on tiptoes to kiss him.

"He told you that?" Aaron's tone betrayed his surprise. His uncle had told him to stay away from Chloe.

"That's right. Nobody knows I'm here. Why should we go out?"

Aaron had met enough homicide detectives to know that wasn't true. They probably knew exactly where she was and would be watching her apartment until a more likely suspect surfaced.

But right now, with her perfume floating in the air and her lips beckoning to be kissed, he didn't care if they had the place surrounded. He bent his head and kissed her long and hard, something he hadn't stopped thinking about since their argument the other night.

Chloe kissed him back, tentatively at first, then with uninhibited passion. He could feel her breasts through the thin cotton dress and thought he would lose his mind. His hands dropped from their safe position at the small of her back to cup her rounded bottom.

"Whoa," she drawled. "You Georgia boys work fast." She stepped back. "I told you, we're eating before we do any serious necking." She brandished a long stalk of celery as a weapon. "That's not negotiable."

Aaron did his best to tamp down his testosterone and let

Chloe call the shots. "I can be patient. I've been waiting for years the way it is. I know you've had a rough couple days." He pulled a stool up to the counter and began coring the green and red peppers that had spilled from the bag.

Chloe lowered her lashes then whispered so soft he could barely hear. "New rules, G-man. No talking about your case tonight or Jason's death or anything that he might have been involved in." When she raised her head, he saw her eyes glassy with unshed tears. "Not tonight. There'll be time for swapping stories. But right now I want to show off what I've learned." She picked up one of the cored peppers and chopped it into uniform pieces in less than a minute.

"Someone's been practicing." He ran a finger up her forearm.

She shook off his touch like a mosquito. "And I've been taking cooking lessons from Jeanette. You know . . . my Grandma. Not the most patient teacher in the world, but she knows more than Emeril about Creole and southern cooking." She attacked a purple onion with gusto. "I'm making gumbo and you better be hungry. Find me your *tante's* biggest pot."

She had no idea how hungry he was, especially after she bent over to rummage in Sophie's lower cupboards. Something was making his heart rate spike and his forehead sweat. It was all he could do to keep from picking her up and carrying her upstairs to the metal twin bed he'd slept in as a kid. How sophisticated was that?

He opted to plead for mercy. "Chloe, please, give me something to do. I can't stand around watching you. It's driving me crazy."

"I don't usually have that effect on men. Hmmm." She laid a finger against her chin as though pondering life's mysteries. "Are you sure you're not coming down with something?" She brushed her fingertips over his forehead then across his temple.

Her touch set him on fire. He grabbed her wrist and pulled

her into his arms. He breathed in the lemony scent of her hair and felt her breath exhale against his collarbone. A certain area of his anatomy gave away exactly how much he desired her in no certain terms.

She extricated herself from his embrace. "You do need something to occupy your mind." Pulling a mesh bag from a grocery sack, she threw it at him. "Get busy on these shrimp. Peel and de-vein them. I've got to make my roux," she announced in a schoolteacher voice. "You may pour us a little wine unless you think it'll send you over the edge." She waved her wooden spoon at him.

Aaron poured the wine, cleaned the shrimp, sliced the baguettes, set the table, tossed a Romaine salad, then folded the linen napkins to look like seabirds—anything to keep his mind off how good Chloe looked up to her elbows in the enormous pot with tomato sauce on her chin. He put on a Stevie Ray Vaughn CD, and they both sang and danced along while they worked.

When the CD had played through for the third time, Chloe finally announced, "Granny Jeanette says this should cook for hours. It's been ninety minutes. I say it's done." The wicked glint returned to her green eyes. "We're still young. We can't wait all day for food. I say let's eat!"

Aaron had just finished carving faces into the radishes. "I'm with you!" He jumped to his feet then pulled the pot off the burner with oven mitts.

Chloe carried the basket of bread into the dining room while Aaron followed with the gumbo. He didn't care if everything was still as raw as her famous asparagus once he noticed her hips sway beneath the silky dress.

But the food wasn't undercooked. His first bite had him thinking about a three-bedroom colonial in the suburbs, with bikes lying in the driveway and finger-paint artwork on the refrigerator. Thoughts like those he hadn't had since Stacey crushed every domestic idea he ever harbored. He reached for the wine and topped off both glasses.

Chloe shook her head. "Easy there. Wine puts me to sleep."

Aaron stopped pouring immediately.

"I've a small confession to make." She picked up her goblet and took a hearty swallow despite her warning. "In college, at Ole Miss, I had quite a reputation for imbibing."

He laughed, never knowing a woman her size that could handle even two glasses of wine.

"Laugh if you want, but it's true. Just ask Mama. She had spies reporting back on my adventures. I wasn't kidding about that." She took another small sip. "But my notoriety was exaggerated if not downright fictitious. Sort of like Jesse James—his story kept getting bigger and better for a hundred years."

"I'm fascinated. You're putting yourself in the same category as the Wild West's most dangerous outlaw?"

"Precisely." She broke off a piece of baguette and dipped it into the gumbo. We—my sorority sisters—would challenge other sororities and sometimes a fraternity to drinking contests. We would always win. Always." She ladled more soup into his bowl and a smaller portion into hers.

"What was the prize? The losers picked up the tab?"

"Much better, although that went without saying. We made them cut our grass for the entire summer, clean out gutters, chores like that. We even got this one sorority to paint our house. Most were afraid to climb ladders, so they made their boyfriends or fathers come weekends until the job was done. It was priceless."

"I see what you mean about Jesse James," Aaron said, watching her mop the bowl with the bread. Even that gesture looked wildly erotic in his current state of mind.

She smiled with pleasure at the memories. "Not that I'd ever do anything like that again. I'm a reformed woman. I've mended my evil ways." She picked up the wine glass and took another swallow.

"What did you do, Chloe?" He finished off his own glass, not imagining how this petite ladylike girl could even enter a drinking contest, let alone win."

"The contests were always rigged, every one of them. We set the ground rules and drank at the same Oxford bar. The bartender liked us. He thought we were cute."

"Apparently an observant man."

She laughed, a joyous wonderful sound. "He would pour the first round of draught so we could toast to a good contest and nobody would smell anything fishy. Then the subsequent rounds for our team would be non-alcoholic beer—the perfect color, the perfect amount of froth. Nobody ever caught on. We could drink them under the table." She finished her wine to punctuate her sentence.

Aaron watched her youthful exuberance, her *joie de vivre,* wishing he'd known her during college.

Chloe's face fell slightly. "Why are you looking at me like that? If you think I'm a terrible person, I'll make amends to every person wronged at Ole Miss. Don't call your buddies at New Orleans Police Department."

"Relax. I'll keep your secret. If that was the worst thing you did at college, I'm afraid you're not in Jesse's league."

He saw her visibly relax and wondered why she'd been so afraid to tell the amusing story. His recent subterfuge made her college prank pale by comparison. "But I've got to tell you, you've made it to the culinary major leagues. That gumbo was the best I've tasted since moving back, and I have tried it all around town."

"Thanks, Atlanta. I've come a long way since the shrimp-with-heads meal. I actually like cooking. Sara and I don't eat near as much food headed for the dumpster."

Aaron wiped his mouth and tossed down the napkin. Comments like that never failed to make him feel like a heel—as though he should do more to help them while they struggled to finish school. He could afford it since his usual after-work MO was to rent an action movie or work out at the gym. But he kept quiet. Chloe wasn't ready for any man to "help" her live her life and apparently, with the mother she had, maybe never would be.

As though reading his mind, Chloe lifted her chin and spoke with pride. "I love taking care of myself and making it on my own. Do you realize that until recently I'd never done laundry or ridden a bus or paid my own bills? My mother's chauffeur drove me to grade school. I thought it neat when the other kids' mothers picked them up after soccer practice. I used to watch my *père* just sign his name at his favorite Quarter restaurants and wondered why that didn't work at Burger King."

"I'm surprised you ever ate at Burger King."

"My brother, Hunter, would take me on Saturdays on the sly. Mama never knew."

"You have lived a charmed life. There's no doubt about that." Aaron reached for her hand. It felt warm and soft in his palm.

"Too charmed. Katrina woke me up. I was on campus in Mississippi, but I'll never forget the film footage of the devastation. People's lives destroyed in a matter of hours. Their homes, their possessions—everything we Americans hold dear no matter what our economic level. Except some things weren't adequately shown on TV. Families banding together to get through the dark days, neighbors helping neighbors, strangers reaching out to assist those who, but for the grace of God, could be them."

Chloe ran her fingers through her tangled curls and sighed. "It changed me. At least, it made me see how lucky I was." She lowered her voice to a whisper. "Mama still believes in . . . privilege. Oh, she's not a racist. She doesn't care what color you are as long as you've got the bankroll to back you up. Money is everything to Clotilde."

"We can't pick our parents, Chloe. We just make sure we don't turn into them." He rubbed the back of her hand, trying not to think about the nasty bruises from Hightower.

"I intend to show her. To make her see I'm made from the same Galen stock as our ancestors. Whatever prosperity they created was through hard work and dedication to their dreams. I'm going to put that kind of effort into my art. Make a splash with my one-woman show in two years. I intend to make a name for myself while I'm still alive and kicking. That's why I desperately need Dr. Graziano's class to hone my skills. I'll make Mama proud of me for the first time in my life." Chloe's dark eyes sparkled with excitement and something else . . . something akin to retribution.

For a moment Aaron wondered just how far she'd go to make her mama proud, then shook the notion away. "Make yourself proud. That's about all any of us can hope for." Aaron stood and walked to her side of the table. "And I'm not real proud of myself for deceiving you, even if it is my job." He touched her soft cheek then turned up her chin to gage her reaction.

It turned out better than he'd hoped. She stood up and threw her arms around his midsection and delivered a bear hug that belied her size. She squeezed tighter than a pro-wrestler on Saturday mornings. "That's another thing on my list we won't talk about tonight. Anyway, I seldom demand perfection in relationships since I've got little perfection to offer in return."

He loved the sound of that, although relationships never held this much appeal for him before. "You're about the closest thing I've run across," he said.

"That's because you're from Atlanta," she teased, tightening the embrace, then releasing him suddenly. "You are from Atlanta, aren't you?" She stepped away from him and peered up suspiciously.

"That's where I've lived for four years. I was born in Mobile, then my mom and I moved here. That part was the truth. I didn't move to Atlanta till after the Academy."

"And your request for tour guide services? 'Show me where the French Market is. What's the name of that big church? Where's this Bourbon Street I hear so much about?' " she mimicked his voice.

"All a devious plot to get you to go out with me."

"And the romantic horse-drawn carriage ride? Just another part of your plan?"

"My scheme was to get you to fall head over heels for me." He reached for her, wanted to draw her close, but she stepped away. "How'd that work?"

"The jury's still out." She perched her hands on her slim hips, pulling the fabric taut across her breasts. "You sound almost as conniving as my brother Ethan. Your uncle told me about the lengths he went to snag Cora. And believe me, reminding me of my older brother is not a good thing." She pushed him away with both palms on his chest. "Now go load the dishwasher with our plates and fix a pot of coffee. I won't have your *tante* coming home to a mess. I'll wait for you in the living room. My work is done."

Aaron did as ordered. He transferred the leftover gumbo into a smaller pot and loaded everything into the dishwasher. By the time the coffee finished brewing, he'd wiped down the counter-tops and hauled out the trash. Carrying a wicker tray with the coffee carafe and two mugs, he found Chloe on the living room couch.

She was curled up under an afghan and fast asleep.

Another Katrina couldn't have woken her from her slumber.

Her hand was fisted by her mouth, her breathing slow and regular. She emitted the tiniest snore every third breath or so.

He knew about the snore because he watched her sleep for an hour, then carried her upstairs to the metal twin bed and tucked her in. She didn't wake; she didn't even stir, while Aaron spent the night in the overstuffed upholstered chair, thinking about missed opportunities, missed chances. And the woman who had insidiously become the most important thing in his life.

Chloe awoke to sunlight streaming through sheer lace curtains. She glanced around the crowded room with Victorian wallpaper and teardrop crystal light fixtures without a clue as to where she was. Then she remembered—Aaron's house, or rather, the house he was staying in. She sat up and tucked her knees under her chin.

But how in the world did I get in this bedroom? And how come I don't remember anything after supper?

She lifted the quilt and saw her favorite pink tank dress. She was still fully dressed. What happened last night? She remembered eating the delicious gumbo and crusty baguettes. Dinner certainly had turned out well. Then she remembered spilling her guts about the sorority drinking contest. Not a smooth move for a woman trying to live down her past. Aaron now knows she's not a former lush—just a manipulative cheater and a liar. One step forward, two steps back. Finally, she recalled getting comfortable on the couch to wait for Aaron. She'd planned to resume the hugging and kissing they'd started in the kitchen.

And that's where her memory and their romantic evening ended.

Drat! This wasn't how things were supposed to turn out. Why in the world did she finish that second glass of wine? Chloe swung her legs out of bed and padded to what she hoped would be a door to the bathroom. She found instead a closet jammed full of summer clothes. Thumbing through the garments, she selected a shrunken jersey and capris with a drawstring waist, not wishing to return home in the same outfit in which she'd left.

She stole a look in the mirror. At least the dark circles under her eyes had faded and some color had returned to her cheeks. Creeping down the hallway like a thief, she located the bathroom and locked herself in, not emerging until she'd showered, dressed and tamed her wild mane of hair. Then she planned to look for Aaron. And find out how she had managed to end up in his bed. She knew nothing had happened—he was too much of a gentleman. A big fat liar, but a gentleman nonetheless.

Chloe's thoughts were of Aaron and good-morning hugs and wet kisses and—

"Ooommmph." She ran headlong into Charles Rhodes as she exited the bathroom.

"Good grief, Miss Galen. Is the house on fire?" Charlie asked.

"No, sir. What are you doing here?" She finger-combed her hair, conscious of the way it stood on end when wet.

"I live here, miss," he said, his eyes crinkling into deep lines. "I thought I'd take a shower if there's any hot water left."

Chloe's cheeks filled with color. "Sorry, but I thought you and Mrs. Rhodes were spending the weekend in Lafayette." Her blush deepened, knowing how cheesy that sounded.

"We changed our mind. We'll go next weekend, when Sophie's brother and his brood won't be visiting at the same time." He laughed heartily, his gut jiggling beneath his white undershirt.

"That's fine," she said. "I mean anytime is fine with me. I don't really have an opinion on the matter. And I don't want you to think I spent the night, or anything." Chloe rambled on, not able to stop herself.

"Are you all right, Miss Galen? You didn't fall down and hit your head, did you?"

"No, no. My head's fine. Everything's fine. I'll just be going now."

"Why are you wearing my Sophie's old clothes? She wears those when she works in her garden."

Nothing witty, nothing clever came to mind so Chloe opted for the truth. "I did spend the night, sir, but it's not what you think. I slept in that room alone," she said, pointing at the room she'd woken in. "I fell asleep after dinner because I drank two glasses of wine. And I have no idea where your nephew is." Her words tumbled out in a rush.

Charlie smiled warmly, genuinely. "My nephew is sitting at the breakfast table. I wouldn't let him come up to wake you. We found him downstairs on the couch when we got back last night. His story pretty much matches yours, so I guess it's the truth." He parried left then right, trying to maneuver past her. "Head down to breakfast, young lady. My wife is cooking up a hearty feast."

"Oh, no, sir. I couldn't eat. If you don't mind, I'll just sneak out the balcony door and run home. I'd rather not have Mrs. Rhodes know I stayed over."

He looked at her curiously. "She knows, Miss Galen, since she closed your window so you wouldn't catch a night chill."

"But I took clothes from her closet without asking." Chloe shifted her weight from one hip to the other.

"Are you sure you didn't slip in the shower? Maybe whack your head against the tile?"

"No, sir. I always sound like this. Just ask Ethan."

His belly laugh filled the hallway. "I can't believe a word that man says. He told me you were a hellcat that bites if a person gets close, and that your hair was purple."

Chloe remembered her coiffure, drying into ringlets as they spoke, and tried to snake her fingers through it. "That sounds like something Ethan would say."

"But I think you're absolutely charming and your hair is the loveliest shade of plum." He gently pulled her from the bathroom doorway so he could enter. "Go down to breakfast, Miss Galen. No one, and I mean no one, spends the night here and then sneaks away without eating Sophie's cooking. My Sophie will chase you down the street wielding her skillet."

Charles Rhodes closed the door in Chloe's grinning face. Her mind had formed the mental picture of Aaron's *tante* running down St. Charles behind her while she stayed at arm's length wearing the woman's clothes. The image conjured a smile she couldn't wipe off if she wanted to.

Aaron was waiting at the breakfast table, looking not quite as amused as the night before. His hair was tousled and a shadow of beard darkened his cheeks. Not much chance to shower and shave with four people in the house and only one bathroom.

"Good morning, Chloe," he said, pulling out the chair next to his. "Have a seat. I know you've already met my uncle downtown. This is my Aunt Sophie. Sophie, Chloe Galen." He took a long gulp of coffee.

Sophie turned to give Chloe an appraising once-over from her incongruous pink high-heels to her Orphan Annie hairdo. "Good morning, dear. Well, look at you. I once had an outfit very much like that." She bustled to the table and delivered three plates of food that could feed the entire street.

"Good morning, Mrs. Rhodes. I hope you don't mind that I—"

Sophie cut her off. "The only things I mind are skinny girls who refuse to eat." She furrowed her brow and glared.

Chloe slid one of the plates over, picked up her fork and stabbed a sausage. When Sophie returned to the stove, Chloe stole a glance at Aaron. Although his head remained buried behind *The Times*, he whispered conspiratorially, "Don't look at me for help. I'd rather take on the Russian Mafia than my aunt." His plate of eggs and sausage was half-finished.

She stifled her giggle then whispered, "I was already warned upstairs."

He glanced at her and mouthed, "The sooner you eat, the sooner we can get out of here."

So Chloe ate. And continued to eat until she thought she would burst. Only after their plates were clean and all leftovers packed up for Sara could they escape. Sophie confessed to sampling some of Chloe's cold gumbo and pronounced it "right fine."

Chloe chattered like a magpie during the drive about her first impressions of his aunt and uncle. She paused in her narrative when he parked under a shady live oak tree near the Audubon Zoo. "Aren't you taking me straight home? I'm wearing someone else's clothes held up with a rope belt," she protested, but decided to put her couture concerns aside after noticing his expression. He looked worn out despite the hearty meal.

"I don't want to chance running into Sara at your apartment after Charlie and Sophie foiled our plans."

"What plans were those, Atlanta? What nasty thoughts did you have in mind?" she asked with feigned innocence.

He threw the gearshift into park and turned on the seat. "I'm sorry I wasn't honest with you, Chloe," he said, running a hand through his hair. "This isn't how I wanted it to go with us." His eyes looked deeply set, attesting to the fact he hadn't slept as well on the couch as she had in his bed.

"Don't give it another thought. I'm familiar with the 'Do as I say, not as I do, mode of behavior.' My family perfected the double-standard."

"I know I deserve that, I just wish . . . things could be different."

"Like if I'd stayed poor like you first thought? It's okay, Aaron. You were undercover, just doing your job. How were you supposed to know you'd meet the woman of your dreams?" Chloe's heart filled with emotion, but true to her nature, she interjected a little humor to run interference.

Aaron covered her hand with his. "I'm sorry about last night, too. I sure didn't think they'd turn around and come home." He brought her hand to his mouth and kissed the back of her fingers.

"And I didn't plan to fall asleep on the couch," she said in a tiny voice.

"Something's come up. I'm going out of town for a few days." He started the engine and pulled back into traffic. "The weekend would have been cut short anyway. But when I get back," he said, turning her chin with one finger, "we'll talk. Something we should have done a long time ago."

CHAPTER ELEVEN

Chloe quietly opened Sara's bedroom door to check on her friend. Sara was curled in a fetal position and sound asleep. Chloe watched her best friend sleep for a few minutes then silently closed the door with a deep sigh. Today would not be a good day for Sara. The man she loved had just been murdered. Throw that atop a pile of difficult courses this semester, a heavy work schedule, and never enough money for even life's necessities, and Sara needed all the sleep she could get.

Chloe hadn't been exactly upfront with Sara lately, but how could she be?

How could she tell Sara that Aaron was an FBI agent on assignment to arrest the love-of-her-life Jason? Then there was the little matter of Jason trying to seduce her when she'd gone to his apartment. Seduce—that being the polite word for Jason's very impolite behavior.

Why does life have to be so difficult? It was a sunny Saturday morning. She and Sara should spend the day at the mall, trying on clothes, picking out new CDs, running into old friends at the food court, then catch the streetcar down to the Quarter for some bar hopping at blues clubs.

Instead, Sara would spend most of the day with her head beneath her pillow, knowing she would never see Jason or hear his voice again in this lifetime. Chloe made up her mind to attend the memorial service with Sara to lend moral support. Sara would need it.

Chloe wasn't much better off. Besides being dishonest with Sara—the one person who'd taken her in when no one else would—there was the situation with Aaron niggling at the back of her mind. Aaron didn't trust her. He didn't trust her enough to let her in on who he was or why he came back to town.

She knew he liked her.

She knew he found her attractive. But he didn't respect her.

Not that she could blame him. Why in the world did she tell him the story about her sorority's adventures? Instead of him thinking her a lush, he now knew she'd lied, cheated and scammed to get her way. She was a manipulator—not a person deserving respect. She'd been as big a phony as he was. At least he got paid to be duplicitous. She was only doing it to get back at her mother. And nothing had changed. Maybe she paid her own bills and lived within her meager means, but deep inside, Chloe still felt like a little girl, waiting to be rescued when the trial period was over.

Pulling Mrs. Rhodes' striped jersey over her head, she held it to her nose and breathed in the faint scent of talcum powder. She'd liked Aaron's aunt. A person knew where she stood with Aunt Sophie. Eat a hearty meal and your stock went up. Be nice to her nephew and your stock skyrocketed. Aaron was lucky to have been reared by such kind people. Maybe it was Clotilde who got the short end when she ended up with her—a spoiled brat always looking for the easy way out. Chloe laughed at the thought, but it didn't mitigate her shame.

Chloe tossed the drawstring capris in the hamper then changed into her own clothes. It was never too late to make a fresh start—another of her *père*'s favorite sayings. And she would start with Jason Hightower. Someone had murdered her old high school friend. He might have been a creep lately, but he didn't deserve to die. Aaron might be the undercover cop, but she had something going for her he didn't. No one would ever suspect her of doing the right thing. She would get to the bottom of what Jason was up to and maybe, just maybe, her stock would go up with Aaron.

The cab ride to Old Metairie turned out to be an expensive waste of time. No matter how much cajoling or fibbing she did, the building superintendent wouldn't let her into Jason's apartment. She told him she'd forgotten her purse during her last visit. She explained her picture ID would prove the purse to be hers. But no amount of eyelash-batting sweet talk would change his mind. Maybe the fact a purse hung from her shoulder had something to do with his skepticism. The super finally shut the door in her face when she refused to go away.

Once out of eyeshot, Chloe took the stairs to Jason's floor, not sure of what she hoped to accomplish. Yellow do-not-cross tape striped his door from one frame to the other, underscoring that a crime had been committed. Jason was really dead; he wasn't coming back when the sixty-minute crime show ended. And she might be the chief suspect. His little cottage industry of duplicating someone else's art was at the heart of his murder. Aaron was right about that. If she couldn't get into his home studio, she knew she could get into where he worked on campus. With little time to spare before her afternoon shift at the gallery, Chloe hailed a cab to Leporte University.

The campus was quiet on Saturdays. Few students loitered on the walkways or read under shady trees. The art department secretary had the day off, but luckily the studios were unlocked—all except the one Jason used. She slipped her campus ID card into the lock, then a straightened paperclip, and finally threw her full hundred pounds against the door, all to no avail.

"Can I help you, Miss Galen?" A voice startled her from her mission impossible. "If that's your assigned studio, it would be easier to use the key you were provided."

She turned a red face to greet Dr. Graziano. He stared down

his nose at her with an overstuffed tote on his arm. Deep creases underscored his eyes, while his skin had taken on a grayish cast. "No, sir. It's Jason's studio, but I'd like to go inside."

His lips thinned into a line as he straightened his spine. "What on earth for? The police were already here asking questions, snooping around. I can't fathom what his work has to do with his . . . death." He imbued the last word with a distasteful inflection, as though Jason had somehow disappointed the professor by getting himself murdered.

"Nothing to do with that," she lied. "Jason and I were close friends and had been since junior high. I'd like to take a look at his paintings to remember him by."

The professor began shaking his head before she finished. "Until I know what this is all about—"

"Please, Dr. Graziano." As though on cue, her eyes filled with tears. "He was my mentor, as well as my friend. He's the only one who ever encouraged me." Two large tears ran down her cheeks. "This is very important to me."

No one can withstand Chloe Galen gator-tears—a favorite expression of Hunter's. She hoped it still held true today.

Dr. Graziano shook his head, then fell prey to her pathetic demeanor. "All right, Miss Galen. I suppose it won't hurt if you look at his work. Jason was a very private person, but I'm aware you two were friends." This time he gave "friends" an odd inflection, as though it were a euphemism. He slipped his keycard into the lock and waved her in, flipping on lights behind her.

She hoped he would leave her alone, but he trailed behind her as she thumbed through stacks of canvases. Some average, some good, some great, but none were Jason's. When she started on the third stack, Graziano apparently grew bored enough to steer her in the right direction.

"Over there, Chloe, against the back wall. There are some

oils he'd done emulating the early Mission Period. Really quite good."

With Graziano watching her intently, she knew better than to peruse the oils too closely. They looked familiar, but definitely not Hightower in style, yet his customary slashed signature graced the bottom corners of the finished works.

"Were these for his fall show?" she asked, her voice echoing in the high-ceilinged room.

"Absolutely. Excellent work—his interpretation of subject, use of light, all quite accomplished."

"I couldn't agree with you more." A lump she couldn't swallow settled in her throat. She stared at the paintings, feeling for the first time a feeling of acute loss for Jason. She forgot what he'd become, including their last meeting when he'd tried to bribe her, then intimidate her, then muscle her into submission. Looking at the sensitivity, the magic of his art, she remembered only the boy who'd loved to paint when all the other boys were heading for the soccer fields. He didn't care what names they called him. He didn't care if his own father labeled him a sissy. Jason loved his art. And seeing his recent work, Chloe thought him truly a great artist.

This time her tears were for real.

"I think you should see his work in progress. It's on the easel by the window. He showed it to no one."

She swiped at her eyes and walked to where he indicated then carefully removed the black cloth drape. She gasped as the lump in her throat plummeted to the pit of her stomach.

"I take it by your expression you didn't pose for him at any time," Graziano said, coming up behind her. He gazed at the painting over her shoulder—the portrait of her.

It was Chloe Galen, without a shadow of a doubt, yet nothing like her. He had captured a woman unknown to anyone but the deepest recesses of his mind. She was no beer-drinking college girl of dubious repute, dressed in baggy jeans and cropped t-shirts with flip-flops on her feet. The Chloe Galen of his artistic imagination was dressed in flowing red silk and stiletto high heels, displaying more cleavage than she ever dreamed about. She looked taller than the real Chloe, with more womanly curves. Her hair was no tousled mop of curls, but an elegant severe coiffure swept back from her face accentuating high cheekbones and a sharp jaw. No spray of freckles across the nose, no lower lip too full to match her upper, no tiny scar by her eyebrow where she fell off her bike racing Hunter down Riverwalk. This mythical creature's skin was absolute perfection.

But it wasn't Jason's liberal embellishment of reality that unnerved her. Most artists improved on what they saw when creating a portrait. It was her eyes. Dark as bayou swamp water, they were cruel, heartless, almost lifeless. They chilled Chloe as though someone opened a window in January despite sunlight flooding the studio with warmth.

Was this how Jason saw her: cold-blooded, pitiless, filled with contempt for the world? She shuddered, then took a step back, but couldn't take her eyes from the painting. "No," she whispered. "I didn't pose for this." She looked to Graziano for answers, for some insight.

"It's a magnificent piece. Not sappy and sentimental as most artists would paint of the woman they loved." The professor drew the black covering over the canvas, blessedly obscuring her view of the haunted visage.

"Loved?" she asked, her voice little more than a squeak. "Is that what you see, Doctor? I see something closer to hate."

He secured the covering tightly with elastic cords. "Love. Hate. You know what they say—a thin line separates the two when a person can't have what he wants." He turned and met her eye with a cool stare.

Her queasy, unsettled feelings ratcheted up a notch. *What had Jason told him about me?* She took another step back, from the painting and from the teacher who could make or break her this year. "Well, I certainly hope this won't ever appear in any posthumous show."

Whatever emotion had taken hold vanished; Graziano lifted the painting from the easel. "It won't, Miss Galen, because I'm giving it to you. Take it." It wasn't a question, or suggestion, but a command.

"Mine? I can't take that." Her voice sounded as though she'd swallowed a sparrow.

"You can, and you will. I've met Jason's . . . family. There's no love of art in that household. They'll put it up for sale titled 'A murder victim's final gift.' Is that what you want?"

For her answer, she hefted the heavy painting and walked across the studio, to make sure no one laid eyes on the hateful thing again. She got as far as the doorway when Graziano stopped her.

"Wait. How did you get here? Streetcar? Bus?" He lifted one end of the canvas, shifting his leather tote to his shoulder. "I'll drive you home, Miss Galen. I was on my way out when I ran into you anyway."

Chloe gratefully carried one end, while Graziano carried the other for the long walk to the staff parking lot. The sooner she hid the monstrosity, the better.

Graziano said little on the drive to her apartment. He seemed evasive when she questioned him about the curriculum of the grad class she'd signed up to audit. When he mumbled, "Let's wait and see" for the third time, she dropped the subject. Unexpectedly he launched into a diatribe against Jason's family. They apparently had little use for funerals, so Graziano had to arrange the memorial service scheduled for Monday. Chloe assured him she would attend as they pulled into the alley behind her building.

His lip furled as he took in the overflowing garbage bins, the car up on cinder blocks and children playing in a shopping cart in one disdainful glance, but he said nothing. The professor left as soon as they carried the painting to her door before her neighborhood rubbed off on his expensive herringbone suit.

Fortunately, Sara wasn't home as she hid Jason's creation behind her luggage in the back of her closet. The lie she invented during the drive home as to why she couldn't reveal what was under wraps sounded lame even to her. The less Sara knew about Jason's apparent obsession, the better. Funny how an unwanted fixation only seemed romantic in television perfume ads. In real life, the memory of their last meeting scared her to the bone.

Chloe glanced at her watch with alarm. Due at work in thirty minutes, she changed into a long cotton skirt and silky top and ran for the streetcar stop. This wasn't the time to get fired with no serious inroad into Jason's murder surfacing at either his apartment or the studio where he worked. She doubted the dapper and dignified Mr. Kurt Shaw would stoop to fraud in a renowned gallery inherited from his father, but the memory of the four Fritzches waiting to be framed troubled her. To acquire one for sale, perhaps two from a collection was possible, but four turning up without a prominent estate liquidation was unlikely. Chloe intended to take another look at them. Few people knew Jason's style and technique as well as she, although Fritzche certainly wasn't his passion.

Chloe stood for the entire ride on the streetcar since the number of tourists had returned to normal. She loved the noisy, dusty old-fashioned streetcars, infinitely preferring them to the short lived air-conditioned Canal Street line destroyed by Katrina's floods. The antique St. Charles line escaped un-scathed, allowing New Orleans again to remain suspended in time. She crossed into the Quarter and ran the three blocks down Royal, arriving panting and perspiring to La Bella.

"I had abandoned hope, Miss Galen. You are late," Kurt Shaw snapped, shrugging into his sport coat. "The gallery has been busy since we opened, and Miss Pierce and I need to grab something to eat." Her boss was already guiding his appraiser-cum-lover toward the door.

"Will you be all right by yourself, Chloe?" Alicia asked, slipping on her raincoat.

Didn't they know it was already seventy degrees outside? Chloe opened her mouth to speak, but Shaw cut her off.

"She'll be fine. Chloe's handled customers solo many times before. We'll be back in an hour," he said, dragging Alicia out the door.

Chloe doubted they would be back in sixty minutes. And doubted even more that they were actually heading to any restaurant, remembering the little scene she'd interrupted. Maybe romance in Shaw's cramped office had grown old hat so his friend at Hotel Provencale set him up with a suite for some afternoon delight. She watched them hurry down the street while a breeze exposed the carefully concealed bald spot on the back of Shaw's head.

She hoped to be married and settled when she reached Shaw's age, not competing in the dating world. Married and settled to whom? Aaron? Living in a columned four bedroom with a sloping lawn down to the waterway in St. Tammany Parish? Maybe they would discuss current cases and evidence over the dinner table while their children made mosaic designs with their peas and carrots. Aaron—the image of his powerful arms crossed over his chest flashed through her mind, warming her everywhere despite the gallery's AC turned to high.

Unfortunately, two families with eight kids between them entered the shop, curtailing her pleasant fantasies of life with

Aaron. She would have her hands full keeping the younger kids from knocking over pedestals and the older ones from slipping small collectibles into their pockets.

A steady stream of lookers kept Chloe on the floor for at least forty minutes until finally a blue-haired matron paid for her Delft vase and left. Chloe hurried to the back room to search for the Fritzches, since none were hanging in any of the gallery's four rooms. She'd been too preoccupied with school to pay much attention to work until now and said a silent prayer that Shaw and Pierce weren't just grabbing a quick sandwich—or a quick anything.

Chloe thumbed through stacks of canvases that leaned against everything in the backroom. Most needed major repairs besides reframing. Art like these could be found in virtually every attic of every antebellum mansion in Louisiana, most warped and water damaged, done by artists of no particular repute. Estate sales also provided much to Shaw, purchased in lots that he could resell to tourists for souvenirs. Every now and then, he got lucky and found a truly valuable piece. Chloe was balanced on the top of the stepstool perusing canvases out of reach when a voice almost cost her a broken limb.

"What on earth are you doing in here, Chloe? No one's watching the floor. Kurt could be robbed blind." Alicia spoke in a hushed voice then looked over her shoulder.

"Where is Mr. Shaw?" Chloe climbed down to the bottom step so she would be at eye level.

"Delayed on the street. He's talking to an old customer. I came back to relieve you. What are you doing?" Her tone implied the question still required an answer.

"A customer asked if we had any Fritzches. I remembered seeing some back here to be reframed." A partial truth usually sounded better than a complete lie.

"What customer? The gallery was empty when I came to look

for you." She stuck her head out the door to see if they were still alone.

"You're kidding!" Chloe tried her best to look irritated. "This sweet old lady asked me to check the back room when I mentioned seeing some a few weeks ago."

"She must've tired of waiting. How long have you been back here?" Alicia crossed her arms over her impeccable linen suit. How come it hadn't wrinkled like every linen garment Chloe ever owned?

"Maybe five minutes. What shall I tell her if she comes back?" Chloe stepped off the ladder and looked up into Alicia's cool blue eyes.

"They're going up for auction at the end of the month with a very healthy reserve. Any customer not wanting to wait can buy one now at the reserve price." She slicked a hand through her long blond hair. "Let's talk out in the main gallery in case Kurt returns. He won't like us both back here." Oddly, she sounded almost afraid of the guy.

"But where are they until the auction?"

Alicia looked for a moment as though she'd forgotten their topic of conversation. "They're on consignment in a gallery in Houston near the convention center. The drunks might be back, but tourists with money to burn aren't. Business in the Quarter is still off except for t-shirts and hurricane souvenir glasses."

She took hold of Chloe's sleeve and pulled her from the storeroom, remembering to lock the door behind them this time. "If your client comes back, tell her to view them on their web site." She jotted the web address on the back of her business card.

"I hope you don't mind my questions." Chloe smiled sweetly at the woman too flawless for her own good.

"Not at all," she said, returning the smile. "It's to our advantage for you to learn the business." Alicia spotted Kurt in the doorway, shaking spring rain from his coat, and hurried to meet him.

Chloe busied herself with her duster and hoped her snooping didn't get back to Shaw. She needed to keep her job, for financial reasons and for the opportunity to be useful to Aaron. Useful and indispensable—two words no one had used to describe her in quite some time. From behind the Grecian burial urn, she watched Pierce and Shaw go in opposite directions as a group of tourists entered the shop. She needed to figure out what was going on. Apparently the answer no longer resided in the back storeroom.

Swallowing her pride, she picked up the phone and dialed Hunter's number. A family with deep pockets might come in handy after all.

Aaron returned from New York in a foul mood. The coffee in the Big Apple proved better than the precinct bitter brew, but nothing had gone smoothly. At first, no judge either in Louisiana or New York wanted to issue a search warrant for the Fritzche recently sold to a collector in the Upper East Side of Manhattan. He drove straight from the airport to the precinct and found Charlie in his office—the first thing to go right all day. He needed to talk to someone and not just about the case.

Charlie looked up when Aaron entered carrying two large coffees and a bag of beignets. "How'd it go, son?" he asked, already reaching into the bag. "You finally get your hands on that painting?"

"Yeah, it's at an upstate lab right now, but it will be a while before tests confirm it's a fake." Aaron settled back in his chair with his own sugary beignet.

"Why the delay? You would think the new owners would want to find out if they got ripped off."

"No, they'd rather quietly resell it to another unsuspecting fool who will hang it up and not notice. It's buyer beware in the art world, and they don't want to be left with the hot potato. Legitimate auction houses usually provide letters of validation for what they sell on commission. But true provenance can be hidden or lied about. Collectors like to think they're buying from a country squire or an eccentric little old lady who kept the piece for years, not some shady estate dealer looking to turn a quick profit."

"I don't get why the value is so arbitrary. Can't buyers check to see what something is really worth?" Charlie reached into the bag for another beignet.

"There's no price book like with used cars. The value of art changes from day to day. Certain artists or styles become vogue or fade from prominence constantly. Fortunes can be made or lost by the increasing number of investors. But fewer patrons buy and hold art for long periods of time, eventually passing it down to heirs in their estates. Everybody wants to make a quick buck. When you throw in unscrupulous dealers, things get even more dicey. Temporary syndicates are formed and dissolved to manipulate and inflate prices. Many players in the art world are marginally dishonest, but most draw the line at outright fraud. If word got around they sold a knockoff as an original, it would threaten the entire business. Collectors might be willing to pay a fortune for the flavor-of-the-month, but not if it wasn't the real thing."

Charlie nodded his head, but his expression remained baffled. "Well, spending so much time to get hold of the Fritzche caused you to miss the memorial service for Hightower. It was on Monday. I went with a couple Homicide detectives."

Aaron looked his uncle in the eye. "Anybody interesting show up? I would've liked to pay my respects." He knew murderers often attend the funerals of their victims.

"See for yourself. I saved you the eight-by-ten color glossies." From his drawer Charlie withdrew a stack of photos and spread them across his desktop. "Taken discreetly, of course."

Aaron bent over the candid shots, picking up one to study closely. He saw Chloe in old Metairie Cemetery, along with her roommate and her favorite art professor. Both women had dressed in unrelenting black, Sara in a mini-dress, Chloe in a boxy little suit.

Charlie leaned forward to see which had captured Aaron's interest. "Both those gals sobbed and carried on at the grave-site. But other than his parents, all the other mourners were classmates, under twenty-five. Not that youth has ever prevented someone from committing murder." He leaned back in his chair, brushing powdered sugar off his shirt.

That was more information than Aaron needed to hear. Why would Chloe cry over a man who'd attempted to rape her the last time they saw each other? Aaron hadn't liked the pompous fool when they'd met in Chaz's and liked the fact Chloe had cried over him even less. But the guy didn't deserve a bullet in the head for arrogance.

"He must have gotten greedy," Aaron said, picking up the photo of Hightower lying on his kitchen floor in a pool of blood. "Maybe someone thought his talent could easily be replaced."

"Who do you think might be his replacement?" Charlie asked.

Aaron swept the photos into a stack and slipped them into the envelope. "That's what I aim to find out. Let me hang on to these for awhile." He rose to his feet and headed for the door. He didn't want to discuss his hunches at the moment.

And he didn't want to think about who might be lined up as Jason's replacement.

When he'd landed at New Orleans airport, he'd called both Chloe's apartment and her cell but gotten no answer. Until forensics was finished on the confiscated painting, he had little else to do but watch Graziano's campus office. After three hours of stake-out his stomach growled, his back had stiffened up, and the car felt like a Lafayette above-ground tomb—the kind that effectively incinerated your mortal remains using only the hot Louisiana sun.

As he was about to give up and get some something to eat, he spotted Graziano leaving the Fine Arts building, carrying an overstuffed bag and a huge parcel. And he wasn't alone. Chloe Galen struggled with the other end of what had to be a painting. His appetite vanished. His need for more caffeine disappeared as he watched the woman of his dreams help load the artwork into the back of a full-size SUV.

She apparently had been busy while he'd been out chasing judges on Long Island, New York.

He'd already received the report that Chloe had tried to enter the crime scene at Hightower's apartment on Saturday. She'd spun a tale that she needed to retrieve her purse—the same purse that had been returned to her when Homicide decided not to book her on suspicion of murder. The same purse he saw hanging from her shoulder as Graziano helped her step up into the truck.

Just how far would she go to make her mama proud?

Aaron thought about Stacey and her sweet, tender lies. The convoluted yarns she'd spun to cover her tracks when she went home for family visits and didn't want him to tag along. He thought about Stacey's innocence, her vulnerability, and most of all, his gullibility, and he wanted run his sedan up the bumper of Graziano's expensive car.

But he was professional law enforcement. They didn't attack suspects under surveillance because of road rage. Chloe could've gone to Hightower's apartment with only morbid curiosity— some fascination of how close she had come to disaster.

And Chloe wasn't Stacey. At least, he hoped not.

He followed the SUV at a discreet distance, not wanting to alert them, then watched the middle-aged man struggle to get the painting into Chloe's apartment. He wanted more than anything to confront Chloe, to give her a chance to explain what they were doing. But without a warrant to examine the artwork, he would jeopardize the evidence. If that's what the painting turned out to be.

And if it was nothing more than a gift for her Grandmère, he jeopardized something much more precious with Chloe.

Following Chloe around like a lovesick kid wasn't going to help. He headed for his office to do more research on the professor. Something had to tie him to the fraud and Hightower's murder. With a little help from the department secretary, he hacked into Graziano's bank records. Although not admissible in court, Aaron found the break he'd been looking for. Fifty thousands dollars had been deposited into his money market account four days ago—a lot of money for a college professor to receive for a speaking stipend or department head bonus. His cut of the sale price? Hush money to look the other way? Payment for a getting rid of a loose end? Aaron found it hard to picture the tweed-suited intellectual shooting someone at close range, but he'd been on the job long enough to know how looks can deceive.

Aaron punched in Chloe's number again. This time she picked up and sounded happy to hear from him. They agreed to meet for dinner at Black Orchids in the Quarter at eight. By the time he left the precinct, his eyes had crossed from staring at the computer monitor. He searched for a cache that the professor had been building for years. He also tracked down three more Fritzches up for auction on a web site for a Houston gallery. Each painting listed a reserve of six figures, but he needed someone with far more computer ability than he possessed to see any current bids. His favorite computer geek promised to hack-in in exchange for club seats at a Saints game.

Aaron arrived at the restaurant early and selected a secluded table on the terrace. He'd been avoiding Uncle Charlie since he knew what the man would say—take yourself off the case; you're far too personally involved to remain objective. Was he personally involved? He thought he might be, but what did the former Garden District debutante consider to be their relationship? An interesting diversion until spring break in Panama City?

Chloe arrived at Black Orchids right on time. He watched as she crossed the outdoor terrace toward him. With his heart racing in his chest, his physical reaction was immediate and definitive. He was too close. She looked like a dream in a mint green sundress down to the flagstones with her pink toenails peeking from the hem. Huge hoops dangled from her ears and thin silver chains hung from her throat and settled seductively between her breasts. Her wild curls, similar to a lion's mane, had been pulled back by an antique headband. Her lush lips were stained deep mulberry, while her cheeks glowed from youth, the sun, and all the aesthetics money can buy.

If he had one college-educated, Quantico-trained brain cell left in his head, he would leap the courtyard wall and run for his car.

"Hi, Chloe. It's good to see you," he said instead.

A dazzling smile became her answer as she slipped into the chair he'd pulled close. "Good to see you, too, Atlanta. Did you bring me a surprise from New York?" she asked, turning up an expectant face.

Even her simple question had him searching for hidden inner meanings. Maybe he was falling in love.

Or maybe he'd lost his mind.

Either way, it didn't bode well for him solving the case.

"How do you feel about those mini bottles of shampoo and lotion?" He waved over the hovering wine steward.

"Perfect. Exactly what I'd hoped for." She glanced at the wine list then announced, "Let's have champagne, my treat. I've got my first credit card based on my employment history. Let's celebrate." She named her selection in perfect French to the sommelier. "And nothing domestic either."

"I found out some information on Dr. Graziano, Chloe. He apparently came into a good deal of money lately." Aaron leaned back in his chair then stretched out his legs, anxious for her reaction.

It proved minimal at best. "That doesn't mean he was in on some fraud scheme with Jason. He might have inherited the money or sold some stocks or bonds he owned. There are honest ways to come into wealth." She leaned forward as the waiter poured their champagne. The edge of the wrought iron table pressed her breasts into an intoxicating expanse of cleavage.

He forced his focus off her chest. "Honest ways? Of course, lots of teachers move around fifty grand between their accounts." He sipped the bubbly—very dry with very small bubbles, not like any he'd tried before.

"He's not exactly a teacher. He's department head of the Fine Arts program at a prestigious university with advanced degrees and tenure. Not the same thing as teaching English in a public school."

"You would understand that better than me. Shall we order?" The last thing he wanted to do was to argue after spending the entire flight back thinking about nothing but kissing her and holding her in his arms.

"Okay. As usual, I'm starving." She flashed him a brilliant smile, then studied the menu, reading several entrée descriptions aloud. "Let's choose different things, then pick at each other's plates. I hate it when I order something and someone's dinner looks and smells better." She slapped her menu closed. "I'm having the grilled shrimp and fish with red beans and rice.

Why don't you get a steak, or am I being horribly demanding?" She lifted her shoulders and cocked her head to the side in an entreating gesture.

No man could resist. For a moment, it was as though Aaron saw all past history with her father, brothers, male teachers, and any man unfortunate enough to cross her path. They would posture and command and she would rebel against their pseudo domination, but in the end, Chloe Galen always got her way.

No man could resist her.

He shook away notions that had no foundation. "Both the steak and sharing dinners sound great," he answered. "Consider anything I have to be yours."

"Anything, Aaron. Anything at all?" she asked, her voice husky as she sipped the champagne. "How 'bout your trust? Are you offering that, too?"

"Look, I just don't want you to get hurt. You have no idea how involved your favorite professor is."

"Maybe, but I think there's more to it than your suspicions of Dr. Graziano." She lowered her voice to a whisper. "You don't trust me, Aaron. And it's you who's been telling tall tales lately, not me."

"Not because I've wanted to, Chloe. I wanted to tell you, but I couldn't risk compromising the investigation."

"You didn't think I could keep quiet about what you're up to? Why you came back to town?" She inhaled deeply, her eyes narrowing their focus on him. "Do you have this low opinion of all women . . . or just me . . . since you found out I'm only temporarily indigent?"

His head hurt, his heart ached, even his stomach felt hollow. He wanted so much to end the secrets between them. "No. I had my reasons for not believing everything a woman says from before I met you in Haiku."

"Really? I'd love to hear your reasons and anything else from

229

your deep, dark past that appears to be blocking our path."

Our path. Why couldn't he believe she wanted a path as much as he did? Why did he assume people with money had no use for happily-ever-after? He shook off the notion, not sure how he'd wedged himself into this tight spot but saw no handy escape hatch.

He exhaled a deep sigh. "I told you once I'd been married before. Briefly. It didn't last." He drank the rest of his champagne, wishing for strong black coffee instead.

"I remember. No big deal. Lots of people have a spring training before graduating to the big leagues," she teased, then started on the salad set before her.

He laughed at her cavalier attitude toward something that had brought him to his knees. "It wasn't simply a bad first marriage. Stacey was married to someone else when she married me. She didn't bother getting divorced when she moved to Atlanta and married me." Once said, the words didn't sound half so embarrassing as they had buried in his mind.

"A bigamist? Your first wife was a bigamist?" She set down her fork, her dark eyes rounded with shock. "Was she a Mormon?"

"No, she wasn't Mormon. There was no logical motivation other than she wanted to marry me and knew husband number one wouldn't give her a divorce. She wanted out of her marriage when she saw a better opportunity. She was selfish and short-sighted, and thought no one would find her in Atlanta, or discover what she'd done in a country courthouse in the Georgia backwoods."

"I kind of feel sorry for her." Chloe's eyes looked a bit misty.

This had to be the dead last reaction he had expected. "Sorry for her? How could you feel sorry for a woman who deceived two men with her lies?" Aaron didn't want to expose his raw feelings, yet out the words came.

Chloe again lifted her thin shoulders, but this time the gesture wasn't the least bit coy. "I don't know, Aaron, but it sounds like she saw something she wanted very much and decided to go for it, despite the poor odds for long-term happiness. She couldn't help herself. It probably broke her heart when she realized she couldn't have you in the end."

He studied her for some hint of mockery or derision, but her face was sincere. He remembered some things Stacey had said during their horrible final fight, and for the first time they made sense. "Maybe so, Chloe," he said gently, "but husbands, wives . . . they're one per customer at a time."

Chloe took another bite of salad. "I understand, Aaron. You had every right to be angry, maybe even distrustful of women for awhile, but my guess is Stacey never wanted to hurt you." She looked him in the eye. "Only wanted something she couldn't have."

The waiter interrupted the poignant moment as he set down their dinner plates. And it was a good thing he did, because Aaron couldn't have remained trapped under her siren gaze much longer.

"Let's eat!" she said, scooting closer to the table. "And we'll talk no more about the nasty bigamist Stacey tonight."

"Fine with me." He dug into his salad, thankful for the diversion.

"But I'll tell you one thing, Atlanta, and you best remember it." She gestured with a speared shrimp. "I'm not her."

Aaron returned to his aunt and uncle's house long after they should've been asleep. He found Charlie sitting in a living room easy chair smoking his pipe, an indulgence Sophie seldom tolerated indoors. He settled into the opposite chair, feeling more tired than his twenty-eight years should warrant.

"Why you still up, Uncle? My *tante* kick you out of the

bedroom?" He lapsed into his old drawl, long buried since his Academy days.

"No, she doesn't find me any more annoying tonight than usual," Charlie said, picking up some papers from the end table. "Some faxes came for you after you left the precinct. I took a look at them, son, since they concerned the Hightower murder as well as your case." He waited, as though expecting resentment at his intrusion.

Aaron was too tired to resent or argue with Charlie. Anyway, the Chief of Detectives had every right to see anything that came into the department. "What did you find out?" He held out his hand for the faxes.

Charlie passed them over. "Your computer friend came through for you. He found out that Hunter Galen is bidding on the two Fritzches up for auction. Hunter Galen, your Miss Galen's brother." Charlie waited for the anticipated reaction.

This time he wasn't disappointed. "I know who Hunter Galen is," Aaron said, turning on a light to read the faxes for himself.

"Looks like someone might be trying to cover his . . . or her . . . tracks."

"Charlie—" Aaron began, then bit off his words. He had no desire to take this out on his uncle. Facts were facts, no matter how bitter the pill. He slammed his fist into his knee, then jumped to his feet and started to pace like a caged animal.

"There's more son. You might as well hear it from me, even if you decide to kill the messenger." His uncle's attempt at humor rang hollow in the high-ceilinged antiquated room.

"What else? Why do I get the feeling this whole investigation is happening all around me?" He tried to scan the second fax still clutched in his hand.

"Forensics is finished on the Fritzche you confiscated in New York. Yes, it's a fake, but you already knew that." He breathed out a bone-weary sigh. "They found two sets of fingerprints on the canvas. There were fingerprints under the framing. They were able to identify because of prints gathered for comparison during the Hightower murder investigation.

Aaron didn't understand why his uncle sounded so mysterious, so cautious. "The prints were Hightower's right? No surprise there." He slumped back into his chair.

"One set were, yes, and the other set—"

"Graziano's!" Aaron interrupted. "That's great. Now we've got something to tie that intellectual slimebag to the crime. I'll pick him up in the morning."

"No, not Graziano's." Charlie Rhodes waited until Aaron met his gaze before continuing. "The prints were Chloe Galen's. Now I'm asking you again—no, I'm demanding that you step back from this case."

CHAPTER TWELVE

Chloe carried three baskets of dirty clothes through the back door of Grandmère's Garden District mansion into the utility room. She'd volunteered to wash Sara's clothes, too, since she would have the house to herself. Ethan and Cora had gone to a favorite B and B in the bayou—a little relaxation before the countdown to their baby's birth. She glanced over her shoulder at her pride-and-joy parked in the driveway—a 1990 purple convertible with only slightly rusted side panels and just one dent in the bumper. It had been love at first sight on the car lot. The dealer had processed her credit application, accepted her one hundred dollars down, and off she drove with temporary tags. She said a silent prayer it wouldn't leak oil onto the freshly power-washed flagstones of the driveway.

Spreading her books, papers and laptop across the massive kitchen table, she would be able to study, too. Her core classes, at first more difficult than Ole Miss's, were finally making sense. And she loved the art program, which was every bit as good as Henderson's.

Adding a load of sheets to the washer, her thoughts turned to Aaron, as they often did. Nothing felt as good as his strong arms around her or tasted as sweet as his kisses. In his embrace, she felt protected, cherished, maybe even loved. Although she would never admit it to Sara, Chloe wasn't all that experienced in the passion department. She'd never met anybody who made sex seem all that irresistible before, usually preferring to hang

234

with a group of friends. Even to her high school prom, she'd gone with a male chum, not a romantic heartthrob. Chloe always had plenty of boyfriends—friends being the operative word. She was their pal, a buddy, good-old-Chloe, just one of the guys. Even when she'd outgrown her tomboy penchant for dress and behavior, the male species didn't treat her any differently. It was as if she was everyone's little sister, not just the controlling Ethan and Hunter's.

Aaron was different in every way. He made her feel attractive, sexy, how the expression aptly expressed it—like a woman. There had been nothing platonic about what he had in mind that night in the Rhodes' kitchen. Her own mind wandered to what might have happened if she'd limited herself to one glass of wine with dinner. But the next time she saw him, at their romantic dinner in Black Orchids, he'd dropped her off with only the barest of goodnight kisses. No ill-masked excuses to come upstairs, no red-hot kissing in the parking lot, not even any heavy breathing down her neck. So much for Sara's promise that the mint green dress would bring him to his knees. She just didn't have that effect on men. She wasn't sexy enough, not as demure—

"Who's in there?" A scratchy voice roused her from her daydream. Jeanette with an upraised meat tenderizer in hand appeared in the laundry room doorway.

"It's me, Jeanette. *Votre petite,*" Chloe said clutching her chest. Her heart rate had soared into triple digits. "Please don't whap me with that."

Jeanette's lined ebony face looked confused but she lowered her weapon. "What are you doing?"

Chloe smiled at the woman. "I think you know, Jeanette."

"Whose books and papers are spread all over my table?"

"Mine," Chloe answered, knowing exactly where this was headed.

"Noooooo," Jeanette said, dragging out the word ridiculously.

"Yeeeessss," Chloe mimicked, while adding detergent and fabric softener to her load.

"You are studying, *ma petite?* Are you overturning a new leaf?"

Chloe decided to let the juxtaposition of words pass. "You could say that." She dried her hands and joined Jeanette in the kitchen. "Would you like coffee? I started a pot."

Jeanette looked skeptically at the sputtering coffeemaker, then placed the tenderizer back into the utensil basket. "Who owns that horrible car parked in your Grandmère's driveway?" She lifted her tiny, turned up nose with disdain. "That . . . that beated."

Chloe had to ponder her word choice for a minute as she poured coffee. "That beater belongs to me. I bought it by myself. The payments are only fifty dollars a month after a hundred dollars down. The first car that I've ever owned." She couldn't help grinning like a game show contestant.

Jeanette looked out the window at the car. "Well, on second look it's not so bad. I have seen worse." She crossed the kitchen, muttering under her breath, "Pulled from the muck after the flood."

Chloe was about to defend her new baby, when Jeanette spotted mysterious containers in her refrigerator. "What are those?"

Chloe peered over her shoulder. "Those are called plastic food containers."

"I know that. What's in them?" she demanded.

"Leftover gumbo in that one. Shrimp Creole here." She tapped each with a fingernail. "And Crawfish Étouffée in the big blue one."

"You cooked all that by yourself?" Surprise, maybe even awe, edged her words.

"I did, and I saved samples so you could judge the results. We'll see if Emeril has anything to worry about."

"Let's see how much antacid we got in the house first," Jeanette said, adding half-n-half to her mug.

"Jeanette! If I didn't know you were kidding, I'd say you were starting to sound a lot like Mama."

The old woman slowly lowered herself into the kitchen chair, her face betraying how much her arthritic knees pained her. "I am proud of you, ma Chloe. You've come a long way." A smile revealed a gold back tooth. "Your mama asks 'bout you all the time. And hangs on every word of my answers."

Chloe opened her psychology book. It was as good a moment as any to delve into precursors of deviant behavior. "Is that right?" Her tone conveyed little interest.

"It is. She asked how your cooking classes were coming along. And looked downright pleased when I told her your apartment doesn't smell like dead mice anymore."

"Mama never did care for the smell of dead mice," Chloe murmured, prodigiously copying notes onto her pad.

"And she said your grades are good and that Mr. Shaw thinks you're a big help at the gallery."

Chloe's head snapped up, while Jeanette's chin dropped, aware she'd let slip something she shouldn't have.

"She's still spying on me!"

"Because she loves you and worries about you!"

"Because she's controlling." Chloe's attention returned to her textbook.

"Because she loves you and worries about you," Jeanette repeated, then added softly, "and she's controlling. All of the above." Jeanette reached across the scarred tabletop to lay a leathery hand on Chloe's forearm. "She's very proud of you, Chloe, very proud how well you've done for yourself since returning home."

Chloe yearned for a snappy comeback, a snide retort to toss out that would indicate how little she cared about her progenitor's opinion. But fate conspired against her. Two big wet tears slid down her checks so fast she couldn't duck into the utility room.

It was the breeze through the window, a relief from the recent humidity.

It was Jeanette's cool, papery touch on her arm.

It was hormones from that time of month.

It was not the fact that obtaining her mother's approval at twenty-one years of age brought her to her knees.

Jeanette's touch tightened as she began to pull Chloe's arm. "*Viens a moi, ma petite.* Come to me."

Chloe did as instructed and allowed herself to be drawn into Jeanette's embrace—a hundred-pound woman sitting on the lap of an eighty-pound woman. But grandma-number-two didn't seem to mind the weight. She wrapped her arms around Chloe and hugged, patting her back like a child while Chloe sobbed on her shoulder.

"What's wrong with me, Jeanette?" she said with a hiccup. "Why is this still so important?"

"Because you're normal. Everyone seeks their parents' approval, whether they admit it or not. Some never find it. You're a lucky one."

Chloe wiped away her tears as she scrambled to her feet. "I am a lucky one, and not just because Mama's finally proud of me." She sucked in deep breaths, like some type of yoga exercise, but didn't let go of Jeanette's hand as she slipped into her own chair. "Why did it take so long?" she asked, her voice barely a whisper. "Why did I have to wait so long to win her respect?"

"You had to learn self-respect first."

So like Jeanette to sum things up like an embroidered proverb on a sampler. "And how do I do that?"

"It's very simple: Always try to do the right thing. Admit it

when you've made a mistake. Take responsibility for your actions. Respect yourself if you want others to respect you. And
trust that a power greater than anything or anyone will make
things right in the end."

"You call that simple?" Chloe laughed and the laughter felt
good.

"Simple, yes, but I didn't say easy." Jeanette struggled to her
feet and walked to Chloe's side, wrapping her arms around her
again.

Chloe's throat burned from holding back tears while a large
lump rose in her throat. For the first time, she thought about
how old Jeanette and Grandmère were and how numbered were
their days left on earth. One day they would both be gone, and
who would spell out life's lessons in mottos and maxims?

Nothing could hold back her tears then. They flowed down
her face while she returned Jeanette's hug with passion.

"My back!" Jeanette crowed. "Are you trying to snap my
spine, *ma petite?*" She extracted herself from the embrace but
not before Chloe spotted wet tracks on her ebony checks.

Always try to do the right thing.

The words echoed through her head like a radio jingle stuck
on repeat as she packed her laundry into the trunk. She might
have brought her grades up. Maybe she'd surprised Shaw how
hard she could work. Maybe she could even support herself on
her small salary, including the new car payment.

But she hadn't done the right thing by her old friend Jason.
Somebody had killed him and as far as she knew, she was still
the chief suspect. She wasn't any closer to figuring out who'd
murdered Jason or the extent of his involvement with the art
fraud than she had been a week ago. She still took the easy,
popular, make-no-waves road.

And she sure wasn't doing the right by Aaron. His cool

detachment during dinner let her know things weren't good between them. Now two days had passed and he still hadn't called. It felt like a lifetime. He was trying to do his job, and so far she'd done nothing but get in his way. If she didn't get to the bottom of this, Aaron would never trust her . . . or respect her.

This was one chance she must take. Aaron told her to stay away from Professor Graziano, but she couldn't. The answer lay with him and she planned to find it. Before she changed her mind and headed to the mall for something nice to wear or maybe a double espresso mocha latte, Chloe Galen jumped into her purple car and drove to the faculty offices of Leporte University.

She could always go shopping later.

Dr. Graziano didn't answer the knock on his door until her persistence threatened to bring every teacher into the hall.

"What is it, Miss Galen?" he snapped when he opened it a crack.

She wedged in her foot and flashed a phony smile. "Something very important, sir. I must talk to you."

"I'm very busy. Can't this wait?" He didn't attempt to hide his irritation.

"I'm afraid not." She threw her weight against the door, but he held firm like a bull holding back a lamb.

He looked over the rim of his glasses as if she'd taken leave of her senses. "What do you think you're doing?"

"I'm sure you don't want to have this conversation in the hallway. It's about Jason Hightower and what he was involved with before he was murdered."

Graziano actually flinched at the word *murdered,* as though it offended his intellectual sensibilities, but he flung open the door. "I'll give you ten minutes, Miss Galen, no more."

Chloe marched into his office with determination in her

stride. Her eyes landed on packing cartons, in various stages of being filled. Cabinet and desk drawers were pulled out while his half-dead geranium sat unceremoniously atop the trash. "Going somewhere, Professor?" she asked, nodding at the cartons.

"Don't go dramatic on me, young lady. I'm moving to a larger office in the Administration Building. This office is too small." He exhaled a bored, impatient sigh. "What did you mean about Jason? Get to your point."

Chloe leaned one hip against his desk for support. "He was murdered. And it had nothing to do with drugs, or love, or revenge. It was for the usual motive. Money."

The professor stopped loading manila files into a box and stared at her.

"Ever notice the watch he wore? Or how 'bout that car he drove? Did you ever check out his loft in Old Metairie? Not exactly like the dorms off of McMann." Chloe wasn't sure where all this was coming from, but on she charged. "Maybe he invited you over for pizza and beer sometime."

His air of arrogance returned. "What is the matter with you? I don't keep tabs on where my students live and usually don't accept invitations to party." He gave the last word a particularly disdainful inflection.

"You met his parents at the memorial service. They and Jason had no money."

Graziano held up a well-manicured hand. "I don't concern myself about how students afford the things they buy. I think you'd better leave now, especially if you plan a future in the Fine Arts program."

That stung—especially since her grades were at an all-time high. The Dean's List had been a distinct possibility.

"I think you do know how he afforded his expensive tastes, since you were in on it with him. You two were selling fakes as early twentieth century works of art."

"Don't be ridiculous." His voice sounded convincing, but a facial tic betrayed his discomfort.

Chloe plowed ahead before she lost her nerve. "He painted the forgeries, because his talent was good enough to pull it off. Then you saw that they received the proper authentication— proper provenance—and sold them to unsuspecting buyers who wouldn't doubt the word of the august Dr. Sam Graziano of Leporte." She crossed her arms over her blouse, mainly to hide the fact her heart might burst through her chest.

He stared at her with his expression changing from shock, to indignation, then finally to resignation. Approaching her slowly, he leaned his hip against the desk, too. When he spoke, his tone was barely audible. "Jason was into things he shouldn't have been. I tried to talk him out of it. But the lure of—what do they call it? Easy money—was too great. He wanted more and took bigger and bigger risks. He couldn't be patient, spread things out so as not to flood the market. Allow demand to build on its own momentum. He wanted everything . . . right . . . now." The professor actually hung his head as though in abject sorrow.

"Patience was never his strong suit," Chloe said stepping away from the desk. His close proximity didn't feel comfortable.

When the professor looked up, his gaze had turned vindictive. "He did most of it for you—rich little girl from a powerful family. He knew he didn't have a chance unless he came up with some serious money. He had big plans for the two of you." He straightened up and took a step in her direction. "I didn't think he had a chance with you, money or not. No matter how talented the guy was, his parents were still trash."

"Don't put this on me. I wasn't the one encouraging him." She retreated from him until her back was against the wall. "And even if he was a . . . a . . . thief, he didn't need to die because of it." Her voice shook, while her palms and underarms began to sweat.

Graziano closed the distance between them. She could smell chalk dust and stale pipe smoke on his jacket. What a cliché of a college professor, she thought. Balling her hands into fists, she prepared to fight for her life with every ounce of strength she possessed.

But the man only lifted down a framed diploma from the paneled wall next to her head. He walked to his packing carton and set it inside lovingly. "You don't really think I had something to do with his death, do you?" He glanced at her with hooded eyes before continuing to pack. "I liked Jason. He had his weaknesses. We all do, Miss Galen. But I agree with you, he didn't deserve to die." He wadded several newspapers to cushion the contents then secured the lid.

With effort, Chloe unclenched her teeth, unaware how posed she'd been for fight or flight. "Who then, Doctor? Who shot him in the head at close range?"

Again a scowl, an uncontrolled flinch at the mention of violence. At that moment, Chloe believed he was telling the truth. "I have no idea, but I strongly suggest you let the police do their job and stay out of it. And if you think you'll find some . . . proof to connect me to this forgery scheme of Jason's, you're mistaken. What I told you, I'll never repeat. And if you start accusing the august professor of fine arts, you'll be sued for defamation of character, and needless to say expelled. Isn't Leporte your third college, Miss Galen, and aren't you still a sophomore?" He gazed down his thin nose with unconcealed contempt.

What happened to my extraordinary talent and real potential?

She lifted her chin and focused her gaze on him, trying to emulate his control.

"Keep your mouth shut, and do your homework. You don't want to end up like your greedy, infatuated friend." He barely looked up from stuffing papers from the desk into his briefcase.

Dismissing Jason so cavalierly goaded her resolve. She left her cowering position by the wall and approached as though she had a big gun in her purse for courage. "Are you threatening me, Dr. Graziano?" Her voice rose with indignation.

"Keep your voice down! Aren't you smart enough to know the difference between a threat and a warning? I'm warning you for your own good. Now get out of here." He lifted his head with a final glare as she fled through the doorway into the hall.

Funny; she'd expected him to look flaming mad, but the pompous little professor looked like he might cry.

Aaron had spent a sleepless night followed by two fruitless days tracking down every lead, every bit of evidence in either Hightower's murder or his fraud investigation. Her fingerprints on the fake Fritzche's were the only evidence connecting Chloe to the fraud ring. And fraud wasn't at the top of his worry list at the moment. Someone had killed Hightower to cover up or protect their investment and until that someone was behind bars, Chloe wasn't safe. Homicide had pulled off the surveillance when she was no longer their suspect. Keeping tabs on her while tracking down any possible leads left him with little sleep and no leisure time. But he'd have time for leisure when a murderer sat behind bars.

Seeing her go again to Graziano's office did little to assure him she would follow his advice to stay away from the guy. He watched the office door for ten minutes. About the time he was ready to kick the door down, Chloe ran from the office, her face a mask of misery. If he hadn't dived behind an office supply cart, she'd have caught him dogging her like a not particularly good gumshoe.

Charlie was right. He had lost his objectivity. But he hadn't lost his compulsion to solve the crimes, both of them, and maybe keep someone special from getting hurt. Because one thing was certain, if he was ever going to trust a woman again and trust himself to fall in love—maybe try the one-on-one relationship thing—this was it. And if he didn't keep her safe, in spite of her protests and demands for independence, he might not get that chance again.

Hunter Galen hadn't sounded very surprised to get his call. Aaron had little trouble tracking him down. Chloe had explained that her brother Ethan headed the family's insurance and investment concerns—conservative, boring investments—while Hunter was a stockbroker. He and his partner managed portfolios of those not easily intimidated by IPO's, Emerging Markets, REIT VIPRs, and aggressive sector funds. Not for the faint of heart, and definitely not for senior citizens who had to live on a portfolio's steady stream of income. According to Chloe, Hunter's customers made and lost fortunes similar to Texas Hold-Em in Vegas. An interesting analogy, but Aaron wasn't looking for a financial advisor. He wanted to find out why Hunter Galen was bidding on fake Fritzches.

And despite Chloe comparing the middle Galen sibling to a poker player, Aaron had found the guy honest and down-to-earth, if first impressions at Cora's dinner party were any indication.

His second impression didn't change his mind. Hunter's secretary said she would clear an opening as soon as he explained who he was, and then the busy stockbroker greeted him at the office door.

"Aaron, Aaron Porter, right?" Hunter asked, pumping his hand vigorously. "Come into my office. I was wondering when you would finally call." He led the way and instructed his secretary to hold his calls.

Aaron followed, wondering if he'd been eating the wrong breakfast cereal. The Galen family seemed to have way more energy than average. "I'm curious as to why you were anticipating my call." He glanced around the well-appointed office, elegant but practical, with a nice view of Algiers across the river.

"You're dating my little sister, right? I know I'd have a lot of questions if I tangled up with someone like her." He threw his head back and laughed like a hyena. It was hard not to like this guy. "She must have you scratching your head and talking in tongues half the time." He pulled out a chair close to his desk. "Please, have a seat. Something to drink? Coffee, coke, double scotch, hemlock?" He settled into his swivel chair and leaned back dangerously far.

"No, thanks, nothing for me. Yeah, your sister keeps me guessing, but this visit is more . . . professional than personal." He leveled his gaze on Hunter.

The other man brought his chair back to a sane position and stopped grinning. "Professional? I thought you were a student at Leporte, same as Chloe."

Aaron pondered for an instant what cards to show, how much to reveal. He decided to trust his gut instincts this time. "I'm FBI from the Atlanta office. I'm back in my hometown to investigate an art fraud ring. Chloe's old high school friend was smack in the middle of it." He let this information sink in for a moment.

"Hightower. And now the guy's dead."

Aaron nodded, deciding to let Hunter take the lead.

"You think his death is connected to the fraud ring?" He rapidly put the puzzle pieces together in his mind. "And you're worried about Chloe?" All vestiges of his recent good humor vanished.

"I am. And trying to keep her away from my chief suspects—"

Hunter interrupted, "Not having much luck there, are you? Telling Chloe to stay away from anything is like waving a red cape before a bull." He jumped to his feet and began to pace in front of the riverside bank of windows.

Aaron watched him carefully for any indications of culpability and saw none.

"What can I do to help?" he asked, facing Aaron from across the room.

"You can start by explaining why you're bidding on three Fritzche's on a Houston gallery website."

"That's easy. Because Chloe asked me to."

"Simple as that? You bid five figures on each of three paintings I believe are fakes just because your sister asked you to?"

"Well, yes." Galen shrugged, his face coloring slightly. "It's what I do—make investments. She said it was a hot tip that I shouldn't pass up if I could get them for the reserve. Since she knows art, I thought I'd get in on the ground floor of the next hot collectible." He looked to Aaron for explanation, but Aaron stared back coolly.

After an uncomfortable interval, Hunter sat back down in his chair, but it remained in the upright position. "I'm confused. Why would Chloe want me to bid on a bunch of fakes?"

"That's what I'm trying to figure out." Aaron didn't like the implication Hunter would draw from this, but he needed to find out exactly what Galen knew.

Hunter drew the conclusion Aaron supposed he would. "You think my sister's in on this . . . this fraud ring?"

"Not directly, but she could have got herself mixed up accidentally, or is maybe covering tracks for someone else mixed up in it. Thinking it's the right thing to do."

The two men stared at each other across the desk like junkyard dogs, then Galen's face relaxed a bit. "Yeah, I could see her trying to cover up something if she thought it was the noble thing. But look, Porter, Chloe is no scammer. She would never willingly dupe or rip off anybody, especially not with art. Art is on the same sacred level as religion with her. And would've surpassed religion, if not for her good Catholic school education."

"Actually, I agree with you." Aaron rose to his feet, stretching out his back muscles.

"What can I do to help? Anything, man. I know . . . you have my sister's best interest at heart."

Aaron shook his head. No way could he admit how much he cared about Chloe, since he was there in a professional capacity for the Bureau. "Your family has a private detective on the payroll?"

Hunter nodded.

"Have him keep tabs on your sister. I can't watch her and go after the bad guys, too." He looked at Galen and offered the briefest of smiles. "I could if it was any other woman than Chloe."

"I understand. I'll have Nate Price keep an eye on her, and keep her out of your way." He stretched his hand toward Aaron. "Thanks, Agent Porter. You won't be sorry you trusted me."

Aaron shook his hand and allowed the brief feeling of camaraderie to wash over him. It wasn't an emotion he often experienced. Then he headed for the door. "Oh, and one more thing. I would withdraw my bids on the Fritzches. Save your money. They're about to be subpoenaed for evidence."

Did he just cross the line, giving Galen the tip about the paintings? At the moment, he honestly didn't know. He guessed he didn't as long as neither Hunter nor Chloe had anything to do with the fraud, and his gut instincts told him they didn't. His dull headache just graduated into a throbbing pain behind his eye as he left Hunter's downtown office. To complete the downward spiral, the light drizzle turned into a deluge, darkening the sky and his mood.

Hunter was right about one thing.

Chloe would never rip people off with fake art. He could

usually read dishonest people—women who lied about their age or what they spent on shoes, and everything in between. She struck him as an honest woman, despite failing to mention her family's wealth when they first met. He had relied on his instincts many times on the job and they'd never let him down before.

And she'd had nothing to do with the murder. Hightower had been her friend. He'd been her boyfriend at one time. Aaron blocked out the statistics regarding how many times people committed heinous crimes against family members or lovers.

Maybe other people, but not Chloe. She had no motive. And not because she was a little rich girl. She'd demonstrated integrity by standing on her own two feet. People of integrity never shoot someone at point blank range, do they?

The vibration of his cell phone on mute was a welcome interruption from his raging internal debate. "Porter," he said on the third ring.

"Where are you, nephew?"

He recognized his uncle's agitated voice immediately and ignored Charlie's lack of protocol. He knew the call wasn't work related since he didn't answer to Charlie on the fraud case, only to his superiors in Atlanta. "I'm downtown, leaving Hunter Galen's office. He just bid on three Fritzches that I know are fakes. What's up?"

"Is Chloe with you? You've gotta bring her in, Aaron."

"She's not. What's going on Charlie? Where are you?"

"I'm at the Fine Arts Building at Leporte. In the late Professor Graziano's office."

"Late Professor?" Aaron asked, incredulously stalling for time as he pulled into traffic and sped toward the campus.

"He's dead—gunshot wound to the head. The gun's on the floor next to the body. It looks like the same caliber, probably the same weapon that killed Hightower. We're waiting for crime lab to bag it."

Aaron nearly sideswiped a concrete mixer changing lanes on the freeway. He didn't know why, but his intuition told him time was running out.

"Any GSR on his hand?" he asked, glancing at the dashboard. The needle of the speedometer passed eighty as he weaved through traffic on the Jefferson Highway.

"That remains to be seen. I bagged both hands."

"What does this have to do with Chloe?"

"I was getting to that. Your Miss Galen was seen entering Dr. Graziano's office by a department secretary. The secretary claims she heard heated voices—those were her words. Then Miss Galen was again seen leaving the building in a big hurry."

"Anybody hear the shot?"

"That's where things get a little muddled. The secretary said she went on break to the cafeteria and didn't hear any shots. The other witness who saw Chloe leave the building was too far from Graziano's office to have heard anything. Two teachers thought what they'd heard was a car backfiring and didn't pay attention to the time."

"Who found him?"

"Another professor who was taking over the office space."

"Graziano was going somewhere?"

"Apparently moving to a bigger office."

"All pretty circumstantial," Aaron said, not liking the situation one bit.

"Very circumstantial, but once again, nephew, Miss Galen was the last person to see the victim alive."

To that Aaron had no reply as he pulled into the Leporte faculty parking lot. He was surprised he hadn't picked up a tail from the metro traffic patrol considering his speed.

Uncle Charlie waited almost a full minute before adding in a somber voice, "I need to question Miss Galen. It's better if she comes in voluntarily before a warrant is issued for her arrest."

"I'm on campus and on my way up now." He climbed the steps to the second floor two at a time.

"That's not a good idea. Homicide detectives are taking statements from potential witnesses right now and they won't appreciate seeing you. The crime lab should be here any minute. FBI has no jurisdiction and I won't pull any strings on this one."

"I don't want any strings pulled, and Chloe doesn't need them. Do you really think she would shoot her faculty advisor?"

"I don't know what I think, but I'm paid to look at the evidence. Either you bring her in for questioning or we will. Take your pick."

Aaron walked into the cluttered office at that moment and locked gazes with his uncle like two hawks vying for the same rabbit. Both men snapped their cell phones shut at the same time, while Aaron felt the glares from lab techs and detectives alike. His presence wasn't appreciated at the crime scene. Hell, nobody even knew if a crime had even been committed, but he felt the temperature in the room drop by twenty degrees.

"I'm not interfering with your investigation," he said quietly. "I'll find her and bring her in for questioning, but right now I've got no idea where she is."

That wasn't exactly the truth. He did have an idea, but a hunch was all it was. He glanced around the room, taking in the dead professor lying on his side in a large dark stain on the Persian rug. His eyes were open and his jaw slack. Spattered blood ruined his expensive starched white shirt and tweed jacket. Several cops were rummaging through his desk drawers and half-packed cartons, as though the clue lay hidden in grade books and class schedules. Campus security watched Aaron carefully as though he might slip some key piece of evidence into his pants pocket.

What was happening to his professional reputation?

What was happening to him? Had he lost his objectivity? He took a final glance around the room, which was rapidly being overrun by personnel and spotted several sheets of paper lying on the rug. He knew better than to touch them without a glove and evidence bag, but he leaned close for a better look. A small, perfectly round indentation dimpled the margin of an exam paper. It probably meant nothing. It could have come from a secretary or even the student taking the test, but it sure looked like a high heel imprint to him. And he'd never seen Chloe wear stilettos.

He let the paper lie when he left Graziano's office and felt a palpable breath of relief from the others in the room.

When did he become the pariah on loan from Atlanta? Without time to contemplate his social position, he punched in Chloe's cell number.

She answered with a whispered, tentative "Hello?"

"Where are you, Chloe? We need to talk." He felt relieved just hearing her voice. With the professor dead, Chloe could as easily be the next victim instead of the perpetrator.

"Can't talk now, Aaron. I'm in the middle of something." Her soft voice sounded as though he'd interrupted her during a favorite *Law & Order* episode.

"This is important. We gotta talk and you've got to be straight with me." He tried not to lose his temper, but his voice rose with annoyance anyway.

"You still don't trust or believe in me!" she hissed. "No matter what I do, you still think all rich people are corrupt liars." He heard her voice crack. "You think only poor people like . . . like Abe Lincoln could be honest? I can never till a lie; I chopped down the cherry tree." A singsong inflection underscored her words.

Aaron heard the pain behind the words despite her hushed

voice. "Let's talk. We'll straighten—"

She didn't let him finish. "Can't. I'll call you later." Four cryptic words and the line went dead.

She had hung up on him. Aaron clenched down on his back molars and almost threw the phone out the car window. No sense trying to trace a mobile call. Somebody else could die before locating her using that method.

Five years of college. Two years of intensive training at Quantico. And he felt as ineffectual right now as if his Aunt Sophie was heading the investigation.

CHAPTER THIRTEEN

The crowd changed imperceptibly in the French Quarter with the fall of night. As arm-in-arm elderly couples and families with youngsters in tow found their way back to hotels, the streets came alive with the young and young-at-heart looking for fun of a wilder sort. The bodies grew leaner, the clothes briefer, the voices louder and the energy level escalated along with the music blasting from open doorways. The tourists who came out at night were more interested in bartering with beads than the history of Jean Lafitte or Marie Laveau.

From her café table where she drained the last of her cold coffee, Chloe could hear the music from Bourbon Street as horse hooves clattered down Rue Royal toward Jackson Square. She checked her watch—almost time to leave her safe haven where she'd been gathering courage as she waited for La Bella Gallery to close for the night.

The ring of her cell phone startled her from her contemplation. She gazed at Caller ID, hoping against the odds that it was Aaron. It wasn't; it was Hunter. Her feeling of foreboding hiked up a notch. "Hello?" she said.

"Chloe, where are you? We need to talk." No identification, no standard pleasantries from her brother.

"Yes, Hunter, I'm fine. Couldn't be better. Thanks for asking," she teased, but her heart wasn't in it.

"I'm glad you're fine, now where are you?" he repeated.

"I'm having coffee in the Quarter. What's so urgent?"

"I just had an interesting conversation with Porter. Where in the Quarter? I don't want to discuss this on a cell phone." He sounded nervous and more than a little upset.

"You talked with Aaron? What about?" Her stomach took a nosedive as she straightened her spine against the chair back. "Did he ask for my hand in marriage?"

"Cut the crap, Chloe. He's worried about you. Apparently, you're in over your head once again."

This wasn't what she had expected, and it certainly wasn't what she desired.

"Let me get this straight. Aaron came to talk to you about what a screw-up I am?" Her voice rose with indignation despite her intentions.

"Pretty much, but tell me what coffee shop. I want to talk in person."

"First Ethan, then Jeanette, now you? Why can't you, Hunter, of all people, believe that I can straighten this out with Aaron? Why can't anyone believe that I can take care of myself?"

"Because you can't." The words couldn't have stung more if they'd been tipped with sea urchin juice and shot into her foot.

"I can," she insisted. "I don't need a man to take care of me. I don't need anyone to take care of me."

"That's not what I meant. I know you can take care of yourself. You more than proved that, little sister. That's not the point."

"Then what is?" she demanded, her feathers unruffling a bit.

"That it's nice to have love in your life—to take care of each other, not because you have to or need to, but because you want to. To love another person is a gift. And chances like yours with Aaron don't come along every day." He sucked in a breath and added in a barely audible whisper, "That much I know."

For a long moment, the old city street grew silent. No raucous music, no enthusiastic tourists, no clatter of hooves on pave-

255

ment. Or maybe the silence was all in her head as she tried to process his words. This wasn't fair. This was unexpected. For this, she had no retort. Tears filled her eyes, as her throat went dry.

"Chloe? Are you there? Where are you? I could be in the Quarter in fifteen."

Her nasal passages had congested so much her voice sounded foreign to her ears. "I'll come by tomorrow, Hunter. We'll talk then. Right now, there's something I must do. Don't worry about me. Everything will be fine." She clicked her phone shut before he could argue or hear the tears in her voice.

She doubted everything would be fine, but Hunter couldn't help. No one could help her but herself.

"More coffee, miss?" a sweet-faced waitress asked, breaking her reverie.

"No, thanks. Time to go to work."

The woman nodded, accustomed to people in the Quarter working all sorts of hours.

Time indeed to put her fears behind her and make things right. Chloe paid her tab and left a healthy tip since she'd occupied a choice table for a while. After tonight, she might not need the rest of her paycheck.

It took only fifteen minutes of spying from a darkened doorway before she saw Shaw and Alicia Pierce lock the gallery door behind them and set off down Rue Royal. Arm in arm they walked, talking and laughing, probably on their way to dinner at their favorite bistro on Chartres. They didn't see her as they passed, or anyone else for that matter, seemingly without a care in their insulated world.

Unlike her. She had plenty of cares in the world. Her headache had grown worse, her stomach felt tied in knots, and her legs barely felt they could support her weight as she left her hiding place and crossed the street. And those were just her physical ailments. Her mother still despised her; her brothers barely spoke to her, and Aaron . . .

Aaron, the only man whose respect she coveted, thought her a thief and maybe a murderer. She'd fallen in love with a man who hated rich people, then everything she'd done since had doomed their relationship.

Chloe slipped her employee key, only recently entrusted to her, into the old-fashioned lock and turned the knob. With a furtive glance over her shoulder at passersby, Chloe inhaled a deep breath and entered the silent gallery.

Things couldn't get any worse in her life anyway.

She let her eyes adjust to the dark then threaded her way between antique étagères holding collectables toward the back room. Only streetlight through the high clerestory windows kept her from knocking over priceless porcelains and other expensive objets d'art. Once in the workroom and adjoining storage area, she flipped on the lights. Since this area had no windows, no one would be alerted to her surreptitious snooping.

Exactly what she was looking for she didn't know. Something to get to the bottom of Jason's cottage industry and his death. Something to tie him to Shaw and his expensive tastes, despite a slumping market for expensive souvenirs. The memory of those Fritzches waiting to be framed played heavily on her heart. Why hadn't she thought that four missing canvases turning up at once and then finding their way to Shaw's shop was highly unlikely. She remembered Dr. Graziano visiting the gallery on her first day as an employed woman, too, although she still couldn't picture the bespectacled scholar as the mastermind of some great swindle.

Chloe riffled through stacks of framed artwork, both upright in metal stanchions and leaning against each other in racks. Some could fetch a pretty penny, but others were so badly damaged they should serve no higher cause than fireplace kindling. After giving up on the storage and workrooms, she turned her attention to Shaw's office. Although his desk drawers were locked, his filing cabinets were open and they yielded some interesting provenance documents. Several were for the same painting, as though he had practiced creating a document with the right amount of yellowed aging. Another metal box contained an assortment of official looking rubber stamps. Chloe selected one and brought up the magnifier to study the inscription.

"What are you doing in here, Miss Galen?"

It wasn't a question, more of an incensed demand. Chloe dropped the magnifier and rubber stamp back into the box and flushed up to her hairline. She gazed into the enraged face of her employer Kurt Shaw. Her mouth gaped open.

"Do you think I gave you that key so you could snoop around after hours?" He pulled the box from her hand and threw it back into the cabinet drawer then stared down his thin, aristocratic nose at her. She'd never noticed before how much he resembled a hawk. "I'm waiting, Chloe. Why are you rummaging around in my office?"

Things had just taken a turn for the worse.

"I'm investigating my friend's death, Mr. Shaw," she answered, trying to appear cool and business-as-usual.

"Your friend's death?" The incredulity in his voice overpowered his normal cultured tone. "Nobody has died in my office or storerooms." He slammed the filing cabinet drawer closed and walked around his desk. There he withdrew a bottle of bourbon and a single glass.

Cocktails, anyone?

"My friend's murder, to be exact." She straightened her spine imperceptibly then blurted half her story without breathing. "Jason Hightower was painting fake Fritzches and selling them through your gallery, sir. I believe you've been duped, and Jason was murdered because someone found out about it. Or maybe someone double-crossed him."

He sighed with impatience, his nostrils flaring unattractively. "Chloe, Chloe," he said, in his patented you've-disappointed-me-once-again voice. "Nobody's been duped. Do you really think I'm unable to spot a fake from the real thing?" He glared with condescension and contempt.

"So you were aware Jason was painting fakes? And you sold them for him? You were in on it?" She tried to act surprised, as though that would somehow improve her chances for survival.

He poured three fingers of bourbon and settled back in his swivel chair. "Do you know how hard it is to make a decent living in the art business?" His inflection on the word betrayed his loathing. "Since the advent of Internet auctions, everyone and his granny wants to buy and resell to make a quick buck. They don't know and don't care about what they're buying, just as long as they can unload it to a bigger sucker for a profit." He took a long sip on the drink. "Few people want to invest in art, hang it on their living room wall and then pass it down to heirs, content that in time the painting will appreciate in value while providing them with aesthetic pleasure."

"I'm sorry the world has lost its refinement for you, Mr. Shaw."

"Are you now? You silly little snob. Your family still has most of the Galen wealth. Isn't it easy for you to act so noble—act with a higher purpose? Your little stint here—working at La Bella—is just some point you're trying to make to your family before you come into your trust fund." He leaned forward in his chair, his hawk eyes flashing with anger. "You have no idea how hard it's been to keep this place going in the Quarter, to preserve what my grandfather started and my father continued. Do you know what the overhead is on this place just to maintain the refined image?"

"Business might be down in the French Quarter, but someone shot my friend in the back of the head." Her hands balled into fists, as though preparing to do physical combat to avenge the man who'd tried to rape her in his living room.

"Well, I didn't shoot him. Hightower served his purpose. He produced a believable piece. I had no reason to kill the golden goose. So look for your murderer in someone else's back room." He jumped to his feet and finished the drink in one gulp. "And you'd better think twice about repeating what I told you about the fake Fritzches. Your fingerprints are all over those canvases. You worked in the gallery. And as you say, Hightower was your friend. What will your mother say when the papers report little Chloe, expelled from Ole Miss, returns home to New Orleans to get caught up in an international art fraud ring? Clotilde Galen will take out a hit on your life." His harsh laughter echoed in the high-ceiling acoustical room. "I can connect you to this mess enough so you'll be indicted along with me, so you'd better just keep your mouth shut." No parental concern shaded his words, only a desperate ultimatum delivered by a desperate man. "Now get out of here and leave the key behind. You're fired."

Oddly, those words stung. Chloe had never been fired before and didn't like the sound of it. But she had little time to ponder the consequences to her resume, since she heard the unmistakable clatter of high heels behind her.

"Don't be a fool, Kurt." Alicia Pierce's words contained no coy manipulation now. "You're not seriously planning to let her walk out of here with just a turn-in-your-key-you're-fired, are you?"

Shaw crossed his arms over his Armani suit coat. "Chloe is no fool. She only worked here to prove something to her family. She's not stupid enough to mess things up with Clotilde considering how much inroad she must've made." He glared at Chloe down his hawk-bill nose, and she imperceptibly took a step toward the door.

"You're willing to take that chance?" The screechiness in Alicia's voice contrasted the usual honey-butter tone. "We need those three pending sales to go through. You know how much money is at stake here?" She looked at Chloe as though she were a roach walking across a five-star restaurant tablecloth.

"For God's sake, Alicia. She's my best friend's daughter. What do you think we can do with her?" He poured another bourbon; the discussion appeared to be growing tiresome.

"She's not my best friend's daughter. I'm not losing everything I've worked for and going to jail for murder."

The stale office air grew chilly. Goosebumps rose on Chloe's arms as no one spoke and no one seemed to breathe.

"What the hell are you talking about—murder?"

"Don't you be the fool, Kurt. I told you not to involve adolescent punks, that they couldn't be trusted. But you wouldn't listen. That creep Hightower got greedy. With every painting he upped his cut, and you let him get away with it."

"Every painting kept getting better and better. The kid was good."

Apparently Mr. Shaw still had some reverence for art left in his soul. Chloe took another step toward the door.

"He was nothing more than a craftsman. So he could copy something. Big deal. I didn't like being shaken down by a punk out to impress his purple-haired girlfriend." She glanced with scorn at Chloe. Until that moment, Chloe hadn't realized Alicia was talking about her.

"What do you mean, shaken down?" Shaw drained his glass and set it down with a thud. "I took care of the negotiations with Hightower."

"Not after he started blackmailing us. I told him we weren't giving him one dime more, that he was overpaid the way it was. He said he would circulate a rumor in art collector chat rooms that the Fritzches were fakes and buyers should beware. Then bidding would stop and we'd be stuck with three unsalable paintings." She picked at the polish on one long fingernail. "I couldn't let him do that—ruin our investment. Former buyers would start doubting the provenance of the art they'd already bought from us. We'd be ruined." She shook her silky blond hair back from her face with a bored, weary expression.

"What did you do, Alicia? He was a kid."

Apparently it took longer for Shaw to realize what Chloe came to terms with ten minutes ago. He was sleeping with a murderer.

"He was no kid. A kid rides his bike and plays video games. Once that creep tried to get fresh with me and didn't like taking no for an answer."

"What did you do, Alicia?" Kurt grabbed her forearms and started shaking her, but Alicia shrugged him off and walked around the desk.

"I went to his apartment to reason with him after his latest demand for more money." She poured herself a drink. "I offered him a sort of bonus plan if the paintings fetched more than our target price, plus a percentage on all future masterpieces." She flashed Chloe a deadly stare. "But apparently, he'd gotten into a little scuffle with employee number two here and was hopping mad. He had an ice bag on his mouth and was talking like Elmer Fudd. What did you do, sweet little Chlo?" The honeyed tone was back, besides her glorious smile.

"Nothing he didn't have coming. What did you do, Ms. Pierce?" Chloe tried to feign bravery she didn't feel.

"Ditto. I tried to bargain with him, but he was in no mood to be reasonable."

"So you shot him in the head?" Kurt's words echoed off the

room's ceiling.

"He wanted ten thousand dollars, said he already owed the money to someone. Probably blew it up his nose."

"You killed him for ten thousand dollars?" Shaw stared at her with disbelief.

"Ten grand per Fritzche. That's forty thousand—money I could better use than that nouveau hippie."

"He was twenty-two years old."

Alicia didn't like this particular response and changed her tack. "Kurt, I did this for us. He would have ruined us, everything we've worked for, just when we were about to hit something worthwhile. The three Fritzches got recent bids of six figures each." She walked to him and tentatively placed her hand on his chest. "We could've gotten out of the Quarter for awhile, let someone else run the gallery for awhile. You said you would take me to Europe, to the Louvre and the Sorbonne." She ran her fingers down his shirtfront toward the waistband of his pants.

Chloe took Alicia's coy-ploy as her opportunity to get away and ran for the door. But Alicia, with her mind apparently on two things at once, pulled a small gun from her jacket pocket with agility that would have made Belle Starr proud.

"Stay where you are, Chloe. You're not running out during our staff meeting quite yet." The barrel was aimed at Chloe's chest, while the glint in Alicia's eye resembled a coyote right before a tasty kill.

Chloe stopped in her tracks, the doorway only inches away. She turned back and fixed her gaze on Shaw.

"Alicia, for God's sake put that gun down. Chloe isn't going to say anything. She's not stupid enough to bring this mess down around her ears." Kurt moved to a position almost in between Alicia and Chloe. Almost, but not quite.

"And I'm not taking the chance that she'll be smart like her nerdy professor."

"What did you do to Dr. Graziano?" Chloe's mouth dropped open. How could a person who dresses like a fashion model be capable of murder? Aren't criminals supposed to be socio-economically deprived?

Alicia laughed, showing off her perfectly veneered teeth. "I didn't do anything. He'd been sweating buckets since the feds started asking questions. Then the idiot deposited his cut into an account with his name on it, offshore but not numbered. You would think an intellectual would know in the computer age hackers can find out just about anything unless you're very careful." She shook her head in disappointment.

"Go on," Shaw demanded, not sounding pleased with his afternoon-delight.

"I paid him a visit. He was leaving town, for crying out loud. Where did he think he was going to go? A man who struggles to achieve tenure and whatever else he deemed to be top of the crap-heap won't be happy living in a bungalow in Costa Rica with other criminal ex-patriots." She swirled the amber liquid in her glass then took a hearty swallow. "I explained that all roads would point to him as the mastermind when this went down. We were merely duped by the professional art expert." Her gaze locked with Chloe's. "He would lose his position, his respect, probably even the closest spot in the faculty parking lot. He did the only right thing."

"Dr. Graziano wouldn't have killed himself," Chloe shouted. "I used to see him at Mass; that's a mortal sin. Anyway, where would he get a gun?"

"I don't know anything about his soul and eternal damnation, but I helped him out with the gun part. Since Katrina, plenty of un-traceables were left behind, and that one only needed a good oiling. But I assure you, Graziano did the honors himself once I pointed out that the paper trail led back to him.

He removed that task from my to-do list. I was already halfway down the hallway." The sparkle in her baby-blues betrayed a frightening sociopath.

"Enough! I've heard enough, Alicia," Shaw shouted. The romantic bedroom eyes were gone for his beloved paramour. "The scam is finished. We're going away until this whole thing cools down." He turned on his heel to face Chloe. "You go home, Miss Galen. Don't disgrace your family and your father's memory anymore than you already have." His words dripped with scorn. "Nothing will bring your friend Jason back, and apparently he wasn't worth you going to jail for, so keep . . . your . . . mouth . . . shut." He walked back to his desk then began rummaging through the top drawer.

Just that quick, Chloe's last staff meeting at La Bella was over. Her eyes filled with tears—not because Graziano committed suicide or because Alicia murdered Jason. It was Shaw's assumption that she would so easily cover their misdeeds to prevent a further fall from grace with her mother. That her ethical code had a self-serving dollar sign assigned to it.

"You said I came to work here because I had something to prove to my family. That's not completely true. I worked here to prove something to myself, Mr. Shaw. And I'm not done yet." She stood up straight and lifted her chin. No cowering, no simpering, and positively no whining.

"How sweet," Alicia cooed. "How do people get to be like you?" Butter melted off her tongue. "Perhaps it's the silver—no platinum—spoon you were born with, while I got fed with plastic sporks." She steadied her handgun with both hands.

Shaw looked up from rummaging in the desk, while Chloe felt some of her bravado drain away.

"Let's go, Chloe," Alicia said. "You and I are taking a drive in your atrocious purple bug. Why in the world did you buy that horrible color? Something to complement your hair?"

Her words teased and baited, much like the banter between her sorority sisters at Ole Miss. But the look on Alicia's face froze Chloe to the bone.

Her gaze had narrowed into one beam of cold pure hatred.

Aaron drove like the devil was on his tail for the second time that night. He headed not to Chloe's apartment, but back to the French Quarter. He had a hunch she'd gone to La Bella. How a person so small could mimic a bull-in-a-china-shop so perfectly he couldn't fathom. She'd been at Hightower's apartment just before his murder. Then she'd blundered into Graziano's office just before his death—accidental, self-inflicted, homicide—whatever it turned out to be. Aaron needed to stop her before her luck ran out. And every gut instinct told him it was about to.

For the second time that night, he dodged and weaved his way though traffic on Route Ten, praying he wouldn't be too late. He wasn't sure exactly when he started trusting her, but he did. He believed she was telling him the truth.

He didn't know exactly when he fell in love with her either. If he'd been expecting some sappy cupid's arrow through the heart, it never happened. It had more or less crept up on him like a bad summer cold. When you least expected it, love brought you to your knees, knocked the wind out of your sails, and every other cliché he never believed until now. After Stacey, he'd spent years running from any woman who might potentially turn into a real relationship. Now he wanted a relationship with Chloe more than anything.

Aaron spotted a parking spot across from the gallery and pulled in headed in the wrong direction. La Bella looked locked up tight, as you'd expect at this hour, but he drew his weapon and looked in the sole unshuttered window. Nothing moved in the dim interior. Only faint light from the street and the glow from neon exit signs provided any illumination. Pedestrians walked the French Quarter streets at all hours, and Rue Royal was no exception. Several stared curiously as he peeked through the window with a drawn thirty-eight automatic. More than a few crossed the street to the other sidewalk.

He tried the door handle, only mildly surprised to discover it unlocked. Stepping into the cool interior of rarified works of art and overpriced pieces of junk, he remembered the time his grandmother got burned by an unscrupulous antique dealer. The shyster had offered her a couple of grand for a houseful of antiques and collectibles, promising to "clean out the junk" in preparation for her move to an assisted living facility. When his mother found out and tried to take the dealer to court, she soon discovered the intrinsic worth was whatever one would pay and the other would accept. The dealer paid his grand-mother less than ten percent of what he later sold the contents of the house for.

He shook off the memory as his eyes adjusted to the dim light, then he made his way to the back through narrow aisles. Just as he reached the end of an aisle of eighteenth century vases and urns, he heard voices, muffled and discordant, com-ing from a back hallway. Aaron paused near the closed door, waiting for a sound while holding his breath. His palm grew moist as he tightened the grip on his weapon and released the safety.

"How sweet. How do people get to be like you?"

The unrecognized female voice chilled him to the bone. Sarcastic, but not funny. Mocking, but not amused. The woman had a major axe to grind and he had a good idea he knew the recipient of her wrath well.

He waited half a minute with his ear held firmly to the door. He heard the ice-woman again, and then the unmistakable voice of Chloe Galen. He couldn't make out Chloe's words, but he would recognize that tone of righteous indignation anywhere. Without time to call for backup or consider other options, he stepped back and threw his full body weight against the door. With the announcing sound of splintering wood, the latch gave way and Aaron hurtled into the room, dropped to the floor and rolled, coming up with his gun drawn. He heard the blood curdling report of gunfire.

"Drop it," he yelled, rising on one knee. He faced his adversary—a tall, big-haired blonde, more congruous in a Miss Omaha pageant than holding a firearm. She was still aiming at an alabaster bust on a pedestal stand, inches from the door-frame he'd just sailed through. The top of the sculpture had been blown off while three holes in the wall indicated the ice-woman had taken three shots to reduce the artwork to expensive shards.

"Have you lost your mind? That piece was worth sixty-grand," Mr. Shaw shouted.

Aaron recognized the haughty, over-bearing gallery owner from previous stakeouts. He heard the man, but kept his eyes and gun on the woman. She turned her gaze from the ruined bust to slowly meet his eye. The hint of a smile turned up one corner of her mouth.

"Drop it! I'm not telling you again," Aaron said calmly and brought his weapon up level with her head. At this short distance, he couldn't miss. Perhaps the idea that her perfect face might end up like the seventeenth-century woman's caused her to slowly lower her small twenty-two. Her smile faded a tad.

Aaron waited until her gun was pointing at the floor before he stole a glance at Chloe. She was crouched down next to the wall, small and compact, with her hands interlocked over the back of her head. She appeared to be expecting a return of the wrathful Katrina.

Good instincts, he thought. "Chloe, are you all right?" he

asked. He scrambled to his full height and yanked the weapon from the woman's hand in one fluid motion.

"It's beyond repair!" Shaw wailed, leaving his position behind the desk to peruse the ruined sculpture.

"Oh, Kurt, shut up." The ice woman glared at Shaw.

Aaron reached down and pulled Chloe to her feet, not taking his eyes off the other two. "Are you all right?" he asked softly.

"I'm fine, Aaron. But I pretty much had the situation under control." She drew an antique dagger from the pocket of her hoodie. Its handle was encrusted with precious rubies and sapphires while the serrated blade glinted dangerously.

"I was waiting for just the right moment for a private girl-talk with Alicia." She slashed the air with the blade. Despite being a couple hundred years old, the knife looked razor sharp and deadly.

Aaron saw Alicia-the-Ice-Woman flinch, but the truly unexpected response came from Shaw. "What are you doing with that, Miss Galen? Handle it carefully. Those stones could come loose." Finally, something had pulled his attention from the shattered alabaster bust.

This man either took his job way too seriously or hadn't a clue what was really happening here.

"Don't worry, Mr. Shaw. I wasn't stealing it. I planned to return it to the showcase when I got finished." Chloe took several steps closer to Alicia, still brandishing the dagger before her.

"Please, Chloe, give me that thing." Aaron gently tugged it from her hand while the two women stared each other down. He slipped the antique into his back pocket.

"She killed Jason," Chloe stated flatly, sounding more like herself once relieved of the weapon. "And she intimidated Professor Graziano into taking his own life. And she was planning to kill me."

Aaron saw the tremble in her arms spread up Chloe's whole body. Soon she was shaking uncontrollably. He drew her against his side, wrapped his arm snuggly around her, then punched numbers into his cell phone.

Commotion in the outer rooms indicated that the passersby on Rue Royal must not have liked his entering a closed shop with a gun drawn and called the police. His uncle identified himself from the hallway and Aaron returned the greeting, indicating an all-clear inside the office. Soon the small room swarmed with patrol cops, detectives, and the undauntable Lieutenant Rhodes.

Charlie pulled the eight-inch dagger from Aaron's back pocket where he'd temporarily stashed it. "The Bureau's gotten truly creative with the weaponry they issue their agents these days." He inspected the magnificent piece before setting in on the desk.

"Only on special cases like this one. When dealing with antiquities, you gotta fight fire with fire." Aaron hugged Chloe close to his side and felt her trembling slow and then stop. Her arm had snaked around his waist. Their embrace felt good— better than good. Better, actually, than anything before in his life.

Rhodes glanced around the room, taking in Shaw and Pierce, both in the process of being handcuffed by officers, the shattered statue, the bejeweled dagger, then settled his gaze on Chloe. "You do seem to find the center of it, don't you, miss?"

"Only since I decided to live a quiet, temperate lifestyle. Then all hell seemed to break loose."

"Chloe solved the art fraud case and your murder investigation, too," Aaron said, tightening his arm around her. He set Alicia's handgun down on the desk. "This was Miss Pierce's. She confessed to killing Jason Hightower to Shaw and Miss Galen."

"You're not pinning this whole thing on me," Alicia screamed. Her perfect poise and manners finally showed signs of cracking.

"I didn't kill anybody," Shaw shouted back. "I didn't know anything about that. That was all you, Alicia." Apparently the idea of life in prison turned his attention away from his devalued antiques for the moment. "And I never would have harmed a hair on Chloe's head." He looked at Chloe then, his gaze softening with sorrow and remembered friendship for her father.

"That's the truth," Chloe said. "He tried to stop Alicia from hurting me."

"You meddlesome little girl. Why couldn't you keep doing what you do best—getting drunk on campus and mooning passing cop cars?"

That got the attention of the officers dragging Pierce and Shaw from the office. Two or three stole furtive glances in Chloe's direction.

Chloe pulled away from her sheltered spot in the crook of Aaron's arm. He saw her blush up to her hairline. She ran to the doorway after the officers. "Hey, Alicia. Your bad day is about to get worse. Besides getting arrested, I'll bet Mr. Shaw plans to fire you over shooting the statue and break up with you. Better turn in your key, too, Missy." She stood with hands on hips shouting at their backs as Pierce and Shaw were led away to patrol cars.

Aaron, Charlie, and the other detectives stared as Chloe slowly unclenched her fists and walked back to them.

Her already scarlet complexion darkened a hue. "Sorry," she mumbled. "Just a small, work-related competition between the two of us."

The detectives strolled from the room, bagging and taking the dagger and Alicia's gun with them. One cast a sympathetic glance at Aaron as he left. Uncle Charlie looked from him to Chloe then back to him. "I'm going to need both of you to issue statements at police headquarters." He glanced at his watch. "But I'm sure tomorrow will be soon enough, if—and only if—you don't leave New Orleans, Miss Galen. In fact, I don't want you to leave Agent Porter's sight. Do I make myself clear?" Rhodes loomed over her.

Aaron bit the side of his mouth to keep from laughing. The color had drained from Chloe's face as she went from rose to paper-white in seconds. "Yes, sir," she said. "I won't go anywhere. And I'll come down to make a full statement tomorrow."

"Good," Charlie said, a little too forcefully then turned toward his nephew. "Do you think you can control her, or do you need the dagger back?" The wrinkles around his eyes deepened into a web of lines.

"I think I've got it covered, but keep your cell phone on." Aaron holstered his gun, brushed off his pants and took Chloe's hand. "Consider yourself in custody, miss," he said to her upturned face.

"Okay, but please don't tell my mother."

CHAPTER FOURTEEN

Chloe awoke to soft light filtering through the slats of her shutters. It took her a minute to remember where she was—her old bedroom at Grandmère's house in the Garden District. She and Aaron couldn't decide where to go last might. Sara would have been home at the apartment. Aaron's aunt and uncle were obviously in town for the weekend. Every hotel in town would be filled. That left Grandmère's with Jeanette in residence. Luckily, Jeanette had been asleep when she and Aaron let themselves in and tiptoed upstairs like kids out after curfew. Luckier still, she'd been asleep when their "I've missed you hugs" and "Let's make up kisses" escalated rapidly into the kind of drama usually seen on late night cable TV.

But it had been long overdue. Chloe nestled back into the crook of Aaron's shoulder, initiating a soft snore from him. She let him sleep. After last night, he deserved it. She tingled, remembering the sweet sensual discovery along the way. Nothing remained hidden between them, no secrets kept them apart. He found out about the rose tattoo on her backside and swore not to tell her mother. All her sorority sisters had gotten one after a particularly crazy pledge weekend.

It seemed like a lifetime ago.

She found out he was ticklish and promised to tell everyone.

But she knew she wouldn't, because she loved him and he loved her. He had told her so last night.

And that knowledge made her weak-kneed and light-headed.

It had nothing to do with fake paintings, unscrupulous bosses or dead ex-friends. She felt a little scared, but very happy.

Chloe kissed his stubbly cheek, then took her cell phone out to the balcony so not to wake him. Today was Sara's twenty-second birthday, and Chloe wanted to sing her the tired old song and make sure she found the two wrapped gifts hidden in Chloe's drawer. One was a bottle of her favorite perfume, and in the other box Sara would find a stunning diamond necklace from Jason, supposedly bought for the occasion before his death. It was a white lie and Chloe wasn't in the lying business anymore, but his one couldn't hurt her newfound practical nature. Sara could sell the expensive piece and pay off half her student loans or keep it as a reminder of her first lost love. Either way, Chloe didn't want it, and Sara could use it more than she.

Aaron padded out to the balcony and wrapped his arms around her as she clicked her phone shut. Her off-key singing had been a hit, but not as much as the presents. Sara at first had been silent upon opening Jason's gift, and then Chloe could have heard her in the Garden District without the phone.

He murmured a husky "good morning" next to her ear. "What's all that yelling about?" he asked, tightening his hold on her. "Another crisis already? It's not even nine o'clock."

His touch was electric. She felt a *frisson* of electricity snake up her spine as she turned within his embrace. "No crisis, just a minor conundrum solved. Sara apparently liked her birthday presents. Could we take her out later today to celebrate? Someplace special?"

"We could. How 'bout Chaz's? I remember she liked that place."

The bittersweet memory of dining there with Jason floated back, along with a pang of sorrow. "No, not Chaz's. Let's try someplace new. Somewhere none of us has been."

"Agreed." His fingers reached up her back under her shirt. "I trust the princess slept well last night." He kissed the top of her head then drew her tightly against his bare chest.

She felt the strength of his pectorals through the thin cotton of her sleep shirt and forgot all about birthday dinners. Or anything else except for how good he made her feel.

"No more princess. I graduated to queen status after last night. And you shall be my king." She lifted her chin to receive his kiss.

"King sounds good. I'll probably need a career change once the NOPD completes their report to the FBI's Atlanta Bureau. I didn't exactly keep them in the loop on this one."

"When did you decide to trust me?"

"About the same time I realized I loved you."

"Was it because of my honest face?" she asked, peering up at him.

"No, it was more or less your hair."

Despite her resolve to behave in a responsible, adult manner at all times, she stamped her foot. "What is so wrong with my hair? I'm starting to develop a complex."

He pulled her tightly against him, stringing kisses through the hair in question. "Not a thing. You, Chloe Galen, are absolute perfection. Come back to bed. I'd like to show you what I really think about you."

"Later, Atlanta, if your uncle doesn't toss me in the clink and throw away the key. Right now, I've got to get ready for church." She glanced up expecting at least some mild derision.

Instead, he simply smiled. "Let me stop home for a change of clothes and I'll go with you."

"Not this time. There's something I must do. My mother never misses eleven o'clock Mass and I'd like to . . . you know, run into her." She felt her cheeks heat with a blush. "I'd like to offer an olive branch, and she couldn't possibly strangle me in

275

front of church-going witnesses." She pulled away quickly before she lost her nerve. No way did she want Aaron to witness another bad scene with the dysfunctional Galens.

Not since he'd told her he loved her.

And asked her to marry him.

"Whatever you say, dear," he said with a sly wink and headed for the bathroom.

Chloe tiptoed downstairs, smelling coffee long before she reached the kitchen. She hoped against the odds that Jeanette had simply set the timer on the coffeemaker. But the clatter of pans and lids on ceramic tile dashed those hopes.

"Good morning, Jeanette. What are you doing?" Chloe asked, seeing two skillets on the stove plus an electric griddle heating up.

Two obsidian eyes glanced skyward then refocused on the pans on the stove. "I work here, Chloe. I'm fixing you and your gentleman guest breakfast." The inflexion on the word gentleman revealed skepticism, not sincerity.

"Oh, that's what you're up to," Chloe replied, taking a cup from the cupboard, but not the bait.

Jeanette's spatula clattered to the countertop. "I hope the man you invited to spend the night in your Grandmère's house has honorable intentions."

"I believe they are." Chloe poured her coffee and took an appreciative first sip. "Honorable, that is." She struggled not to smile. "He has proposed."

Jeanette pondered this, momentarily mollified, then turned on her, even more enraged. "And what about your intentions, young lady? Are they equally honorable? You're not thinking of acting like those vapid tramps on TV, are you?"

Vapid tramps? Who teaches an eighty-year-old woman this stuff?

But Chloe took pity on her stand-in grandmother. "I assure

you, they are equally honorable."

"They'd better be. I don't like the idea of you up to mischief while your brother and his wife are away at that BB."

"B and B," Chloe corrected. "Bed and Breakfast."

Jeanette expertly flipped a pancake while adding spices to the crumbled sausage cooling in a bowl. "Whatever. I have no idea why they're still in the buggy bayou when they've got a perfectly fine bed and me to cook breakfast anytime he wants to eat something other than corn flakes with bananas." She poured more batter onto the hot griddle.

Chloe decided not to answer that particular question and asked one of her own. "What are you making?" She dipped a finger into the batter bowl. It was slightly sweet, just how she liked it.

"Sausage gravy and biscuits, pancakes with fresh fruit marmalades, fried eggs." Jeanette didn't look up from her gravy making.

"Jeanette, could you please stop a minute. I need your help." She turned the burner off under the skillet.

"Help with what?" Jeanette looked more than distrustful as she turned the burner back on.

Chloe sucked in a deep breath before continuing. If Jeanette laughed at her, she might lose her nerve. "Are my old clothes from high school still up in the attic?"

Jeanette poured the sausage gravy mixture back into the skillet. "They're packed away in boxes. What do you want with your old clothes?"

"Is that navy dress up there with the pleated skirt and big sailor collar?"

"I guess so. You hated that dress when your mama bought it for Easter. You took it off as soon as you got home from church. What are you up to, Chloe? And don't lie to me." She waved her spatula to punctuate the threat.

"Today's Sunday. I'm going to Mass. If I'm going to sit with Mama in the pew, I thought I'd wear her favorite outfit."

Jeanette cocked her head up to stare, her forehead furrowed into deep creases. "You're joking."

"I'm not, I swear." Chloe made an X mark over her heart.

Jeanette glanced up at the wall clock. "Go find the dress. Your patent leather Mary Janes and white tights should be in the box, too. I'll cook up your pancakes thin like a crepe so you can roll them up and take them with you." Jeanette topped off Chloe's coffee cup then pushed her out the kitchen. "Hurry! Mass at St. Louis starts in ninety minutes."

Chloe's throat closed with emotion as she kissed Jeanette's papery cheek. "I love you," she whispered, unable to say more.

"*Oui,* and don't spill coffee on the white collar on the streetcar."

Chloe ran up the stairs, but from the bottom she heard Jeanette call, "And tell your honorable gentleman to get down here and eat. I'm not cookin' all this up for myself."

Eighty minutes later, after the streetcar ride to Canal, then nearly running down Rue Royal, Chloe slipped into the third pew from the front in the massive St. Louis Cathedral where Clotilde Galen sat alone. She couldn't believe she'd put on tights with the temperature soaring in the nineties, but let's face it—what are patent leather Mary Jane's without white tights?

"Hi, Mama," Chloe whispered, interrupting Clotilde's rosary beads.

Clotilde Galen looked like she'd seen a ghost.

Maybe the tights were a bit over the top.

"Chloe." Her gaze traveled from the top of Chloe's head—the hair appropriately subdued—down to shoes no one Chloe's age would be caught dead in. "What are you doing here?" Her voice sounded raspy, and for the first time her perfect mother looked every bit her age. Her hands trembled as they clutched the rosary beads.

"I thought I'd start coming to Mass again. I've missed it." Chloe felt her throat tighten and her sinuses already began to close. She sucked a quick breath and forged ahead. "And I've missed you, Mama." She'd willed herself not to cry, not to become overly emotional, not to embarrass her mother, but couldn't stop her eyes from welling with tears.

"And I've missed you, my darling daughter." Clotilde threw her thin arms around Chloe's neck and hugged hard enough to put serious wrinkles in the starched lace collar.

Chloe hugged her back, feeling ashamed, heartened and homesick all rolled into one. "I'm sorry" got lost in Clotilde's hair while Mama's French endearments were drowned out by the choir's rousing processional to begin Mass. The parishioners rose to their feet and joined the singing, providing the two Galen women several precious moments for their reunion.

Unseen by Chloe but spotted by Clotilde, Aaron slipped into the pew on Chloe's other side. "Who are you?" Clotilde asked, dabbing her eyes with a lace hanky.

"Aaron Porter, ma'am. I'm Chloe's fiancé."

"Well, isn't that nice news?" The smile spreading from ear to ear looked downright genuine. "Another wedding."

Chloe shook her head. "Don't get too excited. I haven't said 'yes' yet, and I need to finish college first."

Mama looked at her daughter, gave Aaron a quick once-over, then slipped her arm around Chloe's waist. "I'm betting you will. On both counts."

Aaron wrapped his arm around Chloe's shoulder. "It'd be my fondest hope."

Chloe smiled up at Aaron, trying not to reveal everything in her heart.

"That dress looks great on you," he whispered into her hair.

"Can it," she muttered under her breath. "How did you find me?"

"Grandma-number-two spilled the beans."

The mention of Jeanette triggered a thought. "Did you eat some of her breakfast before you left?"

"No time, didn't want to miss Mass. You know, I believe she swore at me when I was leaving. In French."

"No doubt about it." Chloe giggled. "She's a lot like your *tante* Sophie when people leave without eating."

Clotilde smiled indulgently, but pressed the hymnal in front of her daughter in a not too subtle hint. Chloe sang along for two lines, but couldn't help herself. There were some things she needed to know, and patience had never been her strong suit.

"Did you get married in a church the first time around?" she whispered to Aaron as Mama began singing the refrain.

Aaron looked momentarily confused. "No, a justice of the peace in a small town in Georgia. Why?"

"Oh, no reason," she answered but couldn't stop grinning. She sensed Aaron studying her surreptitiously as she joined in on the next two verses.

Once the congregation sat down and the priest began his announcements, Aaron whispered next to her ear. "Chloe, there's something I gotta tell you. I don't want to keep any more secrets."

She glanced up and batted her lashes. "Yes?"

He returned the sweet, tender look. If they weren't in church, she would've kissed him.

"Abe Lincoln didn't chop down the cherry tree," he said.

"What?" she said, her voice much like the croak of a frog. This wasn't the declaration of love she'd been hoping for. Several parishioners cast them curious glances.

"Abe Lincoln didn't chop down—" he started to repeat, but she interrupted.

"I heard you, Aaron. I just don't know what difference it makes who chopped it down." Her frog imitation changed into a snake's hiss, drawing a stern "shush" from Mama.

Aaron smiled sweetly at his future mother-in-law then waited until the choir began to sing again. "George Washington chopped it down, Miss Galen, and that makes a very big difference. George Washington—the quintessential honest man?" He winked and squeezed her hand. "He wasn't born in a one-room log cabin, having to walk ten miles to go to school. He was rich."

It took her a minute, but she finally got it. And when she did, the little question of matrimony—whether or not she'd marry him—was answered.

After Mass the three walked outside the great cathedral together, pausing on the steps to take in the lively square before them. Artists and musicians were already set up to offer their particular abilities. Tourists with money to burn meandered along the walkways. The sky was clear without a cloud in sight, while the breeze blowing in from the levee smelled surprisingly sweet. Chloe even thought she heard birds singing to punctuate the most perfect moment of her life thus far.

"How do you think I should wear my hair for the wedding, Mama?" Chloe asked, patting her subdued curls. "Something like this?"

"Absolutely not," Mama answered, ruffling it up with her fingers so the top stood on end. "I'm thinking something very wild."

ABOUT THE AUTHOR

Mary Zelinsky has traveled extensively since leaving her schoolteacher chalk and overhead projector behind. Her passion for American history has taken her to more haunted inns and quaint seaside villages than she can count. She, her husband, two cats and a dog live in Ohio but spend enough time in the south, New Orleans in particular, to feel like a native. This is her second novel.